Cupid
and
the
Cowboy
Carol Finch

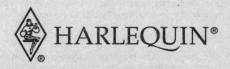

HARLEQUIN®

TORONTO • NEW YORK • LONDON
AMSTERDAM • PARIS • SYDNEY • HAMBURG
STOCKHOLM • ATHENS • TOKYO • MILAN • MADRID
PRAGUE • WARSAW • BUDAPEST • AUCKLAND

ISBN 0-373-75059-5

CUPID AND THE COWBOY

This edition published by arrangement with Harlequin Books S.A.

® and TM are trademarks of the publisher. Trademarks indicated with
® are registered in the United States Patent and Trademark Office, the
Canadian Trade Marks Office and in other countries.

www.eHarlequin.com

Printed in U.S.A.

ABOUT THE AUTHOR

Carol Finch, who also writes as Gina Robins, Debra Falcon, Connie Drake and Connie Feddersen, has written sixty-seven novels in the historical romance, contemporary, mystery and romantic-suspense genres. A former tennis pro and high school biology instructor, Ms. Finch devotes her time to writing and working on the family's cattle ranch in Oklahoma.

Ms. Finch, who received her B.S. degree from Oklahoma State University and taught writing at Oklahoma Community College, Redlands Community College and Oklahoma University's School of Writing, is a member of Romance Writers of America and has been inducted into the Oklahoma Professional Writers' Hall of Fame. She has received nineteen nominations and nine career achievement awards from *Romantic Times* magazine for Historical Love and Laughter, Historical Adventure, Best Contemporary Romance and Storyteller of the Year, and won the RomCon award for Best Romantic Suspense. Ms. Finch has been a published author for twenty years and has 9 million copies of her books in print.

Books by Carol Finch

HARLEQUIN HISTORICALS

592—CALL OF THE WHITE WOLF
635—BOUNTY HUNTER'S BRIDE
686—OKLAHOMA BRIDE
711—TEXAS BRIDE
723—ONE STARRY CHRISTMAS
  "Home for Christmas"
732—THE LAST HONEST OUTLAW

SILHOUETTE SPECIAL EDITION

1242—NOT JUST ANOTHER COWBOY
1320—SOUL MATES

HARLEQUIN DUETS

36—FIT TO BE TIED
45—A REGULAR JOE
62—MR. PREDICTABLE
72—THE FAMILY FEUD
81—LONESOME RYDER?*
  RESTAURANT ROMEO*
105—FIT TO BE FRISKED*
  MR. COOL UNDER FIRE*

*Bachelors of Hoot's Roost

"Better eat while it's hot," Erika said, gesturing toward the covered plate

"You've dropped off the food. Thanks. I can handle it from here."

She didn't take the hint, of course. No surprise there. Her smile doubled in wattage. "What'll it be, Rambo? Water, tea or—"

Me. The word slammed through Judd's brain and sizzled through his body the millisecond before she said, "—coffee?"

Judd was still cursing his betraying thoughts as she uncovered the oversize plate. Tempted past his resistance, Judd sampled the potato salad.

The food triggered memories of family picnics, carefree laughter and summer wind. Judd sorely resented a meal that instantly reminded him of happier times, because he was determined to pay penance for his greatest failure in life.

Judd didn't want this woman intruding into his reclusive life, but she kept burrowing through his defenses, turning him inside out, upside down and backward!

Chapter One

"Damn, here she comes again."

Judd Foster peered through the dusty slats of the mini-blinds and heavy, outdated drapes that covered his living room window.

It was the third time this week that Erika Dunn had shown up uninvited at his ranch house. She was making it difficult for Judd to settle into his self-imposed role as a recluse.

The first time that bubbly female glided up the uneven sidewalk to approach him about selling his old cedar barn and a few surrounding acres Judd had given her a flat-out, unequivocal *no*. But that hadn't discouraged Ms. Cheerful and Determined from making return visits.

Two days earlier Erika had arrived, bearing food from her restaurant in Moon Valley, claiming she had extra portions and didn't want to see food go to waste.

Best food Judd had eaten in years. Not that he had encouraged that perky restaurateur by admitting any such thing, mind you, because Erika Dunn wasn't a woman who appeared to be easily *dis*couraged.

In some ways she reminded Judd of his former self—the self he had turned his back on in order to pay penance at the family ranch. After all, gloom and isolation were what he deserved after what had happened.

Judd squinted against the glaring light of the spectacular Texas sunset that silhouetted Erika's appealing physique. She had the kind of unadvertised and understated beauty that intrigued a man who had been trained to look beyond surface appearances. He reminded himself that he wasn't in that line of work anymore. These days, his only assignment was to try to lead a normal life.

Whatever that was. He wasn't sure he even remembered.

His wandering thoughts trailed off as he watched Erika approach. The woman didn't just walk toward his house; she practically floated, he noted sourly. She was too vibrant, too energized. He didn't want her coming around here, spreading good cheer and flashing that infectious smile.

He just wanted to be left alone.

His attention shifted to the covered dish in her hand. Judd's mouth watered involuntarily. He wondered what delicious, culinary temptation she had delivered this time. More of that melt-in-your-mouth smoked chicken that had been marinated in pineapple juice and coated with her secret concoction of herbs and spices? Or something equally delectable? Apparently, Erika figured the most effective way to coax a man away from his property was to sabotage his taste buds and his stomach.

Judd's betraying gaze focused on the titillating jiggle of her full breasts that were encased in a cotton knit blouse, then dropped to the trim indentation of her waist and finally settled on the sensuous flare of hips clad in faded blue jeans.

Annoyed with himself for being distracted by her feminine attributes, he snapped his attention to Erika's face. Not that it helped. Her face was wholesome and animated and her eyes reminded him of a cloudless sky. Her ivory skin, dotted with freckles on her upturned nose, made her look fragile and delicate—a blatant contrast to her assertive, bubbly personality. She was part bombshell-in-hiding and part girl-next-door. A woman of interesting contrasts and potential. Much too complicated for a man who had sworn off deep, analytical thinking permanently.

He simply wanted to exist and let the world pass him by.

Judd watched Erika balance the covered plate in one hand while she hammered on the front door with the other. Judd knew she wouldn't give up and go away because he had ignored her for a good five minutes the last time she came by. She had outlasted him and outstubborned him, damn her.

Judd opened the door before she pounded a hole in it. "Now what?" he questioned unsociably.

"Hi, Judd. How's it going?"

Erika beamed an enthusiastic greeting as she sailed, uninvited, into his house. The woman was as inevitable as sunrise bursting into a room to scatter the darkness. And worse, the subtle scent of her perfume teased his nostrils. The citrusy fragrance didn't meet you halfway across the room, as if she had bathed in it. Oh, no, it tempted a man closer to inhale a deep, tantalizing whiff.

The instant Judd felt himself leaning impulsively toward her, he withdrew and stiffened his resistance. "The answer is still no," he said right off.

Might as well beat her to the punch and hope she would give up her ongoing crusade to buy his property. He didn't want her to sweet-talk him into signing over that old barn that held fond childhood memories. He didn't want to salivate like Pavlov's dog when the aromatic smoked meat, piled beneath a layer of aluminum foil, whetted his appetite.

Undaunted, Erika thrust the heaping plate at him and smiled radiantly. "No what? *No,* you won't do me a favor by taking this extra food off my hands? *No,* you have decided to stop eating altogether?"

She glanced around the gloomy living room, shook her head in disapproval, and then strode to the west window. "Really, Judd, it should be a criminal offense to keep this grand old home enshrouded in darkness. It looks like a vampire headquarters."

Leaving him holding the plate, she threw open the drapes, jerked up the blinds and opened all three living room windows. Fresh air poured into the room, carrying her scent to him again. Judd winced when blinding sunbeams speared into the room, spotlighting Erika's alluring profile—as if he needed another reminder of how well-proportioned she was.

He didn't. Furthermore, he didn't want to deal with the lusty thoughts her appearance provoked. He didn't want to like anything about Erika Dunn. In fact, he didn't want personal or emotional involvement with anyone these days. Erika was too attractive, too optimistic. Too *everything* for a man who had become cynical and world-weary after years of belly-crawling around hellholes in third-world countries and leading a double life in the process.

Judd wondered what it was going to take to discourage Erika from waltzing in here, as if she owned the place, trying to befriend a man who was completely unworthy of friendship. He hadn't been able to protect the one true friend he'd had the past decade and that tormented him to no end. After that, he didn't want anyone to depend on him or expect *anything* from him.

No one was going to get close to him again. He was just

going to have to try harder to scare off Erika—that shouldn't be too difficult for a man trained in the military's covert ops forces, specializing in the lethal techniques of combat. Just because he had returned to his hometown after an extended stint in the army didn't mean he had forgotten the skills that had kept him alive and kicking all these years.

Erika pivoted toward him, her smile still intact. "Much better," she declared with a nod that made her red-gold ponytail bob and shimmer in the afternoon sun. "You need to stop hiding out here like a hermit, Judd."

"And you need to stop showing up here to pester me. If your objective is to ruin my peaceful day, then you're done. You can leave now," he added with a steely stare.

She didn't so much as flinch. "You know what your problem is?"

"Yes, you," he said.

She ignored the comment. "Your problem is that you have isolated yourself. Everybody in town is starting to think there's something wrong with our local hero. People would roll out the welcome wagon if you would interact with them. You need to renew old acquaintances and make an active contribution to this community."

He snorted, then stared at the air over her head so he wouldn't be tempted to focus on the thrust of her breasts in that passion-pink knit blouse. He was *not* interested in this woman, wasn't interested in getting involved with any woman at the moment. Not interested in rejoining society yet, either.

"I'm not a hero," he countered. "I don't care what people in town think of me. Furthermore, I don't want to sell my barn so you can set up a larger café that will cause traffic jams in front of my home." He made a stabbing gesture toward the plate in her hand. "And I don't need your charity food, so stop showing up here with heaping platters."

To emphasize his point he gave her one of those quelling stares he had used occasionally to encourage men, men who were withholding vital information that threatened national security, to sing like canaries.

Unfortunately, the menacing promise in his eyes didn't seem to faze Little Ms. Local, Helpful and Cheerful. She merely graced him with another one of those hundred-watt smiles that implied that she wasn't the least bit intimidated.

He had to admire her for that—in an exasperated sort of way. Clearly, his previous military training had not prepared him to deal effectively with this particular woman. She was a pushy, bulldozing kind whose engaging smile made you feel guilty for giving her a hard time.

Erika gestured toward the covered plate. "Better eat while it's hot. Today's special of barbecue ribs, potato salad and baked beans is excellent, even if I do say so myself. Fact is, customers have been raving all day."

Standing in precise military stance—spine erect, shoulders thrust back, chin up—Judd looked down his nose at Erika. "You've dropped off the food. Thanks. I can take it from here," he said dismissively.

She didn't take the hint, of course. No surprise there. Her smile doubled in wattage. She mimicked his military stance, offered him a saucy salute, and then turned on her heels to march into his kitchen—as if she owned that, too.

Muttering, Judd stalked after her, watching in annoyance as she flung open the shutters to brighten up the room. Then she rummaged through his cabinets in search of glasses.

Judd's gaze slid to the rounded curve of her bottom, then he snapped to attention. His objective was to discourage Erika from dropping in on him whenever she felt like it. Why was he having trouble remembering that?

Erika wheeled around, a glass in each hand. "What'll it be, Rambo? Water, tea or—"

Me. The word slammed through his brain and sizzled through his body the millisecond before she said, "—coffee?"

Judd was still cursing his betraying thoughts when she opened the freezer to scoop up ice cubes. "Okay, I'll decide for us. We'll have water." She turned back to the sink to fill the glasses, then placed them on the antique oak table that graced the middle of the oversize kitchen. She plucked the plate from his hand and gestured toward the place he was to sit. "I'll get the silverware."

Accustomed to giving orders, Judd couldn't believe himself when he just plopped down in the chair, as if he had been outranked. It was ridiculous, baffling really, the way he responded to this pint-size woman who stood five feet nothing to his six feet plus. He decided he just must be a sucker for this woman who exhibited so much energy and assertive determination—traits he once greatly admired in himself.

Erika leaned over to place a knife and fork beside his plate. Her arm lightly brushed against his shoulder. Judd stifled the thrum of pleasure caused by her incidental touch. He didn't want to enjoy human contact or participate in the slightest emotional involvement. He just wanted to exist on an isolated plane until he had made peace with the recent incidents that haunted him.

His physical response was a hazard of self-imposed celibacy, he assured himself. That was the only reason he reacted to the way she looked, to the sensuous way she moved, to her luring scent, to the smoky sound of her voice and to the lively sparkle in those luminous blue eyes. Unwanted physical reaction and nothing more, he told himself reasonably.

It would pass eventually.

When she uncovered the oversize plate, succulent aromas bombarded him. His stomach growled. His mouth watered. His nostrils flared. Hunger blasted through him, reminding him that he'd had coffee for breakfast and hadn't taken time for lunch.

Tempted past his resistance, Judd grabbed his fork. "No matter how good this food is, I'm still not selling my barn," he declared before he sampled the potato salad.

The food triggered memories of family picnics, carefree laughter, summer wind and young boys racing through the cottonwood trees to reach Moon River and their favorite fishing hole. Judd sorely resented a meal that instantly reminded him of happier times because he was determined to pay penance for his greatest failure in life.

He bit into the smoked rib and his taste buds went into full-scale riot. Man, oh man, Erika Dunn could cook like nobody's business!

When Judd glanced across the table Erika was staring pensively at him. When he noted the hint of sadness in those expressive sapphire eyes he went perfectly still, the smoked rib poised inches from his mouth. When he realized he was being rude by attacking this meal like a starved wolf he pushed the plate toward her.

"Have some." His courteous offer didn't erase the trace of sadness at the edge of her smile. It annoyed him that he was so attuned to her to notice, especially after he had sworn not to let anyone close enough to cause him pain again.

She plucked up a rib. "You still don't remember me, do you, Judd?"

He frowned, wondering how anyone could forget a woman who practically fizzed with effervescence. "No, should I?" he asked nonchalantly.

She shrugged. The coil of reddish-blond curls flowed over her left shoulder and settled on the rise of her breast. Judd looked the other way.

"You were on hand during one of the most crucial, uncomfortable moments of my life," she prompted.

"You had a crucial moment more than sixteen years ago, before I left Moon Valley and joined the military?"

She nodded, then bit into the barbecued rib. "I was twelve years old and you were the big man on the high school campus," she reflected. "A bunch of my classmates circled around me, harassing me because my mother dumped me when I was a kid and left town, headed for parts unknown. The other grade school students were taunting me and chanting that I was good for nothing and my unwed mother didn't want me. When I broke down and started crying the taunts got worse. Then here you came— the football, basketball and baseball superstar from Moon Valley High—to save the day."

When Erika glanced down at the rib in her fingertips Judd noticed a vulnerability that he had rarely seen in her. Apparently, she was exceptionally good at concealing old pain. Much better than he was.

When she glanced up at him from beneath those long, sooty lashes, her smile was back in place. "You marched right up and told the kids to skedaddle. Told them that you better not catch them badgering me again. Then you took my hand, walked me to the café and bought me a Coke."

She propped her chin in her hand and added, "You told me not to pay any attention to those brats. You told me I shouldn't feel ashamed because my mom bailed out on me, that it wasn't my fault she was irresponsible. You predicted that I was going to turn out a whole lot better without her bad influence on my life." Her smile widened. "That was the day you became my hero."

"Yeah?" Judd was sorry to say he didn't recall the incident. But then, there was a mountain of memories standing between his high school years and the present day.

"Definitely my hero," she affirmed. "That's when I fell in love with you. Every boy I dated in high school failed to meet your standard of excellence."

Judd actually chuckled. He hadn't chuckled in months. "So, you're blaming me because you didn't have a steady boyfriend in high school?"

"Heavens no!" Her customary enthusiasm was back in full force. Her laughter seeped into the shriveled places in his soul, warming him. "I'm praising you, not criticizing you. Whether or not I could find a boy who measured up wasn't your fault. I only meant that we used to be acquaintances and that you made a lasting impression on me."

It was nice to know he had made a positive mark on someone's life, he supposed.

"The fact is that folks might forgive and forget what someone has said or done, but they never, *ever* forget how it makes them *feel*. *You* made me feel special during that defining moment of my life. I'm eternally grateful that you came to my rescue and bolstered my sagging self-esteem." She frowned thoughtfully. "I guess that's what you are. You have been rescuing people most of your life, especially during your counterterrorist missions in the military."

Judd supposed she was right. He had retrieved hostages and rescued captured agents from some of the most dangerous places, the most dangerous situations, in the worst armpits of the world because he had been driven by some inner need, some thrill-seeking obsession that he had never taken time to analyze.

Until the day he failed. Until that day six months ago when his skills, instincts and reactions weren't enough to make the difference. Saving the world had lost its appeal. He had shut down his emotions when that last mission went sour.

Forcing aside the tormenting thoughts, he stared curiously at Erika. "This is none of my business, but if your mother abandoned you, what is your connection to Francine Albright? I remember her from my teenage years at the café but I didn't know you two were related. Is she your aunt?"

Erika shook her head. "I was barely six years old when my mother drove through town and stopped at the Blue Moon Café for lunch. She told me she was going to run back outside to get something from the car. She went to get something all right. My suitcase of clothes. It was sitting beside the door."

Her smile faded and she tried to shrug nonchalantly, but Judd knew the incident must have hurt her as much as losing a friend had hurt him.

"That was the last time I saw my mother. Frannie found me standing outside, crying my eyes out. She bustled me back inside and that was the day she became my substitute mother. She put food in my belly, kept a roof over my head and called on the older citizens in town to keep an eye on me when things got hectic at the restaurant."

Judd grimaced. He couldn't begin to imagine what a traumatic experience that must have been for a young child.

"According to Aunt Frannie, folks in a small town like Moon Valley took care of their own," Erika went on to say. "No need to call in outsiders to muck things up. With a wave of her hand and a nod of her head I became her kid and she insisted she was thankful to have me. It was a done deal because she said so. End of story. No legal complications, no time-consuming red tape or string of foster homes. I suspect Frannie made some discreet inquiries, but since I was only six and already hurting, I think she whitewashed the facts to spare me. I came to realize Frannie was more of a caring, responsible adult than my mother. I simply left it alone."

"She just raised you alone, while operating the café," he remarked, impressed by Francine Albright's selfless deed. "And you repaid her kindness by working alongside her."

"Exactly," Erika replied. "Aunt Frannie became my mother and my mentor. She turned over control of the Blue Moon Café to me after I graduated from college. Nowadays she works part-time so she can enjoy her hobbies—gardening, bowling, bingo and volunteer work. She deserves time off and I try to ensure that she has it whenever she wants it. I owe her a tremendous debt. There is no telling where I might have ended up if she hadn't taken me in.

"But enough about that," she said, brushing aside her past as if it were inconsequential—and he knew it couldn't have been. She had been dealt a difficult, demoralizing blow. No doubt about it. "Let's discuss my proposition."

Proposition? His gaze dropped to her Cupid's-bow mouth, then sank to her well-endowed chest. Hell! He was lusting after this tomboyish, freckle-nosed restaurateur who had a sad story to tell—and who was trying to entice him with mouth-watering meals, *not* anything else.

What was the matter with him? Why had he gone soft so fast? He wondered if she had elaborated on that sad tale to set him up so she could milk his sympathy. Keeping that possibility in mind, Judd steeled himself against Erika's winsome smile and held his ground.

"I really want to buy your barn and a few surrounding acres," she insisted.

"No, absolutely not," he said firmly.

For all the good it did him. Erika continued on as if he hadn't spoken.

"Blue Moon Café is bursting at the seams. I have planned and dreamed of expanding for several years."

"The answer is still no," he maintained. "I like my ranch exactly the way it is. I prefer to be surrounded by horses and cattle. Not people."

"I want to make use of the rural setting since your barn is only a mile from town," she went on, unfazed. "I could accommodate customers from all over the county. I'm planning to install bay windows in the barn to provide a panoramic view of the river," she said, enthusiastically warming to the topic. "I want to build pens for small farm animals that will serve as a petting zoo for children and their parents to enjoy after their meal. With good food, a great atmosphere and clean country air the restaurant could be a smashing success."

Very deliberately, Judd replaced the half-eaten rib on his plate and stared at her. "You aren't listening to me. I…do…not…want…to sell that chunk of my property. Not now, not ever."

The flat refusal didn't deter her. Obviously this woman considered *no* to be a personal challenge.

"You aren't using the barn," she pointed out reasonably. "There is a new metal barn right behind this house. That old barn will fall in on itself without repairs. I want to get hold of it before it suffers structural damage."

"Why *that* barn?" Judd questioned, bemused. "Why *my* barn? There are other barns on the outskirts of Moon Valley."

She smiled. He really resented the fact that he was enormously affected by her smile. Everything about her—even the things that irritated the hell out of him—affected him strongly. He sincerely wished he could figure out why because she wasn't his usual type at all. He went for women whose blatant sexuality indicated they were only interested in no-strings-attached pleasures. Which was all the time he could spare when his demanding duties took him all over the world, and at a moment's notice.

"Location, location, location," she replied, then nibbled on the rib. "The paved road is in good condition. Plus, I have been drawn to this place since I was a kid." She leaned over to add confidentially, "When I was feeling low I used to hike out here to regroup and be alone with my thoughts. It was peaceful and comforting and—"

"And you were. trespassing," he interrupted. "I'm surprised my parents didn't send you on your way."

"Your parents? Don't be ridiculous," she said with a dismissive flick of her wrist. "They were wonderful, generous people. They were also regular customers at Blue Moon until their health deteriorated. Besides, I repaid them by delivering food when they didn't feel up to dining out."

Judd inwardly grimaced. In addition to the guilt and regret that hounded him after his last overseas mission, he felt ashamed that he had neglected his parents. For years, his only visits to his hometown came during weekend furloughs. It wasn't unusual for him to be called back unexpectedly and then shipped off to perform clandestine missions.

It seemed Erika had assumed the duty of checking on his parents. He wondered if it was her hero worship of him that prompted her kindness to them.

Well, hero worship was a waste of her emotion. Judd was no one's *hero* these days. He was an incompetent *failure*.

Erika bounded to her feet and strolled to the kitchen window. "Looks like you could use someone to mow your lawn and tidy up around the outbuildings," she observed. "I'll bring Kent Latham out to help you."

"I don't need help," he said, exasperated.

"Actually you would be doing me a tremendous favor by hiring Kent. He could use extra spending money. He sweeps up at the café for me, and I really don't like to send the boy home too early because his mother isn't what you could call a positive influence. Kent doesn't have a father around and you are the prime candidate for his male role model."

Judd pushed himself away from the table and strode toward her. He gave Erika The Look again, but she didn't so much as blink. "I do not need help. I will get to the mowing after I finish constructing the stalls in the metal barn for my horses and cattle. I have no inclination to be some kid's role model!" he said, his voice rising a frustrated decibel. "I just want to be left alone."

"No, you don't." Erika grinned, undaunted. "Kent and I will come by day after tomorrow."

"I won't be here," he replied stubbornly.

"Of course you will. You haven't left the place, except

to buy groceries, for almost two months. You have spent most of your time with your horses and cattle, and you need to interact with folks in town. But not to worry, I'll help you get reacquainted," she volunteered.

"I *like* being alone," he declared.

"No one really enjoys being alone," she contradicted. "It isn't healthy. Besides, you've been a local hero for years. Your parents were so proud of your military honors and commendations. They sent articles to the *Moon Valley Star* each time you were promoted, just so everyone could keep track of your accomplishments."

His parents hadn't really known what he was doing, Judd mused. Most of the time he carried fake ID and falsified background information. He wasn't who his family thought he was. His job had consumed and defined him and now he wasn't sure who he was, either. Besides being a neglectful son, he tacked on.

"Maybe they were proud of me, but that doesn't compensate for the fact that I was halfway across the world when Dad had his heart attack. I was flying back from a mission when Mom passed on," he blurted out, surprised that he confided the information to her.

She regarded him for a moment, then reached out to touch his arm compassionately. Judd tensed. He wasn't a touchy-feely guy and painfully lacking when it came to demonstrating emotion. He had been trained to keep his feelings in cold storage, to respond with skill and intellect. Apparently Erika didn't have this problem displaying emotion.

"You shouldn't feel guilty about that," she insisted. "You were defending our country. Your parents realized that you served a higher, very important purpose."

When she removed her hand and walked away an odd

feeling of emptiness assailed him. Judd didn't want this woman intruding into his reclusive life, but she kept burrowing through his defenses, turning him inside out, upside down and backwards. Some highly trained, kick-ass specialist he had turned out to be. He couldn't save his best friend and he couldn't even get this female out of his house, let alone out of his life.

Ms. Eternal Optimist just damned all the torpedoes he aimed at her and plunged full steam ahead, determined to fulfill her goals, despite any obstacle standing in her way.

But she wasn't getting her mitts on that cedar barn, no matter how many servings of delicious food she delivered. No matter what she offered in exchange…

The thought put a devilish smile on his lips. He wondered how she would react if he came on to her. Maybe she would turn tail and run and finally figure out that not all lost causes—like him—were worthy of rescuing.

When she started past him he caught her arm and drew her backward. In one fluid motion he positioned himself in front of her, blocking her between him and the powder-blue Formica counter. He gave her a suggestive grin, leaned in close and said, "Did you ever stop to think that maybe money isn't the incentive I need to convince me to sell to you?"

Judd was totally exasperated when he noticed the impish smile that spread across her lips. "Is that the best you've got, Rambo?" she teased, her blue eyes sparkling with amusement.

Dumbfounded, he stared at her, trying to figure out where he had gone wrong with his scare tactics.

"Trying to frighten me won't work," she assured him. "I told you that you've been my hero for years."

"Yeah well, that's the thing about hero worship, honey.

It's just an illusion," he countered. "Fact is that I'm rough around the edges, tough as nails and I'm plagued by a mean, nasty disposition."

"That's the most ridiculous thing I have ever heard."

To his absolute frustration she called his bluff by pushing up on tiptoe and pressing a loud, smacking kiss to his clenched jaw.

"You aren't the kind of man who has to offer bargains to attract women." She flashed him a cheeky grin. "Not with that great body and those rugged good looks. So don't think I'm falling for that nonsense."

Judd didn't know why he made no move whatsoever to prevent her from sidestepping him and breezing into the living room. He had let her flit off with the knowledge that, with her, at least, he was pretty much a pussycat. All hiss and no bite.

So much for his former bad-ass reputation.

"Don't bother to come back," he felt obliged to call after her, in an attempt to save face.

"See you day after tomorrow," she answered as she sailed out the door. "'Bye, Judd."

Judd braced his hands on the counter, scowled a couple of times, then closed the shutters. The room plunged into darkness and shadows. Good. That was the way he wanted it. He didn't need that woman bringing light and cheeriness into his home and reminding him how dark and empty his life had become. He had hours of grieving to do, years of guilt and regret to wallow in. Erika Dunn was screwing up everything with her bubbly enthusiasm.

Someone needed to devote some time to getting control of that woman and discouraging her from meddling in other people's lives.

Not him, of course. But someone.

When Judd heard the door click shut he tramped off to close the blinds and pull the drapes. No one was going to brighten his dismal world until he was damn good and ready. He needed to come to terms with his failure and his loss first.

Just because he had returned to the family ranch didn't imply that he intended to socialize. This was just the place to hang his hat, a place to exist. Erika Dunn was not going to blow into his life like a human hurricane and disrupt his plans! He just had to figure out a way to make her keep her distance.

For sure, he had met with failure today.

So what else was new? he mused as he strode off to grab his boots so he could head outside.

Chapter Two

Erika sank onto the seat of her no-nonsense economy car, inhaled a steadying breath and fanned herself to cool off. Whew! Finding herself plastered up against six feet four inches of prime USDA choice male in its finest physical form had sent sensual lightning zapping through her body.

It had been a battle royal not to throw her arms around those impossibly broad shoulders, run her fingers through Judd's shiny raven hair and scream, "Take me, I'm yours!"

If she had, she predicted Judd would have run in the opposite direction. He seemed to have his heart set on making her dislike him, but that simply wasn't going to happen.

Erika chuckled at her longtime fascination for Judd Foster. Luckily, she'd had the good sense not to humiliate herself today. Not only did Judd *not* remember that pivotal moment in her life, but also he really didn't find her attractive—despite what he might have said to the contrary.

She knew he was only trying to drive her away, but he hadn't applied the slightest force and his attempt had been totally ineffective. He had amused her rather than intimidated her. But it was a nice try on his part. At least he had done something besides brood and sulk for a few minutes.

Erika switched on the ignition and vowed that Judd

Foster hadn't seen the last of her. He needed companionship to battle whatever demons were tormenting him. He needed to be surrounded with friends who cared about him. She knew that for a fact because she had suffered her share of torment, loneliness and rejection, and she had discovered that giving of her time to help others held depressing thoughts at bay.

That day, sixteen years ago, when Judd scattered her taunting classmates and showered her with kindness, Erika had realized that just because she didn't have a normal family life didn't mean she was alone in the world. Judd had inspired her not to give up the fight. From that day forward she accepted the citizens of this community as her extended family and made a place for herself in Moon Valley. She had vowed to give something back to the older generation in this town that had rallied around her during her darkest hour.

Those kind, caring folks had made a marked difference in Erika's life. She might have grown up doing homework in the back booth of the Blue Moon Café and learning to cook and clean up after customers, but she had also learned a lot about the elemental good in people in the process. The older generation had looked out for her, accepted her, even if her own mother had dumped her off like unnecessary baggage and hightailed it out of town.

Erika had accepted her lot in life and became the girl-next-door. She had befriended everyone who needed a helping hand and had done her best to link lonely hearts together so they could find the companionship and happiness missing from her own life. Because she had carried a torch for Judd Foster for years, she had refused to waste her time on men who couldn't meet her expectations.

Her curse in life, it seemed, was clinging to an unattainable dream. To shatter the shimmering fantasy, only to discover it wasn't all she had conjured it up to be, was daunting. Yep, she had backed herself into a corner with her hero worship, she realized.

But at least she didn't have to face disillusionment.

Seeing Judd Foster after all these years stirred up the memories that had refused to die. Now Erika was reluctant to reach out for what she really wanted—namely Judd himself—for fear of rejection and disappointment. *Idolizing* him was safe and familiar, and the scars of her mother's rejection were not easily forgotten. Being romantically discarded by Judd would crack the very foundation of her long-held affection and respect for him.

That might sound crazy and convoluted to someone else, but it made perfect sense to Erika. There were some things you changed. And some things you simply left intact.

Erika veered onto the graveled path that led to the old cedar barn, then climbed from her car. That bullheaded, brooding, special ops commando stood directly between her and another long-awaited dream. And by damn, she was going to find a way to transform Judd's *no* into a *yes*.

In order to do that, Erika knew she had to put Judd back in touch with life, with his roots. He was wasting away on this ranch. He spent more time with his livestock than people. Erika was compelled to help him work through whatever was tormenting him—the same way she tried to support her friends who needed her compassion when they were down and out.

Wheeling around, Erika strode to her car. The moment she sank onto the seat the memory of being meshed against Judd's incredibly masculine body assailed her again. The man packed such an incredible sensual wallop that she had nearly drowned in those cocoa-brown eyes fringed with long, thick lashes. She had nearly gotten lost in his appealing scent.

Good thing she was smart enough to realize that he was only putting on an act, in hopes of prompting her to clear out for good. She knew he didn't really want *her*. Why would he? He could have any woman he wanted with just one come-hither glance. Erika knew she wasn't worldly, sophisticated or experienced. She didn't know the first thing about luring and seducing a man, and she wasn't about to experiment with her dream lover, and thoroughly humiliate herself. She did have her pride, after all.

But that didn't mean she hadn't been tempted to fling her arms around Judd's neck when she had the chance and treat herself to a taste of those full, sensuous lips. She really had wanted to know if kissing Judd was as earth-shakingly incredible as she imagined it would be. Yet, she had been hesitant for fear of disappointing him with her lack of feminine wiles. Hence the playful, smacking kiss on the cheek.

She'd had no intention of blowing her secret fantasy to kingdom come. It was all she had going for her.

No matter what else happened—or didn't happen—between them, Erika was not giving up on Judd, even if he had given up on himself. Maybe she couldn't realize her dreams of having Judd return her affection or acquiring the barn to renovate into a spacious restaurant, but she wasn't aborting her crusade to put Judd back in touch with life in his hometown.

The man was going to get off his ranch and emerge from his self-imposed shell, even if she had to drag him kicking and screaming.

Erika grinned at the mental image that leapt to mind. She predicted that was exactly what it would take to ensure Judd regained that vital link to life. And she was volunteering to take on the job—for his own good, *not* to mention hers.

"HEY, RIKI, any luck convincing Judd to sell the barn when you visited him yesterday?" Aunt Frannie asked as she flipped a hamburger patty on the grill.

Erika ambled into the Blue Moon Café's stainless steel kitchen to wash up after making her deliveries. Francine was working industriously. But then, Francine Albright had always been hardworking and industrious. That's where Erika had acquired her work ethic.

Aunt Frannie never whined about working. A young, active fifty-five, Frannie led a busy life and kept her gray hairs covered with a tint that closely matched Erika's natural hair color so they would look more like family. Despite the onset of facial wrinkles and gravity's effect on her feminine body, Francine was still attractive and had always received her fair share of masculine attention.

Francine had never married and Erika felt guilty about that. She suspected she was the reason. Francine had dedicated her life to the café and to raising Erika. But there had been times when Erika caught Aunt Frannie staring wistfully at husbands and wives who fussed over their children. Yet, when Erika questioned her about the possibility of marriage, Aunt Frannie shrugged and claimed she was satisfied with her lot in life.

At least Francine had been satisfied in the past. Lately, Erika sensed restlessness in Francine, as if she was itching to move into another phase, as if something was missing.

Erika knew that feeling all too well. What Francine needed was male companionship, Erika diagnosed. Of course, there wasn't a man on God's green earth who would be good enough for this woman who had raised her.

"Yoo-hoo!" Aunt Frannie teased playfully. "Hello?"

Erika grinned as she scooped up the coffeepot. "Sorry. In answer to your question, no. Judd Foster hasn't agreed to sell the barn. The man could teach stubborn to a mule, I'm sorry to say."

Francine flipped hamburger patties with an efficient precision that testified to years of experience behind a spatula. "Well, if I know you, you won't give up until Judd's convinced that he *needs* to sell the property to you. You keep feeding him and he'll come around eventually," she insisted. "Never saw a man yet who could resist a good meal or… Well, never mind about the other thing men usually can't resist." She winked spryly. "We did have that birds and bees chat some time back, didn't we, hon?"

"Yep, about fifteen years ago," Erika replied, chuckling. She didn't mention Judd's flimsy ploy to scare her off. Aunt Frannie would get all huffy and take the incident the wrong way. "I did manage to line Kent Latham up to do yard work for Judd. Maybe that will help Judd settle into civilian life after so many years in the military. He doesn't know what to do with himself without a crisis to defuse."

"Bet not." Aunt Frannie scooped up the toasted buns and slathered mustard on them. "That's got to take some getting used to. Take me, for instance. Working half days after years of doing double duty at the café is quite an adjustment. I have to invent activities to occupy my time."

"Luckily, you've come up with scads of hobbies," Erika remarked.

Aunt Frannie nodded. "You betcha, girl. Wouldn't miss bingo night for nothin'. Still trying to improve the techniques of my bowling game, too. And those photographers from home and garden magazines will be beating down my door when I get my flower beds in tip-top shape." She nodded toward the coffeepot in Erika's hand. "Better go fill the cups. David Shore has been hanging around for an hour, waiting for you to return from making deliveries."

Erika walked from the overheated kitchen and sighed appreciatively when the whirring ceiling fans provided a blast of cool air. She glanced across the room to see David Shore, the newly hired county deputy, lounging in the corner booth.

"Where have you been so long? I was about to list you as a missing person," he said with a teasing grin.

"Delivering meals." Erika returned the smile as she refilled David's mug.

"Still catering to your elderly customers? Don't know of any other cafés in the county that perform that service."

"Mrs. Jamison was a regular here on Mondays, until her health failed her," she explained.

She didn't add that Wanda Jamison was one of the women who had looked after her while Aunt Frannie was swamped with business. To repay the widow's kindness, Erika delivered food to the retirement center every Monday. In fact, she made deliveries several days a week to the women who had cared for her during her childhood. No way would Erika allow herself to forget the good deeds that had come her way.

David lounged against the black vinyl seat and eyed her speculatively. "I could have sworn I saw your car at the Foster place yesterday when I cruised into town."

"You did," she confirmed.

"Still a hard sell, huh?"

Erika bobbed her head. "Judd Foster obviously has a sentimental attachment to that old cedar barn."

"Absolutely. So…you wanna go play bingo tomorrow night? I'm off duty," David said out of the blue.

Surprised, Erika smiled at the attractive, sandy-haired deputy. "Sorry, I have other plans."

"Why can't you play bingo with me? Got a hot date with Judd Foster?" he asked speculatively.

Erika smirked. "The man rarely leaves his ranch. Besides, he isn't interested in me. He thinks I'm a bothersome nuisance."

"Then he's an idiot. So how about we take in a movie Wednesday night if I can get off duty. You need to get away from the job and so do I. We can keep each other company."

"Sorry. This is a hectic week. Lots of community activities and catered meals to prepare. Wesley Larkin's family is throwing a birthday bash and I'm going to smoke some chickens and ribs for the shindig."

"Well, darn. Looks like I have another lonely week ahead of me," he grumbled.

Erika scanned the café, noting that her high school classmate and best friend, Sylvie Vaughn, was ensconced in the back booth—alone. Although Erika wasn't interested romantically in David, she liked him. She predicted Sylvie would, too. Considering the hassle Sylvie's ex-husband usually caused, maybe *she* needed an introduction to David. Erika mentally kicked herself for not considering the potential match earlier.

Abruptly, Erika snatched the mug from David's hand

and spun on her heels. "Come with me. There's someone I want you to meet."

Eyeing her curiously, David followed in her wake. Sylvie, munching a hamburger, looked up, then blinked in surprise.

"Hey, Syl, how ya doin'?" Erika placed David's cup on the table. "This is David Shore. He recently took a position with the sheriff's department. Dave, this is my good friend, Sylvie. She teaches history at the high school and she's active in the community and is knowledgeable about sports."

Self-consciously, Sylvie touched her napkin to her mouth to wipe off a glob of mustard, then smiled. "Nice to meet you, David."

He cast Erika a bemused glance then eased into the booth. "My pleasure, Sylvie."

When silence descended Erika said, "I presume Matt is still at Little League practice." She glanced at David. "Matt is her six-year-old son. He's got a powerhouse swing like Mark McGuire and he lives and breathes baseball. Unfortunately, he doesn't have a dad around to play catch and attend the games."

Leaving the twosome, Erika strode off to fill the empty coffee cups and chat with customers. She kept a casual eye on David and Sylvie, noting that they appeared to be getting along well enough to carry on a conversation rather than staring awkwardly at their silverware.

After catching up on the latest scuttlebutt from the local gossips, Erika returned to the kitchen to relieve Aunt Frannie. "You can call it a day. The supper rush is over and the teenage hired help has arrived."

Aunt Frannie untied her apron and narrowed her gaze

on Erika. "Playing Cupid again, are you? Why are you matching up Dave and Sylvie?"

"Because it dawned on me that they might make a great couple. David is new in town and he needs companionship. You know Sylvie's ex makes a nuisance of himself by showing up intoxicated on her doorstep every few weeks. It always upsets her when she has to shoo him away. It might be nice for her to have a man like David around occasionally."

"Prob'bly would," Aunt Frannie agreed as she stared pensively at the booth. "But I thought perhaps you two might eventually progress into something more romantic."

"You know what they say, those who can't *do,* teach. Those who can't find love play Cupid." Erika tied her apron around her waist and glanced at the ticket hanging above the stainless steel grill. "Dave is really a nice guy and I like him, but he's not—"

"Yeah, I know," Frannie interrupted. "He's not Mr. Right. I lost mine during the Vietnam War. He was everything I thought I wanted, until God decided to put him on eternal guard duty in heaven." She glanced skyward and frowned.

Erika knew Aunt Frannie had never fully recovered from the loss of her fiancé. She and Frannie had a lot in common, Erika mused. She wasn't too pleased that she had been stuck with a mother who didn't give a hoot about her. It must be true that the Lord worked in mysterious ways because Erika still hadn't figured out why she hadn't been blessed with a large family since that was something she had wanted for years.

"Well, I'm off," Frannie announced. "I'm getting my roots touched up at the Do or Dye Salon, then I'm headed over to the special bingo competition for the over-fifty crowd. Since I'm feeling lucky today, I plan to beat the pants off that ornery loan officer who thinks he's got the Midas touch."

Erika raised a brow. "Who?"

"Murph," she prompted as she scooped up her purse then slung the leather strap over her shoulder. "He got transferred to Moon Valley Bank about three months ago. You know, gray hair, good build and mischievous smile. He does lunch with us three times a week."

A wry grin pursed Erika's lips. "Murph, huh?"

Frannie plucked the hair net off her head and tucked it in her purse. "Yeah, conceited as all get-out, too. Every time he wins at bingo he waves his winning card in my face. This is war! Gimme a month and I'll have him whittled down to size."

"Since when did you start taking bingo so seriously?"

"Since Mr. Hot Stuff rode into town in his Benz," Frannie said as she breezed off. "Never could stand conceit in a man. Once I teach him his place in the pecking order he won't ruffle my feathers the way he's doing now."

Erika shook her head in amusement then donned a hair net that made the shape of her head appear distorted because of the long ponytail wadded up at the base of her skull.

When Erika pivoted to hand an order to the teenage waitress, Sylvie was leaning on the counter, staring at her. "What are you doing?"

"Cooking burgers and fries," Erika replied innocently.

Sylvie's brows flattened in disapproval. The tactic might have worked on her students, but not on Erika. After all, a real pro had tried to intimidate her recently. No one could deliver The Look better than former special ops commando Judd Foster.

"That's not what I meant and you know it. Don't play dumb with me, Riki. Why did you set me up with the deputy sheriff?"

"There's a problem?" Erika asked. "You aren't embezzling from the collection plate at church, are you? Tampering with history grades? Selling dope to students? Are you afraid the cop might catch you doing something illegal?"

"Of course not, but I do have a deadbeat semi-alcoholic ex-husband who occasionally comes by to see his son. What am I supposed to do with a cop?"

"Jeez, Syl, I thought you had figured that out back in college biology when we studied human anatomy and reproduction."

Sylvie flung her a withering glance then snickered in spite of herself. "For your information, I know my way around the male anatomy, thank you very much. Now, tell me why I'm going out with David Shore tomorrow night."

Erika beamed in satisfaction. "You are? Great! You are entitled to some fun. Do you want me to watch Matt for you?"

"I would appreciate that since you maneuvered me into this date. Lord, I haven't dated since I was in college and I can't believe I agreed to this. I'm out of practice. Luckily this is just a get-to-know-each-other kind of date. You know, exchange chitchat for a couple of hours and then call it a night."

Erika smiled in amusement. She and Sylvie went back a long way. Best friends since the seventh grade. Confidantes. In fact, it was Erika who had tried to convince Sylvie that marrying Richard Vaughn was a disastrous mistake, but Syl was in lust and couldn't see past the haze of hormones.

Sylvie had set up Erika with a few dates in college,

which had testified to Sylvie's inability to select decent men. Although Erika had avoided long-term relationships, she considered herself a better judge of men than her friend—not surprising since Sylvie's father had been as much of a lush and all-around dud as her ex-husband.

"I've got to deliver meals to the Smiths and Ralstons," Erika said. "I can drop off Kent Latham for his new job, then swing by and pick Matt up."

Sylvie dug into her wallet to pay for the meal then shifted uneasily from one foot to the other. "Maybe I was too impulsive to agree to this date. Maybe I should have invited David over to the house to watch a rented movie and meet Matt."

"Geez, Syl, relax, will you? You owe it to yourself to let your hair down and socialize with a man your own age."

"As if you heed your own advice." Sylvie scoffed. "You've let this café control you since college. You also bust your fanny doing good deeds for everyone. In fact, your personal life consists of catering to the needs of everyone but yourself. I bet you haven't missed a single visit to the retirement center to play cards with those cantankerous old biddies."

"Hey, those cantankerous old biddies weren't always so cantankerous. They were kind and generous and they helped raise me. The least I can do is visit them," Erika defended herself.

Sylvie held up her hand like a traffic cop. "Okay, Riki, you've made your point. But you can't tell me to get a life when you need one as badly as I do."

Erika shrugged nonchalantly. "I'm just holding out for Mr. Right."

"I would sincerely like to know if Mr. Right is real or

imagined," she said. "You've mentioned him since junior high. Whoever this mystery man is, or *could* be, you'll never find him when you play matchmaker and foist off potential boyfriends on me and our friends."

"Dave only comes in here to get acquainted with the townsfolk," Erika insisted. "Besides, I'm not his type."

Sylvie tossed her curly blond head and smirked. "You could be every man's type if you put forth the effort with nice clothes and makeup. You don't give yourself a chance. I never have figured out why." She eyed Erika speculatively. "In fact, I don't recall that you ever dated anyone for more than a couple of months. Just why is that, humm?"

Erika avoided Sylvie's probing gaze and glanced at her watch. "I better get back to work and you probably need to pick up Matt."

Sylvie nodded. "He went over to a friend's house after ball practice. I'm on my way to pick him up."

When Erika spun toward the kitchen, Sylvie wagged a polished red-tipped finger at her departing back. "One of these days we are going to sit down and discuss your fickle streak, Riki. It wouldn't hurt *you* to have a man in your life, you know. And don't try to feed me that nonsense about being the girl-next-door type. I don't buy it."

Erika didn't have a fickle streak. She simply had exceedingly high expectations—and a fear of rejection that stopped her in her tracks. But she wasn't going to confide that to Sylvie. With a wave and a smile Erika strode off to fill a plate with today's melt-in-your-mouth special and serve up a piece of slice-of-heaven pie.

HERE SHE COMES AGAIN, Judd mused as he stood at the living room window. What really disturbed him was that he had been standing watch for ten minutes. He would shoot himself in the foot before he would admit that to Erika. But he did look forward to her visits that broke the monotony of making ranch repairs and tending his livestock.

Dressed in a colorful buttercup-yellow knit blouse and trim-fitting jeans that subtly defined her feminine assets, Erika strode up his sidewalk, carrying another covered plate. A dark-haired, gangly teenage boy was one step behind her. The kid was so thin that Judd doubted the youngster possessed enough strength and muscle power to push a lawn mower without wearing himself out.

Before Erika pounded on the door, Judd whipped it open.

"Hey, Judd, this is Kent Latham. Kent, Judd." After the quick howdy-dos Erika surged through the door. "C'mon in, Kent."

As had become her habit, she thrust the plate at Judd, then opened all the drapes and windows. Her customary ritual amused as much as it annoyed him. The woman was hell-bent on chasing away the gloom and shadows that surrounded him.

"I'll stuff this plate in the microwave, then we'll get Kent started mowing," Erika announced as she retrieved the food.

When she sailed off like a launched rocket, the kid crammed his hands in the front pockets of his baggy jeans and stared down at his oversize feet. "Riki said you're a military hero," Kent mumbled awkwardly.

"Did she?"

"Yeah." Kent's tousled red head bobbed jerkily.

"I spent a long time in special ops," Judd said evasively.

"Bet you've been everywhere and done everything. Were you one of those SEALS or somethin'?"

"Something like that." That was enough on that subject, Judd decided. And hell! He didn't know how to relate to a kid. It had been two decades since he had been one himself. His experiences in the service had taken the boy out of him PDQ.

"So," Judd said uncomfortably. "How old are you, Kent?"

"Thirteen."

Had Judd ever been that young? That skinny? "I hope you don't mind using a push mower. I don't have the riding mower up and running yet. Ever handled a weed-eater?"

"Nope," he mumbled, head downcast.

Great. At least he didn't have to potty-train the kid. He jerked his head around to see what was keeping Erika. She was opening the shutters so sunlight would glare off the chrome appliances. Well, what had he expected?

"All set, guys. Let's get Kent started so Judd and I can have a chat."

"I hate chats," he mumbled as he followed Ms. Sunshine outside. "The answer is still *no* and it will still be *no* next week, next year, next decade, next century."

Erika smiled to herself. Judd might have been a hard-ass commando, but he had agreed to let Kent do yard work after barking an adamant *no* at her a few days earlier. She would continue to chip away at his prickly armor. Eventually, he would come around to her way of thinking.

And *not,* she promised herself determinedly, in the next century! Despite what Judd thought, he *needed* her intervention in his reclusive life—and he needed it badly.

She watched Judd drag the push mower from the tool shed and give precise instructions for starting and operating the machine. When Kent didn't follow Judd's procedure to the letter, he had to begin again. The man was obviously particular, but Erika supposed strict attention to detail had kept him alive in his dangerous profession.

Erika's betraying gaze drifted over Judd's derriere when he squatted down on his haunches to set the throttle on the mower. Muscles bunched in his powerful arms and strained across the width of his shoulders that were covered by a threadbare white T-shirt.

Erika sighed in feminine appreciation. For the life of her she couldn't conjure up another man who exuded such masculinity and sex appeal. True, Judd's nose looked as if it had been broken at least once and the dark stubble that shadowed his face gave him a bad-boy appearance—but a very appealing bad-boy appearance. Also true, he didn't smile nearly as often as he should. He had a scar from a bullet hole above his left elbow and his raven hair was showing signs of gray at the temples, but still—

"Something wrong, Erika?"

She snapped to attention and felt a hot blush creeping up her neck to splash across her cheeks. Although he had caught her ogling him, she pasted on a beaming smile. "Just thinking."

His thick brows jackknifed, then he frowned. "That sounds dangerous. Try not to do it too often in my presence."

He turned back to give Kent a few more instructions. When Kent shoved the mower forward Judd monitored the boy's progress for a full minute before performing an about-face. His midnight-colored eyes bore into Erika as he approached and she inwardly sighed at the magnificent sight of him. No doubt about it, Judd Foster was a gorgeous hunk with high-voltage sex appeal who inspired all sorts of feminine fantasies.

"The answer is no," he repeated. "So don't even start. Got it?"

"Fine, but I have another proposition for you."

"I don't like being propositioned," he mumbled as he led the way to the house that was now so bright that he needed to wear sunglasses inside as well as outside. "I don't intend to invest or become a partner in your restaurant so don't give me any sales pitches. We're not discussing the cedar barn."

"Fine."

He glanced suspiciously at her. No argument? Now what was this little con artist up to? *"Fine?"* he repeated dubiously.

"Yes, fine. I still think you're making a colossal mistake because I had planned to pay you a premium for the property. But go ahead and shatter my dreams and trample them beneath your combat boots."

He made a stabbing gesture toward his feet. "In case you haven't noticed I traded in my combat boots for cowboy boots. Ranching is the name of my game these days."

"Fine, cowboy, but you are still crushing my dreams." She whizzed into the kitchen. "Do you have Coke or lemonade on hand? You'll want to take Kent something to drink in about fifteen minutes. This month has been unseasonably warm and he isn't accustomed to the heat. He's been working indoors with me."

"I'm supposed to provide the hired labor with food and drink?" he asked incredulously.

"Of course, it's the considerate thing to do."

She rummaged through his refrigerator and Judd cursed himself when his gaze zeroed in on her shapely behind. She had an especially nice, well-rounded butt. He wished he didn't keep noticing that.

"Here's a can of Coke. That will do for a rewarding treat, but lemonade would be better for Kent. Too much caffeine and he'll bounce off the walls. You can pick up other flavored fruit drinks when you go shopping. Or better yet," she said as she spun to face him, nearly blinding him with her radiant smile, "you can have your housekeeper do your shopping for you."

"I don't have a housekeeper," he reminded her.

"You will tomorrow," she assured him. "Thelma Pruitt desperately needs a part-time job to occupy her. She lost her only son in a traffic accident six months ago. Her husband died two years ago. She needs someone to care for, to fuss over."

"You're ambushing me again," he accused. "I've been ambushed before and this is exactly what it feels like, minus the live ammo."

She flicked her wrist dismissively. "Don't be so melodramatic. I'm only asking a small favor of you."

"You are trying to rope me into hiring another employee," he grumbled. "I don't want or need someone fussing over me. For heaven's sake, I'm thirty-four years old and I've dealt with a helluva lot more trouble than battling dust bunnies and planning a meal!"

"Don't get your briefs in a tangle," she teased him.

"I don't wear briefs," he flung back.

"It was just a figure of speech," she said, battling the visual image of Judd in military issue boxers—or better yet, nothing at all. Before she got sidetracked she focused on her topic of conversation and said, "Remember that you're doing Thelma a tremendous favor by giving her a job. She could use the extra money as well as the diversion. A couple of days a week for cleaning, laundry and meals that you can pop from the freezer to the oven won't kill you, will it? This will work great, trust me on this."

"No," Judd said stubbornly. "Absolutely not. I don't want Thelma Pruitt underfoot. Hell, I don't want a kid who's built like a scarecrow to mow the lawn, either!"

Erika shook her head in dismay. "I hope Kent can't hear you bellowing like a moose. He's such a sensitive kid. I have been doing my darnedest to boost his self-esteem. He receives the same kind of razzing at school that I used to endure. So naturally, I'm sympathetic. Anything you can do to teach him pride and confidence will be greatly appreciated."

She glanced at her watch then pivoted on her heels. "Gotta run. I have to pick up my friend's son. I'll swing by to get Kent before dark. That way you and Kent will have time for male bonding and you can tell him which jobs you want him to tackle during his next visit."

"One visit a week will be plenty," Judd insisted begrudgingly.

"No, it won't," she countered. "There's a decade of collected junk that needs to be loaded up and hauled off. But don't toss out any unique antiques that I might be able to use for decoration in my new restaurant. I'll be glad to pay you the going price for the treasures, of course."

He stared at her through narrowed eyes. "There will be no new restaurant on my property and no treasures for you to rummage through…"

His voice trailed off as she strode away. The woman moved faster than a car chase. Plus, watching her whiz around gave him a head rush. Plus, she had more energy than she knew what to do with. *Plus,* she needed a stint in boot camp so she would learn to obey orders.

Judd sighed audibly as he watched Erika move down the

sidewalk. That woman was something else. She never backed down and she never let up. She had bullied him again and he couldn't believe he had allowed her to get away with it.

A housekeeper? If she kept this up, it would be so crowded around here that he couldn't swing a dead cat without hitting an unwanted employee. He would have to pack up and move away to get some peace and quiet!

Yet, despite his frustration Judd grinned reluctantly. He had to admire the woman's spunk and persistence. He didn't have to like it, of course. Which he didn't. Very soon he was going to have to figure out how to stop her from intruding into his secluded world.

Judd walked off to fetch a drink for Kent before the kid wilted in the heat. He had the unshakable feeling he was losing control of his life. He had encountered an infuriating woman who left him torn between impulsively pulling her into his arms and pushing her away before she got too close.

Of all his difficult missions, he was pretty sure that dealing with the human tidal wave that went by the name of Erika Dunn was going to be one of his toughest assignments to complete.

Chapter Three

Four days later Erika climbed from her car and watched in awe as Judd put the roan gelding he was riding through its paces in the corral. Dressed in a body-hugging T-shirt, faded jeans and boots, he moved as one with the spirited horse he was training. The man was such an amazing athlete and so self-disciplined that he was bound to succeed at whatever he did.

She wondered what it was like to be blessed with so many natural talents.

When Judd noticed her coming toward the fence he reined to a halt and furrowed his brows suspiciously. "Now what? Or dare I ask?"

"I was hoping you could do me a favor," she requested.

With casual ease, Judd dismounted then strode toward her. "I'm kind of in the middle of the last two favors," he said as he gestured toward the recently mowed lawn. "Thelma is up at the house, cleaning everything that doesn't move. I had to get out of there before I was scrubbed and vacuumed."

Smiling in satisfaction, Erika ambled back to her car. She felt Judd's curious gaze on her as she hoisted two canvas sacks from the trunk. "Aunt Frannie and I are donating uniforms and new equipment to one of the Little League teams, but I can't take the stuff to practice tonight because I'm catering a birthday party. I was hoping you could drop it off in about an hour."

"You aren't going to give up, are you?"

Erika started when the deep baritone voice came from so close behind her. "You need to wear a bell. You have the uncanny knack of sneaking up on people."

He flashed her a rare grin that did strange things to her pulse. "It's what I do best." He glanced speculatively at the heaping bags that were filled with balls, bats, head gear and catcher's equipment. "This is the very last favor I'm doing for you," he announced.

"Of course, I wouldn't dream of asking anything else of you."

Judd snorted at that. "Doubt it. You strike me as the kind of woman who asks for the moon, expecting to come away with a pocket full of stars at the very least."

She shrugged, then heaved up one of the bags and toted it toward his four-wheel-drive pickup. "This favor is for an excellent cause. The team we sponsor might be short-handed on coaches, but I won't let the kids lack equipment."

"Whoa, whoa, *whoa*." With the second bag slung over his broad shoulder, Judd caught up with her in three quick strides. "Don't think for even one minute that you're going to maneuver me into coaching Little League baseball," he said darkly.

Erika stared innocently at him. "I didn't suggest any such thing. You're just the delivery boy here. If it doesn't matter to you that the youth in your hometown will never have the chance to become the star athlete you were then that's your business. I'm just doing my civic duty so the boys can dress the part, even if they can't *play* the part."

Judd dumped the bags in the truck bed, then rounded on her. "I've dealt with several pushy people in my day, lady, but you take the cake. Just so you know, you aren't going to prey on my conscience because I don't have one left."

Erika couldn't help herself. She chuckled at the stern expression on his handsome face. "You are such a liar, Foster. You care about people, even if I have yet to figure out why you're trying so hard not to. One day you're going to tell me."

"Don't hold your breath, Dunn," he countered.

"Ah, so you *do* admit that something's bothering you. Tell me what it is and I'll find a way to fix it."

"Just because you're the fairy princess of Moon Valley doesn't mean you can fix *me*," Judd murmured as he turned away. "Some things are unfixable."

Erika's heart went out to him, even if she didn't know precisely what caused the pain she saw glittering in his onyx eyes. Sooner or later, she would pry it out of him, for his own good. After all, it was her mission in life to see everyone else's fondest wishes come true. It was her compensation for being unable to enjoy her own whimsical dream of love and family.

The reflective thought caused Erika to shift uncomfortably. That was her problem, she mused. She had given up on her dreams of romance, a real home and a family of her own. She and Judd did have something in common. They had both given up on themselves. In his case, he had turned his disillusionment inward and she turned hers outward to spare others from the disappointment and feelings of inadequacy that niggled her. *She* hid behind a cheery smile; *Judd,* behind a scowl.

"Why are you looking at me like that?" Judd asked.

Erika blinked, unaware that she had been staring at Judd while plumbing the depths of her innermost thoughts. "No reason," she said dismissively. "Gotta go. Thanks again for running this errand for me. You're a real sweetheart."

"I'm nothing of the kind," he said as she turned on her heels and hurried away.

Just because the local fairy princess had tried to shame him into it Judd swore to himself that he wasn't getting involved with Little League. Thanks to Erika, he already had a kid showing up three evenings a week to mow and clean up the barn lot and outbuildings. He had a housekeeper underfoot three mornings a week.

Grumbling at his inability to tell Erika no—and mean it—Judd strode back to the corral to unsaddle his horse. He fed a few square hay bales to his calves, then jogged to the house to shower and change after Thelma left for the day.

An hour later he found himself surrounded by fifteen excited six-year-olds that were bouncing around him like Mexican jumping beans, anxious to get a look at their new uniforms and equipment.

Judd felt a tug on the hem of his shirt and glanced down into the familiar face that was capped with blond hair.

"Hi. Remember me? I'm Matt Vaughn. I was at your farm with Riki when we picked up Kent from work. Are you our new coach?"

Suddenly fifteen expectant young faces peered up at him. Judd heaved a defeated sigh. The do-gooder had struck again. "Yeah, I guess I am."

While the boys oohed and ahhed over the equipment

Judd glared at the mental image of red-blond hair, twinkling blue eyes and freckled nose that floated above him. "You're going to pay for this, *Riki,*" he muttered under his breath.

LATER THAT EVENING, Erika was flipping hamburgers when the bell over the café door jingled and a dusty, sweaty version of Judd Foster walked inside. She bit back a triumphant grin, aware that Judd hadn't been able to resist that endearing group of boys whose former coach had been laid up with a broken leg.

"Supper is on the house," Erika called as she pointed her utensil toward an empty booth. She watched in satisfaction as several of her customers stopped Judd to express their delight in having him back in the community. She was thankful that he had taken the initial steps to rejoin civilization rather than holing up on his ranch.

"Sit," Judd demanded when Erika turned the cooking duties over to Aunt Frannie and brought him a cold drink.

Erika sat. "If you plan to chew on me, why not try the bacon burger and fries instead?" she suggested. "Nothing like a hearty meal and cool drink to wash the infield dust from your mouth."

Not to be deterred, Judd wagged his index finger in her smiling face. "I—"

Judd clamped his mouth shut when Matt Vaughn and his mother halted beside the booth. "You probably don't remember me, Judd," Sylvie gushed as she reached out to pump his hand. "I was in Erika's class. I just wanted to stop by to thank you for coaching Matt's team." She glanced down to smile at her son. "He says he learned all sorts of cool stuff at practice."

Matt beamed and nodded enthusiastically. "We've got the best coach in the whole town."

"And the coolest uniforms, thanks to Erika and Frannie," Sylvie prompted.

"That, too," Matt chimed in. He flung himself into Erika's arms to give her a grateful hug then smiled at Judd. "See ya at the next practice, coach."

As mother and son walked away, Judd raked his hand through his disheveled hair and slumped tiredly in the booth. "You owe me, big time, for this."

"Admit it, Tex. Helping those kids gives you a warm fuzzy feeling," Erika challenged.

When she tried to rise, Judd grabbed her free hand, then released it abruptly because touching her gave him the warmest, fuzziest feeling of all. But he didn't want to get attached to the local do-gooder, even if he did lust after this woman who downplayed her femininity and had made no attempt whatsoever to encourage his attention.

Honestly, Judd didn't get it. He couldn't figure Erika out. She claimed she'd had a flaming crush on him during childhood, but she didn't seem interested in anything except taking him on as another of her charity cases. She even admitted that she thought he was attractive. He had never had trouble luring a woman; he just wasn't interested at this low point in his life. But still, what was with her?

"One last thing, Mother Theresa," Judd said as he watched Erika rise to her feet. "I'm finished being the extension of your goodwill. I have a ranch to put back on its feet and fields to work before planting crops. Thanks to you, I'm looking at three ball practices and a game night every week for two months. Do *not* do *me* any more favors that monopolize my time."

When Erika frowned pensively Judd squirmed on his seat. He could almost hear the cogs of her mind cranking—and that never boded well for him.

"You know what you need?"

"Yes, some peace, quiet and time to myself." He squinted at her. "But thanks to you, I'm not getting it."

She ignored his complaint. Nothing new there. "I have a few friends who would make great company during a night on the town. I could introduce you to—"

"No." He rejected the idea immediately.

"Just for dinner and a movie—"

"No," Judd butted in once again.

As usual, Erika wasn't easily discouraged. She gestured her head toward the attractive, well-dressed brunette who was eating alone. "Zoe Radburn operates the local driver's license and vehicle tag agency. She moved here about five years ago. She is really a nice lady."

"Good for her."

Erika called his attention to a shapely redhead who was chatting with an older man. "That's Patty Barker. She owns the flower shop and is raising two small children alone. You would like her, too, and her kids are really adorable."

"What about you?" Judd asked. "Who takes *you* out to dinner and a movie?"

She chuckled lightly. "I don't *do* movies, because I'm busy making dinner for everyone else. I'll be back with your food in a jiff."

And off she went, leaving Judd to wonder what kind of man a woman like Erika might find appealing. Not that he cared one way or another, he quickly reminded himself. He was just curious.

AUNT FRANNIE SMILED wryly when Erika returned to the kitchen to fill Judd's order. "Very impressive work, girl," she praised. "You have our local war hero out in public and socially involved."

"It wasn't easy," Erika confided as she dropped a patty and bacon on the grill.

"Better make that a double order," Frannie advised as she stared through the doorway to size up Judd. "I think a man like that can put away a lot of food."

He certainly could. Erika knew it for a fact. She dropped a second patty on the grill.

Frannie crossed her arms and ankles and leaned against the doorjamb to study Judd speculatively. After a moment she said. "He's The One, isn't he?"

Erika's usual precision of flipping burgers failed her. The patty ended up on the floor. "Well, damn."

Chuckling, Frannie grabbed a paper towel to clean up the mess. "That's what I thought. So what are you going to do about it, girl?"

"Nothing, just try to be his friend." Erika concentrated on her chore so another patty wouldn't end up on the floor. "If I can keep Judd from closing himself off from the world entirely I will have done my good deed for the month."

Frannie's gaze narrowed.

"You're twenty-eight. Just how long do you plan to live through the satisfaction of your charity cases?"

Erika was in the process of flipping the burger when Frannie's on-target insight caused her to flinch. The burger launched upward, hit the ceiling then plopped back to the grill. "Well, shoot."

"Gimme that utensil," Frannie ordered as she elbowed

Erika out of the way. "Check the fry basket and try not to dump the whole batch on the floor. Now then, take my advice and go after what you want with the same sense of purpose you apply to your good deeds."

Erika's shoulders slumped. "Why contend with defeat and rejection? It's safer this way. Less complicated."

Frannie pivoted toward her, looking more serious than Erika had ever seen her. "Don't make the same mistakes I did," she cautioned. "I used raising you as my excuse not to care or to get involved with anyone else after losing my fiancé. I took the safe way out, too, and all these years later what do I have to show for it? If I hadn't closed myself off you might have had a brother or sister and a real home life."

Erika tried to imagine what that might have been like.

"In retrospect, I realize I wasn't doing you or myself any favors," Frannie continued. "Don't wait until you're my age to realize you should have taken the risk. Here." She handed the utensil back to Erika. "My date has arrived and I'm going for the gusto while I still have some gusto left."

While Frannie peeled off her apron and hair net, Erika glanced toward the front door. Looking freshly shaved and scrubbed, Murph strolled over to ease onto the stool at the counter. His eyes lit up and he smiled when Frannie emerged from the kitchen. Erika could almost feel the sparks flying. Frannie's fashionable new do and a carefully applied coat of makeup appeared to have met with Murph's approval.

Frannie was putting out the effort, Erika realized as she watched the older couple exit. She wasn't sure she could do it, having never tried to attract a man. Her gaze landed on Judd, who was sprawled leisurely in the booth sipping his soda. The very thought of using her feminine wiles on him gave her a bad case of the jitters.

What feminine wiles? she asked herself as she toasted the hamburger buns. She would end up making a fool of herself if she made a romantic play for Judd. Besides, he would be a hard sell—whatever demon was hounding him made him as hesitant and reluctant to love as she was.

"Angie?" Erika called to the teenage waitress. "Deliver this order to Judd Foster."

Angie glanced around the café. "Who?"

Erika smiled in amusement as she pointed at Judd. *She* barely noticed anyone else while he was in the café. But at sixteen, Angie couldn't see past the two high school boys who were wolfing down burgers at table four.

While Angie delivered the order, Erika scraped off the grill. Since no new customers had arrived she ambled over to join Judd. And darn Frannie for putting romantic notions in her head. Now she felt like a nervous teenager and casual conversation escaped her. She didn't know how to interact with Judd. Thus far, she had been asking favors of him and he had stubbornly protested. What was she supposed to talk about? The weather? How lame was that?

"Good burger," Judd said between bites.

He wouldn't think so if she had served him the one that had momentarily stuck to the ceiling. "Thanks."

That's it? That's all you can think to say? Jeez, this was too hard. She fell back to more familiar ground. "Do you remember Ivan Snyder? He farmed north of town for years."

Judd eyed her warily. "Vaguely, yes. What about him?"

"Well, I was thinking—"

"I thought I asked you not to do that around me," he grumbled, then popped two French fries in his mouth.

"He's widowed and retired. His son and daughter live

out of state and rarely come to visit. He's such a dear, sweet man and he's lonely out there all by himself," she said, warming to her sudden inspiration. "Now that you're involved with baseball, Ivan is the perfect candidate to check on your livestock. He's a wealth of knowledge when it comes to animals. I could bring him by your farm and he could—"

Judd flung up his hand to demand silence. "Stop right there. How many more charity cases do you have lined up for me?"

Erika thought it over for a moment and said, "This is the very last one, I promise. Ivan is wonderful company. I'll bring him out in the morning when he comes in for coffee break." She beamed enthusiastically. "This will be perfect. Ivan can show up the same days as Thelma and the three of you can dine together. It will give Ivan and Thelma a chance to get to know each other better and you'll still have your privacy four days a week."

"I don't need a built-in family," Judd muttered. "Why are you so determined to give me one?"

Because it's what I would wish for myself if I hadn't already made this community my extended family. Erika kept the thought to herself and shrugged. "Because it will bring you out of your blue funk, cowboy. And now might be a good time for you to tell me what is really bothering you and has kept you isolated at your ranch."

"No," he said very deliberately, "it's not. There will never be a good time for that."

"Fine then." Erika popped up like a jack-in-the-box. "But at least top off supper with a piece of slice-of-heaven pie. Sugar, whipped cream and chocolate is a surefire deterrent for depressing thoughts."

Judd muttered under his breath when Erika trotted off, her ponytail bobbing behind her. Hell and damnation. He'd let that woman pawn off another dependent and he had barely put up a fuss this time.

At least Ivan Snyder would serve a useful purpose. Judd was the first to admit that he had been away from the ranch for years and that agricultural practices had changed. Ivan could update him. The man probably knew a lot about repair and maintenance of machinery. With ground to work in preparation for the fall wheat crop Judd could use a tractor driver—like young Kent Latham—and someone—namely Ivan—to train him while Judd was coaching baseball.

Heaving a sigh, Judd slouched in his seat and asked himself how he had gotten in so deep so fast. He hadn't had enough time to himself the past few days to brood over the loss of Steve Carlton, a friend who had become closer than his own brother. They had been together through thick and thicker for a decade. It wasn't right to let his memory go in just a few months. Especially when it should have been the other way around. It was Steve who—

His gloomy thoughts scattered when Erika returned with her heavenly antidote for a man who was wading through his hellish past.

"This will make you feel better." Erika set the mouthwatering dessert in front of him. "Guaranteed."

Judd took a bite and swore he had never tasted anything quite like the fluffy pastry that melted on his tongue and had his taste buds offering a standing ovation.

"My specialty," Erika declared, staring anxiously at him. "You like?"

"Mmm," was the best he could do at the moment. He swore she had added some sort of euphoric ingredient. Although his mother had been a good cook, she couldn't compete with this. "I think I'm addicted," he murmured after the third bite.

"Enjoy." Erika spun around when the bell jingled over the door, signaling the arrival of another customer. "I'll see you in the morning."

Judd didn't object. Couldn't. He was too busy devouring the most scrumptious dessert he had ever tasted. Erika's culinary talents almost made up for her habit of dumping dependents on his doorstep to crowd his private space.

Almost.

THREE DAYS LATER Judd was in the process of replacing the rotted boards on the corral when Ivan Snyder reported for work, driving his old pickup with a trailer attached to the bumper. Frowning curiously, Judd set aside his hammer and walked toward Ivan.

"Hey, Judd, gorgeous day, isn't it?" Ivan climbed from his pickup and adjusted the straps of his pinstriped bib overalls. Then he gestured his gray head toward the corral. "You might want to reinforce that fence with steel panels," he recommended. "You know how nervous cattle get when you pen them up and sort them out in confined spaces."

"Good idea, I'll do that." Judd glanced toward the trailer. "What are you hauling, Ivan?"

"Riki asked me to drop off a horse for her." He shrugged casually. "She said something about this mare being part of her restaurant's petting zoo. She also said you would know what she was talking about, even if I didn't."

Silently fuming at the woman's audacity, Judd stalked around the trailer to get a better look at the animal Erika was trying to pawn off on him. His eyes widened in shock when he found himself staring at an aging swaybacked gray mare.

"I'll unload her in the pasture," Ivan offered as he climbed back into his pickup.

"Unbelievable!" Judd darted forward before Ivan could back the trailer to the gate. "Where is she?" he muttered in question.

"Who? Riki?" When Judd nodded curtly, Ivan hitched his thumb toward town. "She's at Moon Valley Park. The community garage sale is Saturday. She's delivering donations. This is the annual fund-raiser to purchase protective suits for our volunteer fire department."

"She is not going to get away with this," Judd vowed as he whipped around and stamped toward his pickup.

He was going to drive to the park and lay down the law to that presumptuous female. Erika had erroneously presumed that he was eventually going to sell his barn to her and that he wouldn't object to stabling that pitiful excuse of a horse until then.

She had browbeaten him into hiring unneeded employees, but she wasn't going to pull *this* fast one on him, he promised himself as he whizzed into town.

Bounding from his pickup, Judd panned the park to see Erika's red-blond ponytail bobbing behind her as she carried a box to one of the tables that had been set up beneath the pavilion. Neck bowed, he cut through the crowd, nodding silent greetings to former acquaintances as he made a beeline toward her.

"I *told* you no more favors," he breathed down her neck. "That swayback horse belongs in a glue factory."

Erika squawked in surprise when he barked at her abruptly. "Oh, hi, Judd." She pivoted to flash him one of her trademark smiles, but he refused to reciprocate.

"Don't 'Hi, Judd' me," he muttered.

He grabbed the box from her arms, then carried it over to drop it on one of the tables. Then he clutched her arm and steered her toward a shade tree so he could bite her head off in private. Before he could lay down the law to her, she flung up her hand to deter him.

"First of all, I know that horse doesn't look like much—"

"I'll say it doesn't," he cut in caustically.

"But Old Nell is reported to be the gentlest, most well-mannered mare in the county, so naturally I bought her," she explained. "She is perfect for kids because she was owned by a family with four children."

Judd braced his arm against the tree and leaned forward. Big mistake. He caught a whiff of that tempting perfume she always wore. Then his traitorous gaze dropped to those soft, lush lips—and he scowled at his inability to remain focused on the reason for his hasty trip into town.

His blood pressure shot up immediately when he noticed Erika was paying the same fascinated attention to his mouth.

He let out his breath with an irritated sigh. "What in the hell am I going to do about you?" he said, more to himself than to her.

Erika barely heard the question. He was so close she was practically breathing him in. His nearness elevated her pulse in the time it took to blink and she suddenly had trouble swallowing. Honest to goodness, she wanted to kiss him so badly that she could barely stand it.

This was irony for you, she thought. Even though Judd would never be interested in her, she had never been interested in anyone but him. To make matters worse, Frannie had been harping at her all week to make a play for Judd. The last thing Erika needed was to be reminded that her Mr. Right was right under her nose—and just a kiss away.

Shaking herself loose from her rambling thoughts, Erika focused on the subject at hand. "I will gladly pay you to keep Old Nell at your ranch until I can make other arrangements," she squeaked, her voice nowhere near as steady as she would have preferred.

"It goes without saying that you will be expected to make other arrangements," he said, a hitch in his voice.

When he pushed away, Erika half collapsed against the tree. This man had such a potent impact on her senses that it took the longest time to recover after having him so close.

"I'll keep that horse temporarily," he said grudgingly as he looked the other way. "But this is not permanent."

Impulsively, Erika pushed up on tiptoe to press a fleeting kiss to his clenched jaw—and told herself to be satisfied with the slightest physical contact. It was all she would ever get from him, she knew. "Thanks, Judd…and since you're here…"

He eyed her suspiciously as she turned to retrieve the pup that was tied up to one of the park benches. Judd had the sinking feeling that she intended to foist off the ugly mutt on him, too.

"Hold it right there," he insisted.

Erika stopped short and cuddled the pathetic excuse for a canine to her chest. "You can look into these sad eyes and say *no* to your future watchdog? And what about those two adorable kittens I purchased in hopes of ridding your barn of mice?"

Judd glanced toward the box she indicated to see two

yellow feline heads rising above the rim of cardboard. His shoulders slumped and he huffed out an agitated breath. "Well, hell."

"You know I have a soft spot in my heart for rejects, being one myself."

She smiled hopefully at him and, idiot that he was, he caved. But pride made him say, "Okay, but this is it. I'm not kidding around. No more employees. No more pets. I want your promise right now."

Erika smiled triumphantly at him. "Sure, whatever you say, Judd."

"Whatever I say? Hell!" He scowled as she handed him the mutt that had paws the size of coffee mugs. The animal was going to grow up to be as big as a Shetland pony, he was sure.

"I'll provide all the feed needed," she insisted before she strode over to pluck up the box of kittens.

Laden down with pets that he didn't want, Judd spun toward his pickup.

"I'll bring food for your supper and a stockpile of feed tonight," she called after him. "And Judd?"

He halted to glance over his shoulder and saw her smiling radiantly at him. That smile of hers was his Waterloo, he thought defeatedly. "What?"

"Thank you. I really appreciate this."

"Yeah, sure. Can't wait to get home and trip over my new pets."

Having said that, he stalked off.

Fifteen minutes later he wheeled into his driveway to see that Ivan had taken up the chore of hammering new boards to the corral posts. Ivan glanced up and grinned wryly as he watched Judd tote his new pets to the barn lot.

"You really told her off good, didn't you?" Ivan said while he stared pointedly at the dog and kittens.

"Damn sure did." Judd snatched up the hammer and took his frustration out on the nail that he secured in the two-by-six. "That'll teach her to mess with me."

Ivan snickered as he went back to work on the corral. "Good thing you put your foot down—quick and hard. Otherwise, this place would be crawling with a dozen dogs and cats. I'd say you got off lucky, son."

Judd decided Ivan was probably right.

Chapter Four

Two weeks after the community garage sale, Erika was ready for a vacation that took her miles away from Moon Valley—and Aunt Frannie in particular. Since the night of The Lecture, as Erika referred to it, Frannie had been on a personal crusade to push Erika at Judd and to mention his name in every other paragraph of conversation.

If that wasn't bad enough, Frannie had decided that a change in Erika's appearance might draw Judd's attention.

"This is a bad idea," Erika protested as Aunt Frannie shoveled her out of the kitchen and frog-marched her through the dining room of the café.

"It's an excellent idea," Frannie contradicted. "The appointment for your makeover has been set up and paid for. It's my birthday gift to you. Now go!"

"My birthday isn't for another month," Erika reminded her.

"And we're going to see the new you before you turn twenty-nine. Don't argue with me." She flashed a determined glare. "Maybe you can alter your stick-in-the-mud behavior if you alter your appearance. It worked for me."

Erika tried to object, but Frannie closed the door in her face and lurched toward the kitchen.

This was not going to work, Erika mused as she hiked down the street to Do or Dye Salon. She had been wearing the same ponytail since she was ten years old. It was familiar. It was comfortable. It was timesaving.

Hesitantly, Erika stepped into the salon to see Roxanne Dorche, the local cosmetology expert, waving the tools of her trade like Edward Scissorhands.

"Park it, hon. Boy, do I have a do for you!" Roxanne said as she champed on her gum. "I've wanted to get my hands on that hair of yours for years." Beaming with anticipation, she gestured toward her assistant, Twila Franks. "Then I'm turning Twila loose to give you a makeover that has been a long time in coming. 'Bout time we had the chance to repay you for all the nice things you've done for us through the years."

Wondering if she would recognize herself when the cosmo-duo finished with her, Erika reluctantly parked herself in the chair. "Nothing too drastic," she requested.

Roxanne glanced conspiratorially at Twila. "Right, hon. Whatever you say."

And then she went to work.

SHELL-SHOCKED, Erika emerged from the salon two hours later. She had sat through a highlighting session that left so much tin foil in her hair that she swore she was picking up satellite signals. She had inhaled perm vapors until she was light-headed. Her red-gold hair—which had hung straight down her back for years—was now a riot of curls that brushed her shoulders and glistened with strands of platinum blond. Coiled corkscrews surrounded her face, which had expertly applied makeup that concealed the freckles on her nose and accentuated the length of her lashes and the color of her eyes. Roxanne had even insisted that she put on a clinging cotton blouse that accentuated the fullness of her breasts and exposed her midsection.

The beauticians had raved over the transformation, but Erika barely recognized the reflection staring back at her in the mirror. She looked seductively glamorous, but that had never been the look Erika strived to attain.

How were you supposed to *act* when you didn't *look* like yourself?

"That's what I thought," Frannie exclaimed when Erika came through the café door. "A diamond emerging from the rough. You look fabulous!"

Erika was eternally grateful that it was early afternoon and the café was empty. She was not prepared to face customers who would undoubtedly ask who she was trying to fool with this ridiculous transformation.

"I feel like an impostor," Erika muttered as Frannie studied her critically then gave her two thumbs up.

"You look like a million bucks," Frannie insisted.

When the door opened, Erika inwardly flinched and refused to spin around to offer her customer the usual greeting smile. She wanted to dash to her apartment, wash the permanent from her hair before it set and scrub her face squeaky-clean.

"Good afternoon, Judd. What can I get for you?" Frannie asked, grinning wickedly.

Erika, her back to the door, wished the floor would open so she could sink out of sight. Of all the customers who might have arrived, why did it have to be *him?* Humiliated and self-conscious beyond words, she scurried toward the kitchen.

"Erika? Is that you?"

She halted in her tracks. It took all the gumption she could muster to turn around and face him. She expected Judd to burst out laughing at the outrageous transformation that didn't suit her. Inhaling a fortifying breath, Erika pivoted around and lifted her chin, double-dog-daring him to comment.

Judd's dark eyes popped and his brows nearly rocketed off his forehead. He gaped at her for a long moment, then he said, "What the hell happened to you?"

Thoroughly crushed, she watched Judd's astonished gaze turn into a pained grimace when Frannie elbowed him in the ribs. "What was that for?" he croaked.

"For sticking your cowboy boot in your mouth," Frannie muttered sourly. "I gave my daughter a birthday make-over and that's the best you can come up with?" She glanced at Erika. "Put a lethal dose of poison in his order. I'll gladly pay for his funeral." She threw up her hands in annoyance. "Men!"

Judd could have kicked himself all the way into next week for blurting out that thoughtless comment. He hadn't believed it possible to hurt Erika's feelings because she usually came on like gangbusters, despite what he said to her. But in his defense, he had been totally unprepared for the startling transformation from cute girl-next-door to out-of-this-world hottie.

Truth was, he didn't want to see her as a knockout because he had been unwillingly attracted to her from the moment she came to his ranch. That had been bad enough. This was worse. She looked sexy and sultry and that strapless thingamabob that showcased her cleavage and midriff put all sorts of unacceptable ideas in his head.

When Erika spun around and disappeared into the

kitchen, Frannie elbowed him again, harder this time. "Don't stand there, you dummy," she scowled. "Go tell her she looks gorgeous and that you approve of her makeover. If you don't I'll take you apart with my bare hands, former hotshot commando or not!"

Since Frannie looked as if she meant to do him bodily harm—and knowing she had access to a kitchen full of sharp knives—Judd went after Erika.

"GIVE ME YOUR ORDER," Erika said without turning to face him.

Judd noticed that she had slipped a denim shirt over that skin-tight garment that accentuated her shapely physique. Thank goodness.

"I'm sorry," Judd said awkwardly. "It's just that I had this certain image of you—and wham. It changed so abruptly that you caught me off guard."

She glanced sideways at him and he noticed the hint of tears in her eyes before she snapped her head around. He felt like a world-class heel. Maybe he should be mollified by hurting her feelings after she had exasperated him repeatedly, but he wasn't as mean-spirited as he had wanted her to think when she began dropping by his ranch to make an offer for his barn and pester him out of seclusion.

"What do you want to eat?" Erika demanded, and he thought he heard a muffled sniffle in the middle of the question.

"For starters, fried crow and humble pie. No kidding, Erika, I'm really sorry. You look…uh…" He scrambled for the appropriate compliment. "Breathtaking."

"Right. Moon Valley Barbie. Restaurant debutante," she

muttered as she slapped several burgers on the grill. "I'm making this order *to go*."

"Good. I'm feeding the family you rounded up for me. Thelma is washing miniblinds and windows. Ivan and Kent are helping me inoculate and brand cattle."

She slapped several more patties on the grill, then stalked over to dump an oversize pile of fries in the basket. She didn't look in his direction or say another word. Judd shifted awkwardly from one booted foot to the other, then glanced over his shoulder to see Frannie poised by the door, glaring pitchforks at him.

"Have dinner with me tonight so I can make it up to you," he said impulsively.

"No. Absolutely not."

Damn, she sounded as stubborn as he once had.

"C'mon, Erika, just this one small favor," he cajoled. "It's not as if I haven't done several favors for you lately."

"Give Patty Barker or Zoe Radburn a call." With swift precision she flipped the burgers, then smeared butter on the buns. "I'm adding an extra hamburger for Kent. We need to fatten him up."

"Erika…" he said with a sigh.

"Frannie! Get him out of the kitchen," Erika called out suddenly. "Surely we're violating several codes by having him in the work area." She hitched her thumb over her shoulder. "Get out and stay out."

Judd got out. When he passed Frannie she tried to vaporize him with another nuclear glower. He was definitely out of practice in dealing with females, he mused. All the more reason that he should have kept to himself.

It was Erika's fault. She had dragged him back into society before he was damn good and ready. Now look where it got him. In trouble with the town's do-gooder.

Five minutes later, Frannie exited from the kitchen with three brown paper sacks—and another murderous glare. "I'm charging you double for the order," she growled menacingly. "Got a problem with that?"

"Uh...no," Judd mumbled, then ventured a placating smile. "Which burgers are laced with poison? Sure would hate to serve one to my hired hands when it was meant for me."

To his relief, Frannie's ruffled feathers settled back into place and she managed the semblance of a smile. "I let you off easy this time, bud. Consider yourself *very* lucky."

Judd wheeled around and hurried away, mentally kicking himself all the way to his pickup. He was going to have to figure out how to compensate for his blunder. Having Erika mad at him felt unnatural. And damn it, he didn't really want to be at odds with her. The fact was that he liked her, even if he was careful not to let it show or to act on his lust.

ERIKA WAS ENORMOUSLY GRATEFUL that the other customers who showed up for the evening meal offered only complimentary comments about her new appearance.

Too bad the one man whose opinion mattered more than it should have wasn't impressed with her new image. *What the hell happened to you?* His words rang in her ears and cut to the quick. Damn it, he could have talked all day without saying that!

Frannie's early-bird birthday gift had accomplished one thing, Erika thought as she served up another platter of mesquite-flavored brisket. She knew for a fact that Judd

Foster wasn't physically attracted to either version of herself: girl-next-door or Moon Valley Barbie.

This was a shining example of why you shouldn't tamper with unattainable dreams. Erika knew she should stick to cooking because she was a shameless failure in the romance department. This was the absolute last time she was going to allow herself to think in terms of love, marriage and family with Judd—despite Frannie's recent lectures.

"Done with romance," Erika murmured as she closed and locked the front door of the café for the night. She might look different, but that didn't change who she was on the inside. She had always been everybody's friend and no one's lover—she just had to deal with it.

Still mentally sticking pins into Judd, Erika walked outside to clean the large smoker housed in the shed behind the restaurant. Hunched over, vigorously scrubbing the metal racks, she heard a shuffling noise behind her. Suddenly the overhead light flicked off, plunging the shed into darkness.

"What the—?" Her voice dried up when two darkly clad figures pounced on her. Her breath came out in a whoosh and she groaned when she was knocked off balance. She skidded across the concrete floor, ripping her jeans and skinning her knees.

Erika's attention shifted from the pain in her knees to the spitting end of the pistol pressed against her neck.

"Get up, lady," the man said in a gruff voice.

Before she could react the man jerked her upright abruptly. His hand bit into her forearm. He kept the pistol barrel pressed against the base of her neck while he shepherded her into the café. In the dimly lit room she saw two faces, concealed by black-and-orange ski masks, looming over her.

"Where do you keep the money?" the other intruder demanded as he pointed his handgun at her face.

"Under the counter," she said shakily.

Her life kept flashing before her eyes until the burly-looking thief lowered his pistol. He darted around the tables to rummage beneath the counter. A moment later he raised the zippered leather pouch, then tucked it inside his dark jacket in triumph.

Erika's heart sank. There was three days' worth of cash in the bag. She hadn't had time to make a bank deposit because she'd been away from the restaurant, catering several parties this week. These thugs had picked the worst of all possible nights to rob Blue Moon Café.

"What's that?"

Erika realized belatedly that the man holding her at gunpoint was gesturing toward the leftover brisket she had wrapped in aluminum foil. "Just food."

"We'll take that, too," her captor told his partner. "And get that pie while you're at it. And don't forget her purse. It has to be around here somewhere."

Quick as a scurrying rat, the second thief rounded up the food and grabbed her purse from under the counter.

Erika waited with a sense of fatalistic gloom, wondering if she had done enough good deeds to gain entrance into the Pearly Gates. This was it, she predicted. The curse of the birthday makeover had struck full force. She was a goner.

Her captor pulled a roll of duct tape from his pocket and ripped off a strip. He covered her mouth, then bound up her wrists and ankles. Anchored to a chair in the middle of the café Erika watched the thieves sprint out the back door. She heard two car doors open and shut, but no headlights glared off the windows as her car, and the get-away car, peeled down the alley.

Her mind raced, trying to remember what victims were supposed to do when their wallets were stolen. Checkbook, credit card, social security number. It was all gone and she couldn't get to a phone to call for help or stop payment. She would probably become the victim of identity theft, too.

A sob escaped her lips as pent-up emotion erupted like Old Faithful. She had been scared half to death by those thugs—only a few hours after being thoroughly humiliated by Judd's reaction to her makeover.

"Perfect ending to a perfectly miserable day," she mumbled into her gag.

Chapter Five

Sprawled in his recliner, his hand curled around the remote control to the TV, Judd jerked awake when the phone blared. Bleary-eyed, he glanced at the clock. Who was calling him at eleven? This was only the second time his phone had rung since he had moved in.

"'Lo," he said drowsily.

"Judd, this is Francine Albright," came the urgent voice. "Is Riki there?"

"No." Judd levered himself upright in his chair. "Did she tell you that she was coming out here?"

"No, I just thought she might have decided to strangle you after she closed up the café," Francine replied. "I called her apartment after Murph and I came back from our date, but she didn't answer. I called ten minutes later, in case she had been in the shower, but I got voice mail again. I wanted to make sure she was okay after you made fun of her."

"I did not make fun of her," Judd said succinctly.

"You didn't do anything for her self-esteem, either," Francine snapped.

No, he hadn't and he had been chewing himself down one side and up the other for demoralizing Erika.

"Well, maybe she decided to work off her frustration by cleaning the café from top to bottom. Murph and I will run downtown and check it out."

"No, I'll go." Judd vaulted from his chair and grabbed his keys. "It will give me a chance to apologize without you breathing down my neck."

"Call me the minute you get there so I'll know she's okay," Francine demanded.

Judd tossed the phone on the chair and hurried off. During the short drive to town Judd rehearsed his apology. Admittedly, he didn't know all that much about women. His former career hadn't been conducive to meaningful relationships—not unless you counted a three-day weekend visit twice a year as a relationship.

How Steve Carlton had managed to have a wife and child when he was out of the country so often was still a marvel to Judd. And now there would be no more long-awaited homecomings for Steve.

Judd squelched the depressing thought and focused on his upcoming encounter with Erika. He assumed there would be a certain amount of groveling required if he was to return to Erika's good graces.

Wheeling into the empty parking lot, Judd strode to the front door. Dim light illuminated the café. He could see Erika in the middle of the diner, her head down on the table. He rapped on the glass door to gain her attention.

When she raised her head he saw the gray tape over the lower portion of her peaked face and he erupted in foul curses. Fear and concern plowed through him as he hiked up his foot and kicked at the door. When that didn't work, he grabbed the wooden park bench beside the oversize flowerpot and used it as a battering ram. The whole time

Erika shook her fuzzy head at him, but he was too intent on getting to her to puzzle out her signal.

On the third heave-ho glass shattered around him. He reached through the jagged hole to unlock the door. Judd rushed toward her, noting she was still shaking her head at him and gesturing her bound hands toward the back door. Judd skidded to a halt, crouched down, then glanced in the direction she pointed. He reflexively reached for the handgun in his shoulder holster—and remembered he wasn't armed because carrying concealed weapons was part of his *former* life.

The back exit was standing wide open. He had demolished Erika's front door for no good reason. Well, there was a good reason, he silently amended as he hurried toward her. He had been frightened for her and getting to her immediately was foremost on his mind. Plus, she looked so rattled and betrayed that it blew him wide open. He felt the overwhelming need to comfort and protect her.

Judd peeled the tape off her mouth. The blotchy condition of her face indicated she had been crying. "Are you okay?"

"No, I'm not okay," she muttered as she held up her bound hands to him. "I was robbed!" Her voice hit a shrill pitch. "They took my purse, my car, my money!"

Tortured blue eyes lifted to him as he quickly freed her wrists. "Why'd they do that?" she asked in a quaking voice. "I would have given them whatever they needed, just for the asking!"

"Everything's okay," Judd soothed. "Just calm down."

"Calm down?" she howled. "*Calm down!* I thought I was about to die! *You* might be used to staring death in the face, but *I'm* not and I can't stop shaking!"

Mascara bled down her cheeks. Her hair was a ball of frizz

thanks to the humid spring air. Judd had never seen Erika look quite so vulnerable. Or adorable. He felt the instinctive need to hug her close and console her, but she shrank away from him, as if she just remembered that she was aggravated with him for hurting her feelings this afternoon.

"Go call 911," she demanded as she raked a trembling hand through her fuzzy hair.

"In a minute." Judd sank down on his haunches to unwrap her ankles, then noticed the rips in her jeans and caked blood on her knees. His alarmed gaze flew back to her splotchy face. "What did they do to you?"

"Shoved me down on the cement floor in the smoker shed and stuffed a pistol in my neck," she said, and scowled. "Who were those guys? Don't they know this is the first place they could come for a handout if they needed food or money? They didn't have to rough me up!"

When her voice broke on a sob, Judd pulled her to her feet and into his arms. He held her close, aware that she was still shaking violently in the aftermath of the terrifying assault. He had the uneasy feeling that it would be a while before Erika-the-do-gooder recaptured her trusting, kind-hearted spirit.

"Everything is going to be fine, I promise," he murmured against the crown of her curly head. "If I get my hands on those bastards I'll pound them into putty for robbing and scaring you."

Erika's attempt to hold on to her crumbling composure failed her completely. She disgraced herself by collapsing in Judd's comforting embrace and accidentally smearing mascara on his white T-shirt. Tears overcame her again and she burst into sobs.

It occurred to her that her secret dream of being held in

Judd's embrace had not once in all these years entailed her blubbering all over him while he offered compassion. Her fantasy had shattered like the glass on her front door.

"I'll go make the calls," he murmured as his lips grazed her forehead. "Sit down and I'll bring you something to drink."

Humiliated, disillusioned and on a downhill adrenaline slide, Erika wilted back to the chair—or tried to. She would have sprawled inelegantly on the floor if Judd hadn't grabbed her arm to guide her to the seat.

Mortification avalanched on her and her shoulders slumped. She was falling apart. She almost never fell apart. She wasn't helpless or clumsy. Not usually. But she had gone to pieces and Judd was here to bear witness.

Damnation, could anything else possibly go wrong today?

"Take a deep breath," Judd insisted when he returned with a cola.

Erika did as she was told without raising her gaze. She couldn't bear to see another round of sympathy in Judd's dark eyes. To him, she was only one of the hapless victims he had rescued over the years. God, could she *feel* any worse?

"Now drink."

Dutifully, she took the cup and gulped.

"Now take another deep breath."

This was just too much on top of everything else. Her emotions were all over the place and she couldn't take it anymore. She raised her watery gaze and visually skewered him. "Leave me alone and go make the damn calls. I don't need you telling me when to breathe and when not to!"

A wry smile quirked Judd's lips as he rose from a crouch. "You're back to being mad at me. Good. I'd rather deal with that." He brushed his thumb over her cheek, rerouting the tears. "I'm really sorry about what I said this afternoon. You really do look cute."

"Cute?" she snorted, highly offended. "I look hideous. Mascara has to be forming dark circles under my eyes. My makeup is undoubtedly smeared every which way on my face and the half bottle of super-duper styling gel that Roxanne caked in my hair feels as sticky as chewing gum. And you have the nerve to tell me I look *cute* after I've been robbed? How naive and gullible do you think I am?"

"Well, not *now*," Judd amended hurriedly. "But earlier. You were real cute."

"Cute is for kittens and puppies," she snarled at him.

All that saved her from hurling her cola at him was the fact that he had the good sense to lurch around and dash to the phone. Simmering like a pot of stew, Erika gulped down her drink and glowered at Judd while he made the calls to the sheriff's office and Aunt Frannie.

On wobbly legs, Erika headed for the rest room to wash her face and tie a band around her frizzy hair. She was definitely going to wash out this perm from hell before the recommended twenty-four hours. She could not deal with this hairdo disaster on top of everything else.

"ROBBED?" Francine howled when Judd gave her the news over the phone. "I've only been robbed once in my twenty-nine years in business. Is Riki all right? Did they hurt her?"

"She's fine." More or less, Judd silently amended. "Scraped knees and ripped jeans. She's a little rattled and hugely disappointed in humanity, but that's only to be expected."

"I'll be there in two shakes," Frannie said.

The line went dead. Judd heaved a sigh and wished he could get his hands on the thugs that had upset Erika. He hoped the cops caught the bastards pronto. Too bad the cops couldn't turn them over to him for a few hours. He would like to give them a crash course on the wrong end of special ops training.

His spiteful thoughts trailed off when Erika emerged from the rest room. Her face was devoid of makeup. The freckles on her nose were visible again. Her hair was bound up in a lopsided ponytail and the knees of her jeans were wet from dabbing water on her scraped skin. She shot him a quick glance, then flounced on the chair to chew the ice in her cup. Judd kept his distance since that seemed to be what she preferred.

A few minutes later, the shattered door opened and Francine, with Murph hot on her heels, exploded into the café. "Oh, baby, are you okay?"

While Francine fussed over Erika, and Murph gave her a there-there pat on the shoulder, Judd watched flashing lights reflect off the plate glass windows. The county deputy strode inside to introduce himself to Judd. Then David Shore headed toward Erika.

No doubt about it, Judd mused. The cop had a sentimental attachment to Erika. There was nothing impersonal about his manner. Although David was professional about taking the statement, the consoling pats indicated he knew Erika personally and was fond of her. But then, who wasn't? The woman was the pulse beat of this community. The fairy godmother of Moon Valley.

"Cordon off the café?" Erika wailed in response to the deputy's comment. "Aren't you overreacting here? What evidence could they possibly have left behind? And what

about our customers? I have two dinners to cater this weekend. I can't cancel at this late date!"

Judd strolled over to interject a comment. "We can handle that at my ranch. The old smoker in the barn isn't state-
of-the art, but it still works. You can also use my kitchen."

Erika shot him a disgruntled glance. "Thanks, but no
thanks."

"Great idea," Francine enthused. "And I don't think
Riki should be left alone tonight either. Do you, Judd? She
had quite a scare. She might as well stay at your house if
she's going to be cooking out there in the morning. I'll
swing by her apartment and grab a suitcase of clothes
while Dave is wrapping up this investigation. Murph and
I will take care of everything. Be right back."

Judd frowned, bemused by the faint smile on Frannie's
face, but she hurried off before he could figure out what
the smile meant.

"You could stay with Sylvie," David suggested gently.
"She will probably insist when I tell her what happened."

"It's late. No need to bother anyone else," Judd inserted.
"I'll take care of her."

"Why? You don't even like me that much," Erika
pointed out. "I'll just stay with Aunt Frannie."

"I like you fine," Judd declared.

He liked her a lot more than fine. That was the problem.
He had been fighting the attraction from day one. Sure, he
had shrugged it off as a lust attack, caused by his self-imposed celibacy. He hadn't wanted to get involved with anything or anyone until he worked through his guilt and grief.
Yet, Erika had been there for him—whether he liked it or
not—and now he would do the same for her.

"As soon as we can re-enter the café, I'll clean up the

mess I made of the door and help you do whatever needs done." Judd waited a beat then said, "C'mon, Erika, you can't stay with Francine. In case you haven't noticed, there's something going on between her and Murph. For sure, he wants to be there to console her. You know I have plenty of room in the house. You can even fling open all the blinds and take over the place the way you usually do when you come barging in."

The comments prompted a hint of a smile. He could tell she was giving his offer consideration.

"After all, what are friends for?" he added.

"Okay," she said eventually. "But you'll have to stay out of my way while I'm cooking."

He held up his hands in supplication. "No problem. I can do that."

"Are you sure about this, Erika?" David questioned as he flicked Judd a wary glance. "This is a good way to incite gossip in a small town."

Judd wanted to kick the cop in the seat of the pants for planting seeds of doubt. But he didn't want to spend the night in the slammer for assaulting a police officer. He stared at Erika, silently willing her to agree. Gossip be damned.

Erika peered up at Judd, aware that he felt sorry for her, aware that he felt guilty about hurting her feelings earlier. She should go home alone and tough it out. But the offer to cater from his spacious kitchen was logical and sensible, even if she had to deal with his unwanted sympathy. It beat the heck out of trying to prepare two large meals in her cramped apartment.

"Just don't complain when I take over, cowboy. Remember, *you* offered," she said.

David requested her attention again, asking her for a description of the robbers. When the ordeal of rehashing the incident, in detail, was over, Erika breathed a wobbly sigh and struggled to regather her composure. After Frannie delivered the suitcase, Erika walked over to retrieve her purse from under the counter. Her hand stalled in midair when she remembered her purse was gone, along with her car and the till.

Judd apparently noticed her distress and guessed the cause of it because he strode over to take her arm and grab the suitcase. "Don't worry about anything right now. We'll take care of the necessary calls. You can borrow my truck whenever you need it."

"Don't be so nice to me," she grumbled as he escorted her outside. "I don't know how to respond."

He stopped short and glanced down at her. "Was I really that bad?"

She wanted to tell him that even while he was being distant, remote and impossibly stubborn she still thought he was wonderful. But the words refused to tumble off her tongue. She felt too self-conscious and unsure of herself as a woman to blurt out her feelings. Better to stick with what she knew best. Playful teasing.

"You were worse than a grizzly bear. If not for my strong constitution I would have run scared when you growled at me."

Judd chuckled good-naturedly as he scooped her up and planted her in the cab of his truck. "Glad to see you're back to your usual feisty self again. I was worried there for a while."

She watched him go around to the driver's side, then pile into the pickup. "Judd?"

He turned toward her, his face a study of angles and shadows in the dim light of the dashboard. "Yeah?"

"Thanks for being there. Thanks for your offer to help out tomorrow."

"No problem. I've grown accustomed to doing you favors," he said, and grinned. "It's becoming second nature."

"Then sell me your barn so I can move from the cramped spaces of the café," she requested.

He barked a laugh. "I offered you free run of my house and put myself at your beck and call. Don't push it."

Erika settled against the seat, oddly content. She decided to forego her injured pride and accept his charity.

And *charity* was all she would ever get from him, she reminded herself sensibly. Judd was never going to see her as a potential sweetheart. She might as well take what she could get—the use of his kitchen, his truck and the pleasure of his temporary company. It was better than nothing. But it was still disappointing, because it was a far cry from what she really, secretly wanted from him.

"YOU TAKE the master bedroom and private bath," Judd insisted as he followed Erika through the front door of his house. "While you shower, I'll have Murph place the calls since he probably knows proper procedure, then I'll fix a snack."

"I'm not hungry."

Judd eyed her curiously. "Did you take time to eat supper?"

"No, I was busy and then those men scared me half to death. If that wasn't enough, I embarrassed myself by crying on your shoulder and soiling your shirt." She indicated the mascara stains on his chest. "That kills the appetite, believe me."

"You're going to eat, regardless," he said firmly. "We have Thelma's leftover meat loaf and scalloped potatoes."

Her shoulders sagged. "They took my brisket and pie," Erika blurted out of the blue. "I was going to drop it off as a treat for my friends at the retirement center tomorrow."

"Just goes to show you how ungrateful and inconsiderate thugs can be," Judd replied as he laid his hands on her shoulders and turned her toward the hallway. "Go shower. You'll feel better."

"Will I?" She glanced back at him, as if he had all the answers.

He didn't. He wished he could wave his arms and magically erase her disillusionment, but he couldn't. Miss Dogooder had had an in-your-face reality check this evening. Up until now, she probably thought kindness was always repaid with kindness. But she hadn't been exposed to the world where he had lived and worked for more than a dozen years. Judd would have spared her the brutal truth that bad things could happen to good people if he could have.

Ill-advised and inappropriate though it undoubtedly was, Judd felt the need to cuddle Erika to him and offer moral support and comfort. He turned her in his arms and pulled her close. She reminded him of Little Orphan Annie and she looked as if she needed to be kissed.

Or maybe the truth was that *he* needed to kiss her. Whatever the case, his lips moved upon hers, testing the soft texture of her mouth. He drew her petite body tightly against his masculine contours and savored the taste and feel of her in his arms.

Desire and lust, the damnable curses of all men everywhere, sizzled through him. He delved deeper to sample the dewy sweetness within. She tasted of tears and innocence, and he could get lost in her if he let himself. Before he made matters worse, Judd reined in his burgeoning need and stepped away.

He should say something. But what?

"A charity kiss to make it all better?" she asked with an unsteady breath, her gaze searching his.

"No, I—" He heaved a gusty sigh and lifted his hands helplessly. "I don't know why I did that. I just wanted to—" Exasperated, he struggled to find the words to explain what he couldn't explain to himself. Finally he gave up and turned away.

"It was…nice," she murmured. "Thanks. I needed that."

When she left the room, Judd walked into the kitchen and banged his head against the refrigerator a couple of times, hoping to knock some sense into himself. He had stepped over the line tonight. He couldn't afford to make that mistake again. If he messed with the fairy princess of Moon Valley and wound up hurting her, the whole town would be out for his blood—local military hero or not.

"We're just friends," Judd chanted as he retrieved the leftovers. "And don't you forget it again, pal."

THE SHOWER WAS just what Erika needed. The hot, pulsating water pelted her skin, easing the lingering tension. She washed her hair thoroughly, repeatedly, hoping to undo the coiling effects of the perm. All the while, she contemplated the sweetest, most tantalizing kiss she had ever experienced.

Too bad it hadn't continued for several minutes before Judd realized whom he was kissing and stepped away.

Having had her life flash before her eyes while staring at the spitting end of a pistol, while another weapon poked into her neck, Erika had realized there were glaring gaps of experiences in her existence. Even if she never had a husband and family, she desperately wanted to know—and feel—passion.

The man with whom she wanted to share her desire was presently standing in the kitchen, reheating leftovers. He could probably list a dozen women he would rather fall into bed with. She doubted she would ever be on his list. Just her rotten luck.

Erika frowned pensively as she rinsed her hair. What if she used the excuse of vulnerability and threw herself at Judd? What if they shared his bed, if only for one night? They were both consenting adults. And David Shore was right: speculation and gossip would be flying around town. Why not enjoy what everyone predicted she was doing?

But how did you seduce a man who perceived you as a pain in the patoot? Prey on his sympathy? Catch him off guard? Just come right out and ask him? *How?*

Even as several possibilities chased each other around her head Erika felt herself getting cold feet. Trying to act provocative to seduce a man was not her style. Heavens, she didn't even *have* a style.

The depressing thought followed her from the bathroom and into Judd's masculine-looking bedroom—with its spacious king-size bed. "Forget it," she muttered at herself. "It's not going to happen."

Erika scooped up her suitcase and set it on the end of the bed. Discouraged, she rummaged through the clothes Aunt Frannie had hurriedly tossed in the bag to locate the oversize T-shirt that served as her nightgown. Even after she carefully double-checked she came up empty-handed.

Aunt Frannie had apparently been so rattled about the robbery that she hadn't been thinking clearly when she threw together a bag for Erika's overnight stay at Judd's. It looked as if Frannie had grabbed the first things she had laid her hands on. Erika was overstocked with underwear and socks. The low-cut cotton camisole that she usually wore under a jacket was all she had for a blouse to wear tomorrow. The cutoff denim shorts that she wore around the house—and never in public because they were as skimpy as Daisy Mae Duke's—were all to be had.

Grumbling, Erika dropped the towel and stepped into her panties. Then she refastened the towel around her and padded barefoot to the bedroom door.

"Judd! I need a favor," she hollered at him.

Chapter Six

The instant Erika called out Judd was out of the kitchen and down the hall in a flash. He stumbled to a halt when his gaze landed on his half-naked houseguest. Her wet hair was banded atop her head, emphasizing the slender curve of her neck and silky, bare arms. The towel concealed the swells of her breasts—partially, but not enough to divert his speculations of what lay beneath the terry-cloth wrap, he was sorry to say.

Desire sizzled through him as his betraying eyes drifted lower to survey the sleek, well-toned length of her legs that were marred by scraped knees. Oh jeez, he did not need another vivid reminder that Erika was all woman. How was he supposed to portray the Good Samaritan when carnal thoughts were playing hopscotch in his head?

"Remind me never to send Aunt Frannie to gather clothes for me while she's upset," Erika said, breaking into Judd's wayward thoughts. "She forgot to send sleepwear." She rolled her eyes, then added, "Not that tomorrow's out-fit is practical." She jabbed a finger at him. "And if you poke fun at the getup I have to work in tomorrow, I will skin you alive."

When Erika clutched modestly at the towel, Judd realized his attention had drifted back to the exposed rise of her breasts. Willfully he raised his gaze. "You need a T-shirt nightie?" he croaked, then cleared his throat. "No problem."

He eased past her, his arm brushing her bare shoulder. "Over here. Take your pick of my T-shirts."

Judd pulled open the drawer and heard Erika snicker when she noticed that his garments were neatly folded and stacked.

"You even fold your socks and boxers?" she said in amazement. "You have entirely too much spare time on your hands. Or at least you did until I dragged you back into society and got you involved in the community."

"This is the way we did it in the army," he defended himself as he grabbed a T-shirt off the stack, then draped it over her bare shoulder—for his benefit. He had seen way too much of her satiny flesh for his peace of mind already.

"This ain't the army," she said impishly. "No one is going to put you on report if you cram your underwear in the drawer. You wouldn't believe how disorganized my laundry system is. Good thing *I* don't have to pass inspection."

She already had, Judd mused as he cast her a discreet sideways glance. He approved of everything he had seen—and he wouldn't object to seeing more.

The betraying thought lent testimony to the fact that being "just friends" wasn't working for him. He could definitely imagine what it would be like to see Erika naked, to have the chance to commit every curve and swell to memory.

Better yet, he would like to *get* naked with her.

Judd put on the mental brakes and banished the arousing image. He was treading on dangerous territory here and he'd better watch his step. He had become emotionally involved already and he had gotten in even deeper when he had come to Erika's rescue after the harrowing robbery ordeal. He had become protective of her so quickly that it made his head spin. That wasn't good.

Erika had made him *feel* again, *live* again. He hadn't wanted that to happen until he had made peace with the guilt and regret of Steve's untimely death.

Judd started when Erika reached out to touch his arm. "Hey, are you okay? Why so glum?"

For the first time since the tragedy Judd wanted to confide his anguish to someone instead of bottling it up inside. But not here and now. Not in his bedroom with a half-naked woman who had begun to appeal to him on too many levels.

"Put on the T-shirt and come eat," he insisted as he wheeled toward the door.

Erika watched Judd beat a hasty retreat, wishing he hadn't suddenly shut her out. She really wanted to know what haunted him. Had she said something to trigger unpleasant thoughts? How was she supposed to function under the same roof with him if she didn't know when she had accidentally hit a raw nerve?

Pulling the oversize T-shirt over her head, Erika followed Judd down the hall. She found him in the spacious kitchen that boasted vintage blue linoleum. Blue to match his mood, she mused as she took a seat at the antique oak table.

Despite her lack of appetite, Judd directed her attention to the heaping plate he had prepared for her. "Eat."

She gave him a mocking salute, then plucked up her fork. "Yes, sir."

After she had taken two bites of the meat loaf Judd let out an audible sigh and said, "There was this guy. He was my best friend. His name was Steve Carlton."

Erika was relieved that he had finally decided to put it all out on the table and confide in her. His expression was so bleak that Erika reflexively reached over to take his hand. She could tell that breaking his silence was difficult for him. She wanted to offer her support, just as he had been there for her to lean on after the robbery.

"Tell me about Steve," Erika encouraged him.

His tortured expressed eased up slightly. "He was fun-loving. A real prankster at times. Hardworking and reliable. A dedicated patriot. We started basic training together and were assigned to the same special ops unit," he continued.

"From there Steve and I decided to join a highly classified force that I could tell no one else about, not even my parents. There was no one I could discuss information and assignments with except Steve and a handful of operatives. We became such close friends over the years that we could almost read each others' minds and anticipate each others' reactions to specific situations."

"You were fortunate to have formed such a strong relationship," Erika remarked as she lightly stroked his clenched fist. "Sylvie and I were kind of like that once. But not as close as you and Steve, of course. I will probably never experience that kind of special bond again. But I do know that when things change it leaves an emptiness in your life that is difficult to fill."

"This one was even closer and makes it even more difficult." Judd shifted restlessly in his chair and stared into space, as if gazing through the window of time. "When you crawl through hell together, with enemy guerillas trying to riddle you with bullets, you have to know that you have someone right there who is willing and capable of guarding your back while you guard his. It's like being joined at the mind and the soul. You end up placing absolute trust in someone else's abilities while they are doing the same to you."

And Judd felt as if he had lost a vital part of himself, Erika diagnosed. No wonder he had closed himself off and struggled to adjust to a new lifestyle, and more importantly, to the loss of his closest friend.

"I didn't see it coming," he muttered, his eyes dark with regret and self-loathing. "I *should have* seen it coming. I was trained for moments like that. It wasn't that we hadn't been in situations like that before, because we had. Dozens of times, in fact."

He clenched and unclenched his jaw. "It was like a mental bleep, a moment without instinct or reaction. I saw the movement off to my left and it seemed to take a second to respond. I lunged to cover Steve…but it was too late."

He squeezed her hand so tightly that it cut off circulation and pinched bone. But Erika didn't complain. The gesture was the outward manifestation of the internal turmoil that rocked his soul. "You tried to take the bullet for him," she said softly. "That in itself was a mark of courage."

"I failed." The admission burst from him like a punctured balloon. "It should have been *me* who was hit, damn it. *I* shouldn't be here. For years I purposely took all the one-man assignments so Steve could be home as much as possible. *I* did it because *I* wasn't the one with a wife and five-year-old daughter waiting for me. *I* wasn't the one who had everything to live for, someone waiting for me to come home. *He* was."

Compelled toward him, Erika slid off her chair and curled up in his lap to cradle his head against her shoulder. Her frightening ordeal didn't remotely compare to the depth of turmoil, grief and regret that assailed Judd.

When the dam of grief broke, Judd clamped his arms around Erika. He absorbed the weight and feel of her body nestled comfortingly against his. He held on to Erika for the longest time, waiting for the storm of anger, anguish and remorse to pass. He didn't want Erika to see him wallowing in the depths of despair—no more than she probably wanted him to see her fall apart at the café earlier this evening. But tangled emotions just came pouring out of him after suppressing them for so long.

Judd could feel the wetness in his eyes, feel the lump clogging his throat. He wanted to scream away the unjustness and curse the unfairness of losing his friend who was also a caring husband and father and had so much to live for.

"Would Steve have died to ensure that his wife and daughter were free and safe from harm?" she asked quietly.

"Without a doubt," Judd relied, his voice crackling.

"Would he have been willing to take a bullet to save his closest friend, just as you would have done?"

"Of course, but that's not how it was supposed to work," he muttered. "*I* was supposed to be *his* guardian angel who brought him home safely to his family."

After a moment she asked, "What's it like to have someone love and respect you that much?"

"Reassuring…until you make the kind of misstep I did," he said, and scowled.

"This fun-loving, trustworthy, brave and honorable friend would expect you to close yourself off from life for him?"

He knew what she was trying to do, but he wasn't prepared to accept the answer to that question. His guilt demanded that he continue to mourn Steve Carlton for months to come.

Abruptly, Judd set Erika to her feet then stood up. "I'm going for a walk."

Judd pelted across the living room in hurried strides. The moment he stepped onto the porch he braced his hands on the porch railing and hauled in a cathartic breath. He tried to corral the jumble of emotions stampeding around his mind, but they kept coming at him from all directions at once. In addition, he felt guilty for pushing Erika away. She was fighting her own demons tonight and she had endured the fright of her life. He should be there for her right now.

Some friend he was. Some friend he had always been.

He heard the door swing open behind him and smiled ruefully. Had he really expected Erika to back off? Had she ever?

"Come with me," she insisted as she clutched his hand.

She didn't say another word as she led him across the lawn and down the hill to the old wooden barn. As if she could see in the dark, she headed unerringly toward the east corner, then huddled down beside the spot where three missing boards provided a peephole to the outside world.

A full moon hung over the river that rippled like mercury in the evening breeze. Only the distant chirp of crickets and the croak of frogs broke the silence of the night. Fireflies winked in the shadows of the underbrush.

It was peaceful. Soothing.

"This is where I used to come when I was a kid," she confided. "When the world crowded in on me and I got to wondering why I was on this planet, I would sit here and try to reconcile my existence." She groped for the wooden stool that had once been used to milk the dairy cow Judd's parents kept while he and his brother were in school.

"Make your peace with what you can't change, Judd," she implored. "Look for the best and try not to focus on the worst. It worked for me, even if I never faced the kind of torment you do." There was a smile in her voice when she added, "This place is magical and it's right here on your property. Make good use of it."

And then she evaporated into the darkness like the good fairy she was. All she lacked were wings and a wand, Judd mused as he stared after her.

There, alone, by the light of the moon, Judd came to grips with the anger, grief and resentment that had been hounding him. He encountered each tormenting emotion, one by one, instead of allowing the turmoil to defeat him full force. He told himself to accept what could not be changed and focus on Steve's endearing traits. For once he recalled all the good times they had shared and counted their successful missions while they had worked in tandem.

That had been his problem, Judd realized as he stared out the peephole to admire the serene setting that was right in his own backyard. He had dwelled on the worst of all possible moments. He had disregarded and overlooked a dozen years filled with all the rewarding and glorious moments they had shared in their efforts to make the world a safer place.

An hour later, or perhaps two, Judd felt the heavy burden lift from his soul. He had finally let go of the bad times and clung to the good ones.

He came to his feet and ambled back to the house, noting that Erika had put away the supper dishes and had gone to bed. He moved silently to his bedroom and stood staring down at her shadowy form.

Judd felt as though he had just found his new best friend. Erika had been there for a while now, waiting for him to reach out to her. But he had refused to accept her offered friendship and dodged her attempts to ease his suffering.

No one else had dared to risk his surly disposition, but *she* had come barreling into his life to shake him out of his blue funk, no matter how many times he tried to push her away.

Judd leaned down and braced his hands on the edge of the bed. Impulsively, he brushed a kiss over her cheek. Need blasted him at the first touch of his lips on her satiny skin. She stirred slightly, then woke. Judd was overcome by the fierce need to be close to her, just the way he had been when she climbed onto his lap, offering him an anchor to cling to during that storm of emotion.

"I need to hold you," he admitted to her. And to himself. "Is that a problem?"

Her quiet laughter engulfed him as he heel-and-toed out of his boots. "Not a problem. I could use a little comforting myself." She drew back the sheet so he could stretch out beside her. Then she draped her arm across his chest and gave him a reassuring hug. "Better?"

"Much," Judd murmured as he absorbed the scent and feel of her body nestled protectively to his. "How about for you?"

"Just what I needed, too," she said with a drowsy sigh and a sleepy smile. "Who would have thought that just cuddling could make a person feel so much better."

A FEW HOURS LATER, Judd was jolted awake when Erika's flailing arm caught him right in the nose. He barely had time to register the painful blow when she shrieked in his ear, then shoved him away.

His best guess—when his mind began to function— was that memories of the robbery had invaded her dreams. He couldn't interpret her mumbling, but he predicted that she was reliving the traumatic ordeal.

Judd knew exactly what that felt like.

He gave her a gentle nudge and noted her clammy skin,

her trembling body and the rapid expulsion of her breath. "Erika… Hey, it's just me. Wake up."

She flinched. Her eyes flew open, looking wild and enormous in the shadows. When she recognized him, she half collapsed on her pillow. "God, I think your experience with Steve got tangled up with mine in a nightmare," she said with a seesaw breath. "There for a minute I thought you were one of the bad guys who was trying to hold me down." She glanced worriedly at him. "Did I hurt you?"

Judd examined his nose with his fingertips. "Naw, it's already been broken once. What's another dent?"

He saw her teeth flash in the moonlight that streamed through the window. "Sorry about that."

He waited a beat, then said, "Do you think you can go back to sleep?"

"Maybe. If you sing me a lullaby the way Aunt Frannie used to do," she suggested wryly.

He snorted at that. "I couldn't carry a tune if you stuffed it in a paper bag."

"That's okay." She rolled onto her side, her back to him. "You're a man of so many impressive talents that it just wouldn't seem fair if you could sing well, too," she murmured.

The distance between them felt like a mile. He liked having her body cushioned against his.

He would like to have her body cushioned *under* his.

Judd shoved aside the traitorous thought. "You think I have talents?" he asked as he propped his head up on his hand and glanced down at her.

"You're lousy with them," she affirmed. "Makes me envious just trying to list them all."

"Yeah? Then name one."

"You are an incredible athlete," she pointed out.

"Name two," he challenged playfully.

She rolled to her back to peer up at him. "You're exceptionally good company…when you aren't biting my head off," she said teasingly. "Other than the fact that you talk entirely too much in bed, you're an all-around swell guy."

Talking was not what he really wanted to do while he was in bed with Erika. He was more than ready to take their relationship to an intimately personal level. If she hadn't noticed that his body had responded favorably to having her so close then she wasn't paying attention.

"So…you don't like to sleep with men who jabber too much. What else don't you like?"

I don't like it that we're in bed together and all you want to do is talk, as if I were just a pal. You are destroying my fantasy here!

If this wasn't an indication that Judd viewed her as a friend and not a potential lover, she didn't know what was. Nothing was happening between them, even when opportunity was staring him in the face. Erika sighed in defeat. She definitely wasn't cut out to be a seductress and he obviously didn't find her the least bit sexy.

How depressing.

She shifted her hips and turned her back on him again. "Go ahead and yammer if it makes you feel better. Just don't take it personally if I nod off. I've got a busy day ahead of me tomorrow."

She was hugely disappointed when he patted her head like a puppy, then got to his feet. "I'll go sleep on the sofa so you can get some rest," he murmured. "'Night."

Erika watched him stride from the room, then huffed out

a frustrated breath. "You are such a loser," she told herself before she pulled the pillow over her head to smother her disappointment.

JUDD AWOKE to the smell of freshly brewed coffee and bacon cooking on the stove. He scrubbed his hands over his face, then levered himself up to a sitting position on the couch. His back ached. His legs were cramped from sleeping in tight quarters. But he hadn't trusted himself to sleep beside Erika last night. Getting naked with her had begun to monopolize his thoughts because his perception of her was changing rapidly. She wasn't the nuisance who kept bugging him to socialize and participate in community activities. She had become his confidante and friend…but that wasn't quite enough to satisfy him anymore.

Cool your heels, cowboy, he scolded himself as he stood up to work the kinks from his back and legs. When he caught movement out of the corner of his eye he glanced toward the kitchen—and forgot to breathe.

Sex goddess extraordinaire was smiling at him as she poked her head around the doorway. Her red-gold hair caught flame in the morning sunlight. The smattering of freckles on her nose crinkled as her blue eyes twinkled with lively spirit. He could get used to seeing that cute…er… adorable face every morning.

But what he couldn't get ready for was that spaghetti-strap knit top that accentuated the full swells of her breasts and emphasized the trim indentation of her waist. And then there were those extremely short shorts that exposed her shapely legs—and two skinned knees.

Judd felt his pulse rising as he appraised her thoroughly while she stood against the backdrop of sunlight. He might as well pitch out that "just friends" garbage with the trash, he decided. He was never going to be able to look at this perky, vibrant female again without remembering how appealing she had looked wearing nothing but a towel last night and how seductive she looked in the Daisy Duke getup this morning.

She shook her forefinger at him. "I told you not to make any wisecracks about the clothes Aunt Frannie packed for me." She half turned, making him swallow hard when he appraised her alluring feminine profile. "Now come eat breakfast before I start gathering up stuff for the catered meals. C'mon, Tex, put it in high gear. We need to get moving."

When she turned a full one-eighty, Judd admired the rear view and inwardly groaned. There was no way in hell that he could ever consider Erika the girl-next-door type again.

"You have a ball game tonight, right?" she asked as she placed a steaming plate of eggs, bacon and biscuits on the table. "Six-thirty?"

He nodded as he plopped into his chair. His hungry gaze bounced back and forth between her arresting physique and the appetizing food. "Right."

"Is it okay if I drop you off at the ballpark, then borrow your truck to deliver the meals?"

"Sure. Anything is fine," he murmured before he sipped the coffee that tasted ten times better when she prepared it.

"I need to run back to town to pick up the meat stored in Aunt Frannie's freezer, then swing by my place to change into a more presentable set of clothes. I'll also need the sacks of potatoes and cans of beans that I left at my apartment."

"I can pick up all that stuff for you if it will save you time," he volunteered between bites. He stared directly at her. "But don't change that getup on my account."

She halted in midstep, her plate in her hand, and frowned at him. Then she glanced down her torso. "You're kidding, right? I look like a second-rate floozy."

He waggled his brows rakishly as he bit into a crisp slice of bacon. "Don't sell yourself short. Definitely first-rate."

She swatted him on the shoulder, then sank into her chair. "Don't make fun. These clothes are all wrong and yesterday was a hellish day. I would like to put it behind me."

"I wasn't poking fun." He cast her a fleeting glance, then looked away. "You look hot."

She snorted at that. "Nobody ever accused me of that before."

"Then they weren't paying attention. Any man with eyes in his head would approve of the way you look."

She stared straight at him. "Even you?"

"Didn't I just say so?"

"But I didn't look hot last night in a towel or while I was sleeping in your T-shirt in your bed?" she questioned. "I'm dying to know what it takes to attract a guy like you. This is it? Daisy Duke shorts?"

The image of Erika wearing nothing but those high-riding shorts exploded in his mind and got him hot and bothered in nothing flat. Judd willfully tamped down the roiling desire that accompanied the lusty fantasy.

"Last night doesn't count," he mumbled into his coffee cup. He really did not want to have this conversation, for fear he would blurt out something that might offend her. He had done that several times yesterday.

"Whaddya mean last night didn't count?" she asked, puzzled.

"You were stressed out and I was dealing with my own emotional baggage. If I, being a normal, red-blooded man, would have come on to you because of our close proximity, you would have hated me this morning."

"Wanna bet?" she challenged with a grin.

Stunned, Judd gaped at the mischievous sparkle in her eyes and in her smile. God, she was adorable and vibrant...and *hot*. Why hadn't he allowed himself to acknowledge that weeks ago? Because he had been butting his head against the insurmountable wall of guilt and grief until last night, he reminded himself. Thanks to Erika's gentle prodding and constant distractions, he had stopped mourning Steve's death and had begun to celebrate their friendship.

Judd leaned back in his chair and returned her grin. "Five bucks says that if I had put a move on you last night you would have walked out of here this morning and refused to speak to me again."

Erika cast him a withering glance. "Put the moves on me? That sounds *soooo* romantic. Don't know how I could have resisted you and your smooth moves. Especially since I was so shaken up and vulnerable last night."

"I would have relied on my tact and charm," he assured her.

She scoffed at that. "You don't have any."

"Wanna bet?" he challenged with a devilish smile.

"Sorry, I don't have five bucks. The thieves stole practically everything I had."

"I'll float you a loan, sugar britches," he cooed.

"Cut that out." Erika popped up from her chair and strode over to wash the skillet and plates. It rattled her to realize that she and Judd were actually flirting with each other. She liked it a lot, but...

But what? It's what you've always wanted, remember?

Don't be afraid to go after what you want before it's too late. Seize the moment. Aunt Frannie's words rolled through her mind and she glanced sideways to study Judd speculatively while he devoured his meal.

Maybe she could flirt with him off and on during the day. Sort of test the waters, improve her skills. Not that it would get her anywhere, she mused defeatedly. She would be back in her own apartment tonight. She would be knee-deep in her own life and Judd would be back in his. She probably wouldn't see much of him.

Her thoughts trailed off when the phone rang. And it continued to ring off the hook for a solid hour. Apparently word had spread around town that she had been robbed. Friends and acquaintances knew exactly where to call to offer their condolences and assistance. Yep, folks were probably wondering about the relationship between her and Judd. Too bad that nothing had happened between them.

After Judd had showered and dressed, Erika ignored the phone that was ringing—again—and followed him out the door.

"We'll get what you need from your apartment, then swing by to pick up the meat at Francine's," Judd suggested as he piled into the pickup. "When we get back here, I'll clean up the smoker while you're peeling potatoes."

"Sounds like a plan," she agreed.

Erika mentally ticked off every item on her to-do list as they drove to her apartment. When she walked inside, she screeched to a halt and gaped in disbelief at her ransacked living room.

"Well, hell!" Judd erupted from behind her.

"What is happening?" Erika howled in frustration. She took stock of the upturned tables and chairs. The kitchen cabinets were standing wide open and several items were strewn on the counter and the floor. Nothing appeared to be damaged, just lying around like casualties of battle.

Then she noticed the TV, the CD player and disks were missing. So was the microwave. Outrage and frustration pelted her all over again.

"The thieves must have gotten your keys and the address from your wallet. Looks like they decided to stop in to see what else they could make off with after Francine and Murph stopped by last night," Judd ventured. "Francine would have locked up after she left, wouldn't she?"

Erika nodded numbly as she took another disbelieving look around her crackerbox apartment.

Judd examined the door. "The lock wasn't tampered with. It's obvious the intruders used your key. They must have waited until we were convinced they were long gone and posed no threat."

"I don't have time to clean up this mess!" she burst out with exasperation. "Wasn't robbing the Blue Moon and taking my purse enough? Why did they have to rummage through my place, too?"

"Definitely a double whammy," Judd agreed as he nudged her toward her compact bedroom. "Just grab several changes of clothes, and whatever else you might need, and let's go," he ordered. "We'll worry about this mess later." He glanced around the place again. "This apartment doesn't have much room to move around. I would be climbing the walls if I lived here."

"This is just the place where I shower and change clothes," she explained as she veered into the bedroom. "The café is very demanding."

Cursing the burglars that had wrecked her apartment,

Erika stepped over the clutter in her room. "Thank goodness I made copies of all the information in my wallet so I'll have the account numbers to give a detailed report of the theft," she called back to Judd.

"Smart woman. Grab the copies while you're here."

Erika peeled off her clothes and grabbed another pair of shorts and blouse. Hurriedly, she picked up the supplies she would need for the catered meals. It upset her that someone had invaded her personal space, small though it was. For sure and certain she was going to scrub this apartment within an inch of its life to erase all memories of those robbers that had scoured her home for valuables.

When she walked back to the living room, Judd clutched her hand and led her back to his pickup. "I called David Shore and told him to swing by here while we're at Francine's. Let's just try to stay focused on getting your catered meals together right now. Okay?"

He offered her an encouraging smile and Erika slumped back on the seat. Lord, it felt good to have Judd here to lean on, to help make decisions while she was feeling rattled and frustrated.

"I'm glad I spent the night with you," she murmured. "If I had insisted on going home alone after the fiasco at the café I would have gone into cardiac arrest, especially if those hoodlums had been here when I showed up."

The prospect of Erica walking in on another robbery in progress made Judd grimace. He didn't want to consider the worst-case scenarios Erika might have encountered.

This was the last straw. He wasn't going to leave her alone until her life was back in order and he knew without a doubt that those burglars couldn't return.

"You are staying with me until they are arrested," he said

adamantly. "No way am I sending you back here until I'm convinced that you aren't in the slightest danger."

"You're overreacting. I can make the place livable after I deliver the meals this evening. I appreciate your offer, but it isn't necessa—"

"Yes, it is," he cut in, then shot her a silencing glance. "Don't argue with me. I'm not backing down on this. We are going to be roommates until this case is wrapped up, so don't waste your breath objecting."

"Boy, you can be really pushy when you want to be, Tex," she remarked. "People are going to talk if we spend more than one night together. Count on it."

"Let 'em talk," he said as he sped down the street. "Better that the whole town thinks we're having a wild passionate affair than to risk those criminals showing up, *while you're there,* to pick off anything they might have missed the first time."

Erika forgot to listen after he mentioned a wild, passionate affair. Ah, if only she could be *that* lucky!

Chapter Seven

"Ransacked and robbed your apartment?" Aunt Frannie howled in outrage when Erika gave her the news. "Talk about adding insult to injury!"

Erika nodded in agreement, then glanced down the hall in Frannie's home to see Murph exiting the bathroom. She cut Judd a quick glance and noticed he was flashing her an I-told-you-so grin.

Judd was undoubtedly right, Erika mused. It was barely eight o'clock in the morning and Murph was here. There was definitely something going on between Frannie and Murph. They weren't just bowling and playing bingo together these days.

Camping out at Frannie's until the perps had been apprehended would cause a major interruption in the romance brewing between these two, she realized.

"That does it. You are staying with Judd until those thugs are behind bars," Frannie declared.

"That's exactly what I said," Judd chimed in. "David Shore is checking her apartment and he doesn't want her going back there, either."

"Well, good for you. I'll rest easier knowing Riki is safe and protected. I don't want her near that place until we know she's out of danger and new locks are installed. Leave that to me. The locksmith is a friend of mine and I'll have him take care of it as soon as he can. But I'm not making any promises, so you need to make use of Judd's hospitality until I have this resolved."

Murph joined them in the living room, then curled a possessive arm around Frannie, who was smiling for reasons Erika didn't understand and didn't make time to question. "Don't worry about your bank accounts, Erika. I'm on my way over right now to double check after the calls I made last night. I've taken care of the credit card account, too. If you need a loan, then consider it done."

Erika smiled gratefully. It was nice to have a new friend at the local financial institution. Otherwise, those thugs might have cleaned her out—but good.

When a squad car drove in the driveway to park behind his pickup, Judd wheeled toward the door. "Erika, why don't you and Frannie gather up everything you need while I speak with the deputy."

Judd walked outside to nod a greeting as David Shore stepped from the car. "Any leads?" he asked without preamble.

David shrugged. "Not many. We found the abandoned get-away car ten miles from town on a gravel road," he reported. "It took us a while to track down its owner. The license plate had been removed. It was stolen three days ago from a neighboring county."

"Not just your run-of-the-mill thugs on a Friday night joy ride, I take it," Judd muttered sourly.

"Nope, veteran criminals," David replied. "My guess is that Erika's car, being an older, nondescript model, is just what they needed to remain at large. I suspect someone else

in the area will soon be reporting switched license plates...
if they even notice."

Judd doubted anyone would. How many times did he
glance at his own tag before he hopped in his pickup?

"About Erika," David said, a somber expression on his
face. "I don't want to see her hurt in any way because she's
been displaced after these robberies...if you get my drift."

Judd definitely caught the way David was drifting. "I
have her best interests at heart," he declared.

"You'd better," David replied. "When I moved here less
than two months ago, Erika was the one who made me feel
welcome and appreciated. Most folks keep their distance
from cops, whether intentional or not. But Erika is something special, and I don't want to see anyone take advantage of her vulnerability right now."

Judd met Dave's pointed stare without blinking. Erika
was right. People in town must be assuming that there was
something going on between them.

"Sylvie is upset and worried about Erika," David continued after a moment. "She told me to extend a personal in-
vitation for Erika to stay with her and Matt as long as
necessary."

"There's no need," Judd insisted. "I have plenty of room
to spare. She's fine right where she is."

Dave eyed him assessingly. "Plenty of room isn't what
concerns me, Foster. Put two adults in the same space, especially when one of them is stressed and upset, and things
might happen." His gaze narrowed on Judd. "Sylvie confided that Erika isn't very experienced with men. Do not
take advantage of the situation. I'll consider it my personal crusade to make your life miserable if you make
things worse for her."

Judd didn't have to be a rocket scientist to know Erika wasn't into one-night stands and reckless flings. But Dave was staring him down, as if he were Erika's overprotective big brother and Judd was the big bad wolf. Judd might have found the deputy's lecture amusing if he hadn't been battling his growing feelings for Erika and had to fight temptation hourly.

"Hi, Dave," Erika greeted as she exited the house with an armload of food. "Any report yet?"

Dave shook his head. "Sorry, no. But I'm on my way back to your apartment to have another look around. I'll have a patrol car keep tabs on your place, as well as the café, until the old locks have been replaced."

"Thanks, Dave, I really appreciate it," she said sincerely.

"Sylvie said to tell you that you're welcome to stay with her and that she's coming out to Judd's farm to help you get the catered meals together this morning." He glanced back at Judd. "Since Matt's team has a game tonight, we'll be there to cheer him on. If I can help out, let me know."

"You can," Judd replied. "I need a third base coach. You've been elected." He tossed the cop a teasing grin. "Just don't hand out speeding tickets when our runners round the bases at blazing speeds."

The comment coaxed a reluctant grin from Dave.

"Excellent idea," Erika enthused. "That will give you a chance to get acquainted with some of the parents."

Judd smiled to himself. Erika was always finding ways to get people involved in the community. Dave, it seemed, was another of her special projects.

"I need to get to work," Erika said as she strode over to load her supplies in the pickup. "I don't want anything to ruin Elsie Simpson's eightieth birthday party. Her entire family is coming to town for the celebration at the retirement center."

David cast Judd another meaningful glance. "Don't forget what I said, Foster," he said confidentially, then he spun on his heels and headed for his squad car.

Right, don't mess with the fairy princess of Moon Valley, Judd mused as he hurried over to help Erika arrange her food and supplies.

"What was that all about?" Erika questioned as she climbed into the truck.

"Man talk," he hedged as he stabbed the key into the ignition.

Erika rolled her eyes. "You don't have to be so secretive. I'm a big girl. I can take it. What did he say?"

Judd backed from the driveway. "He said to watch my step with you because you're one of his favorite people."

"Well, darn," she said, and grinned impishly. "We can't fool around? Some friend he is if he doesn't want me to have a bit of fun."

Judd kept his mouth shut and his eyes on the road. Unfortunately, his mind was buzzing with *fun* ways to spend their second evening together. Erika might be kidding around, but Judd found himself taking the prospect seriously. Having Erika in his bed again—and doing nothing about it—would torment him to the extreme. The honor system he had previously relied on could take a direct hit if he didn't watch his step.

ERIKA WAS AMAZED at the number of vehicles parked in Judd's driveway when they returned to the farm. Ivan Snyder, dressed in his usual attire of bib overalls, had already rolled the old smoker from the barn and was in the process of giving it a good scrubbing. Sylvia Vaughn was toting extra food into the house and another dozen friends and acquaintances were hauling in gelatin salads and scrumptious desserts.

Erika glanced uncertainly at Judd, expecting him to be annoyed that people were invading his domain. "I'm sorry. I never dreamed—" she began.

"If I didn't know better, I would swear you called in reinforcements yourself to crowd my space," he cut in.

She relaxed considerably when she noticed the teasing smile that twisted his lips. "Darn, you've found me out. Nothing gets past you, cowboy."

The careless comment was out of her mouth before she could think to bite it back. After what Judd had told her last night, she expected she had hit another raw nerve. A bullet had gotten past him before he could protect his friend and he was never going to forget that.

His smile faded as he looked over at her. "Some things get past me, when I don't see them coming until it's too late," he murmured.

"Judd, I'm sorry," she said softly.

"It's okay," he assured her as he parked the pickup. "I'm learning to live with it, slowly but surely."

"Erika! Oh God, of all the rotten luck!" Sylvie exclaimed as she waited on the sidewalk. "Hi, Judd, nice to see you again." Her gaze leaped back to Erika. "And now your apartment. That is just too much!"

"What happened at her apartment?" Margaret Gordon, the woman holding a cherry pie, demanded.

"They broke in over there, too," Judd reported, taking command of the briefing. "They cleaned her out. The place is a mess."

A collective groan wafted across the front porch. Sympathetic gazes locked on Erika. She tried to smile, but the expression wobbled on her lips.

"Don't you worry about a thing, hon," Brenda Cullen spoke up. "Our local war hero will take good care of you until your stuff has been replaced. Won't you, Judd?"

"Absolutely," he confirmed as he strode over to unlock the front door. "My home is her home. Whatever Erika needs she gets, no matter how long she needs it."

Erika suppressed a startled stare—barely. Judd was being entirely too generous and helpful, at least until this rescue brigade retreated. Then he would probably lay into her for causing this traffic jam in his front yard.

With a sweeping gesture of his brawny arm, he motioned the women into his house. "Can anyone help transport food to the two catered parties this evening?"

"I will."

Erika glanced over to see one of Elsie's cousins smiling at her. "Thank you. I appreciate it."

"I'm going to the party anyway. I can haul food, paper plates, napkins. Whatever you need," she added helpfully.

"I'm going to Frank and Natalie Gresham's fiftieth anniversary party," said Donna Parsons, who was toting a scrumptious-looking Italian cream cake. "I'll swing by to pick up stuff for you, Erika."

Two other friends volunteered to help transport items to the parties. Erika smiled appreciatively. Thanks to the volunteers, she wouldn't be running around like a beheaded chicken, trying to make deliveries and set up for the dinners simultaneously.

Erika lost track of Judd while people milled around his house, trying to cram cold food in the fridge and rearrange his counters to accommodate the desserts. She suspected he had sneaked off for a few moments of long-awaited privacy. Because of *her,* he had been invaded and had likely retreated to the barn to enjoy some peace and quiet.

"Well, look who's here." Sylvie smirked as she stared out the living room window. "It's Juanita Barlow and she's making a beeline toward Judd. I didn't know she was back in town."

Erika came to stand beside Sylvie—in time to watch their well-endowed former classmate give Judd a zealous hug. "Juanita came into the café about ten days ago to announce that she had divorced her second husband and was moving in with her parents for the time being."

Sylvie rolled her eyes in dismay. "Looks like Juanita is up to her old tricks. Judd must be her next victim. Poor guy."

A stab of jealousy skewered Erika as she watched Juanita rub against Judd like a purring cat. Then she intentionally brushed her bosom, which was showcased by a skintight blouse with a diving neckline, against Judd's arm. Erika silently seethed as Judd smiled at Juanita. If he fell for Juanita's practiced charms she would be tempted to skin him alive. Surely he had better taste than that!

Oh sure, as if you *have the right to feel possessive,* Erika chided herself. But she didn't have to stand here and torture herself by watching Juanita tempt and seduce the man that Erika couldn't work up the nerve to go after herself.

OUTSIDE, JUDD WAS doing his damnedest to avoid the brunette who kept clinging to him like ivy. When he voiced the excuse that he needed to gather wood for the smoker, Juanita hooked her arm in his and trotted along beside him. In fewer than five minutes Judd had heard her life story and learned the names of her two ex-husbands—which was definitely more information than he wanted to know.

"I married twice for money," Juanita told him, unabashed, then cast him a provocative glance. "Now I'm just interested in a good time. How about you, Judd?"

Judd was sorry to say that there had been times in his life that he might have taken Juanita up on her offer. He had only been looking to blow off steam between overseas missions. But the prospect of scratching an itch with Juanita, whose sticky sweet perfume was about to choke him down and whose face boasted such a thick coat of makeup that it looked as if it had been applied with a trowel, didn't hold the slightest appeal.

These days, he preferred a woman with a natural, wholesome look.

"I could come out to your place tonight," Juanita cooed as she brushed her hand over his forearm. "After all this furor dies down, we could have some fun of our own."

"Sorry, Erika is staying with me until the thieves are taken into custody," Judd said as he disentangled himself to scoop up chunks of firewood. "We're sort of a couple now," he blurted out impulsively.

Juanita's face puckered to such extremes that Judd wondered if her makeup was going to crack like bad plaster. "You took pity on plain little Riki? You're too kind, Judd. But I guess that's to be expected from a military hero like you. Still, you can call me when you get tired of her." She flashed him a provocative grin. "I think you and I would really hit it off."

Judd didn't think so. He watched Juanita turn and saunter away, one rolling hip at a time, and felt only relief that he could breathe fresh country air again.

"WELL, THIS IS an interesting setup," Sylvie commented after the crowd of women had exited the house. "A sleepover at Judd's. David tells me you're staying here until your apartment has been put back together and you have dependable locks installed."

Erika took note of Sylvie's wry smile and tried to divert her attention. "Sounds like you are in constant contact with Dave these days."

"Yes, we are," Sylvie replied. "Cell phones are wonderful gadgets. You should get one." She leaned close. "Judd is quite a hunk, you lucky girl, you. I might be envious of this living arrangement if Dave hadn't been so darn nice to me. Plus, Matt adores him. Dave drops by the house to play catch with him during breaks. Now that school is out, Matt has been bugging Dave to take him fishing, too."

"Sounds like Matt is ready for you to marry Dave."

Sylvie nodded her blond head. "Matt keeps asking if that's how real dads are supposed to act and he wants to know why his own dad never shows up when he says he will."

"Poor kid," Erika murmured as she peeled potatoes.

"Yeah, I just hope Matt isn't too disappointed if it doesn't work out between Dave and me."

Erika glanced at her friend who had volunteered to help process the potatoes. "Why can't it work out? Dave is a great guy. Reliable, dependable, good-looking. Don't tell me you're holding out for another deadbeat."

"Funny," Sylvia muttered as she sliced up a potato, then dropped it into the pot of water. "The problem is Dave seems to be getting serious already. After my divorce I swore I wasn't going to get married again. Once was plenty. If not for having Matt, whom I adore, of course," she added emphatically, "I wonder if I wouldn't have been better off by following your practice of dating a guy a few times then backing away."

Erika studied her friend curiously. "Okay, level with me, Syl, why are you hesitant to get serious about Dave?"

"Because Matt is becoming the kid Dave never had," she confided. "He includes Matt in everything we do."

"And this bothers you…why?" Erika prodded.

Sylvia focused on peeling a potato and didn't glance at Erika. "I'm afraid Dave cares more for Matt than he does for me. Isn't that pathetic? But when you are uncertain of yourself as a woman, having your date's face light up when your kid walks into the room doesn't do much for your self-esteem."

Having a few concerns—make that a *lot*—in that department, Erika understood where her friend was coming from. "Maybe if I have a talk with Dave—"

Sylvie flung up her hand. Erika reflexively backed away from the knife in her friend's fist. "No, you won't. I will handle this myself. You have enough problems to deal with right now. Besides, you should be concentrating on getting something going with Judd. Too bad you're so fickle."

"I am not fickle," Erika quickly denied.

"Of course you are," Sylvie insisted. "You aren't getting any younger, either. If you want to have kids, you're going to have to make a serious attempt to find a husband. Either that or locate a sperm donor."

"I don't need a sperm donor," Erika objected. "And there is nothing wrong with being particular."

"Fine, be particular…*about Judd.* You're under the same roof with him—that's a step in the right direction. I say go for it. Be reckless and impulsive for once in your life."

Erika cast her friend a disgruntled glance. "Can we talk about something else, please?"

"No," Sylvie said, grinning mischievously. "I'll get married if you will. We'll have a double ceremony."

Erika snickered. "Can it wait a couple of months? I'm kinda busy right now. I have other weddings to cater in June, you know."

"That's always your excuse," Sylvie teased as she went back to work on the potatoes. "Too many good deeds left undone. Too many—" She flung her arms in an expansive gesture. "Whatever. You never take time for yourself."

"Over the last five years, I haven't noticed a string of men lining up to propose, whether I am busy or not," Erika pointed out.

"Of course not. You divert them elsewhere. Like David to me. And he is fond of you, by the way."

"I'm fond of Dave, too. In a good friend kind of way," Erika amended.

"Okay, so scratch Dave off your list. I'm getting attached to him, wise idea or not. So that leaves Judd as your most likely prospect." She smiled, warming to her previous inspiration. "He's got all the right qualifications. He's single and so are you. He's hometown born and bred and ditto for you. You can cook like nobody's business and I don't know a man who doesn't love to eat. And sex is always fun." She frowned momentarily. "That is, if I remember correctly. It's been a long time, but I vaguely recall enjoying it."

"How's it going in here?" Judd asked, jostling Erika and Sylvia from their private conversation.

"Going fine," Sylvia said. "We were just discussing sex. Are you for or against it?"

Erika's face exploded with color as she glared at her friend. "Sylvie, what *is* the matter with you?"

"Not one thing." Sylvie grinned wickedly as she glanced at Judd, who looked as if he had swallowed a watermelon—whole. "I was just telling Riki that you two should get married. Heck, you're already living together. What do you think of the idea?"

Judd held up his hands in supplication. "I've recently discovered that I don't say the right thing around women. I think I should decline to answer."

"Sylvie!" Erika wailed in embarrassment. "Stop fooling around. You know Judd is just doing me a favor after the robbery. Stop tormenting him."

Sylvie went on as if Erika hadn't spoken. "Riki would be a great catch. She's a splendid chef and she's cute, too." She arched a challenging brow. "Don't you think she's cute?"

"Cute is for puppies and kittens," Judd recited precisely as he had been taught the previous night. He smiled conspiratorially at Erika who felt herself turning another humiliated shade of red. "She is beautiful, not cute."

Sylvie's astute gaze bounced back and forth between Judd and Erika. "Isn't she though?"

Erika squirmed beneath Sylvie's speculative stare. "Thanks for your help. Isn't there some place you need to be right now?"

"Yes, as a matter of fact." Sylvie dropped the knife in the sink, then washed her hands. "Matt is at a friend's house and I need to pick him up. But I'll be back later."

"Don't bother if you can't control that tongue of yours," Erika muttered darkly.

Sylvie ignored the comment and spun to face Judd.

"You're a good guy. Thanks for helping out my best friend in a pinch."

"*Ex*-best friend," Erika corrected.

"Glad to do it," Judd replied, then shot Erika a pointed glance. "I was obliged to repay her for all the favors she's done for me lately."

"Oh? What kind of favors?" Sylvie questioned with heightened interest.

Erika wanted to whack Judd upside the head when he grinned wryly and said, "That's a private matter."

When Sylvie's brows shot up, unsure whether he was kidding or serious, Erika frog-marched her toward the front door. "Thanks for dropping by, Syl. I do appreciate it. Too bad you have to leave so soon."

Shutting the door behind Sylvie, Erika pivoted. Her hands fisted on her hips, she stared bewilderedly at Judd. "Are you deliberately trying to incite gossip with that suggestive comment?" she demanded. "Syl was bad enough, tormenting me the way she was. But you—"

Judd waved her off. "I just got through fending off Juanita Barlow outside," he interrupted. "If you don't mind, I prefer that she thinks we've got something going between us. Since the whole town is speculating about what we're doing out here I can head off Juanita, if you'll help me out and play along."

Erika was so relieved that Judd didn't seem to be interested in Juanita that she was prepared to forgive him for putting ideas in Sylvie's head. "So now *we*'re an item? Are you *sure* that's what you want?" she felt compelled to ask.

Judd nodded his dark head. "What I *don't* want is to have Juanita lurking around here, trying to pounce on me. As far as Sylvie is concerned, listening to the two of you reminds me of the banter Steve and I used to share so I joined in. I miss having a friend. So now *you*'re it and you can help me out with Juanita-the-barracuda."

He smiled wryly at her. "Need I point out that *you* owe *me* a few favors? I *need* a pretend girlfriend and you fit the bill."

The thought appealed to her—probably more than it should have. But she kept hearing Francine and Sylvie's reckless advice ringing in her ears. *Go for it.* And why not? This was the man of her dreams and she should enjoy every moment while she had the chance.

"Well?" he prodded.

She looked into those dark, thick-lashed eyes and felt herself caving in. "All right. I'll run interference for you."

He smiled in relief and her heart flip-flopped. "Good. Thank you. I'm in your debt." He gestured toward the window. "The smoker is fired up and ready to go. I'll put on the beef to cook while you finish the fixings for your side dishes. Any instructions?"

Erika retrieved the meat. "I'll be out in a few moments to check the grill."

Judd's comment about being reminded of the banter he and Steve shared assured her that Judd had turned a crucial corner in his grieving over the loss of his friend and compatriot. Judd was beginning to recall the good times he had shared with his friend. That was a step in the right direction.

That magical corner of the old barn worked every time, she thought as she turned back to the pot of potatoes and shifted into high gear to make preparations.

The only thing that worried her was Judd's impulsive decision to pretend to be an item to ward off Juanita Barlow's advances. He obviously didn't know Juanita very well. She was like a heat-seeking missile when she targeted a man that she decided to seduce.

Not that Erika would mind cozying up to Judd and pretending they were a couple. The prospect had tremendous appeal. She just had to be careful and remind herself that it was just an act staged for Juanita's benefit. If she didn't watch her step, she might start believing in impossible dreams.

That will get your heart broken, Erika reminded herself sensibly as she went to work.

Chapter Eight

"Have you ever seen a community get behind one of their own the way Moon Valley has rallied around Riki?" Ivan Snyder asked as Judd placed the meat on the grill.

"Actually, no," Judd admitted. "It is amazing the way people turn out in droves to support Erika."

"You can't help but like that girl," Ivan said as he leisurely propped himself against the metal barn. "I was immediately out the door when the news of the café robbery came down the grapevine this morning. But then, when someone helps you out as many times as Riki has been there for me, it's only natural to return the favor, ya know?"

Judd nodded, then listened to Ivan yammer for another ten minutes after Erika had come and gone to check the meat in the grill. Ivan, Judd had discovered, had the gift of gab. Give the old man an opening and he was good for an hour. As Erika had said, Ivan was lonely. Fortunately, he was an excellent mentor who had been filling Judd's head with all sorts of practical and useful tips about agriculture and livestock. If Judd didn't turn a profit on the farm, it wasn't because of Ivan, who had suggested dozens of cost-cutting practices.

When another vehicle—that looked to be at least a decade old and was the size of a tank—drove in, Judd frowned curiously. Four elderly women, who looked vaguely familiar, climbed out. One was on a walker. One carried a cane and two ambulated under their own power.

"Here comes trouble," Ivan announced.

Judd stared inquisitively at Ivan as the foursome made slow progress toward him. "What kind of trouble? They look harmless to me."

"Those four old biddies helped raise Riki," Ivan reported. "If you cross any of them, you'll wish you hadn't. My guess is they have come to check out the situation with you and their ward. If your intentions aren't honorable they will gang up on you."

Judd chuckled. "I've faced a lot worse in combat."

Apparently Ivan didn't think years of intense military training prepared him to take on the four old women. Ivan shot Judd a sympathetic glance, then hightailed it into the metal barn, voicing the excuse that he suddenly remembered something he needed to do.

Judd appraised the four senior citizens in orthopedic shoes and outdated polyester pantsuits. "Hi, ladies," he greeted them, flashing his best smile.

Four wrinkled faces and assessing gazes zeroed in on him. "You don't look much different than you did in high school," the woman with gunmetal gray hair said. "We hear that you're keeping our girl out here after the robbery."

"Not *keeping* her," Judd clarified. "But she is staying here until she can get her life back in order."

The white-haired woman narrowed her gaze on him. "And where has Riki been sleeping? Answer me that, boy."

"In my room. I camped out on the couch," Judd added hastily.

The woman with the cane jabbed it at him. She sized him up then stared him down. "You expect us to believe that? We may be old, but we aren't blind and stupid, sonny boy."

"No, ma'am," Judd said respectfully. "Erika and I are friends." He suddenly remembered that he had asked Erika to pretend they were an item until Juanita-the-diva backed off. "Well, more than that."

"How much more?" the woman on the walker snapped in question. "You better keep in mind that Riki is a good girl. She's smart and kind. She also has a nice figure, which you men seem to consider important. But that doesn't mean you can take advantage of her."

Judd looked around, wishing he would have had the good sense to beat a hasty retreat with Ivan. "I wasn't planning to," he was quick to assure them.

"Why not? You gay or something?" the gray-haired harridan hurled at him. "If not, why aren't you married already? Or were you married and got divorced?"

Judd choked on his breath. No matter what he said, these old witches tried to play the devil's advocate. "I have never been married. The problem is that no one wants me. Too hard to live with, I guess."

"We could whip you into shape if we decide you're good enough for our Riki," the lady with the cane offered. "I never had trouble lining out Harold, God rest him."

"Yoo-hoo!"

Judd nearly collapsed in relief when Erika appeared on the porch to wave a greeting to the geriatric firing squad that had him cornered and had been blasting away at him.

"Well, that's all…for now, sonny," the white-haired woman said dismissively. Then she gave him the evil eye.

"Just watch your step with Riki, hear me? We eat marines for lunch."

"I was specialized army," Judd said.

"Served them up for supper," the woman on the walker said with a flash of false teeth. "You only get one mistake and wham. You're in the frying pan. And we mean business."

Judd was eternally grateful when the old women turned around and headed toward Erika. Ivan Snyder was right. Judd's training had not prepared him to deal with that brood of outspoken old hens.

ERIKA FROWNED curiously when Wanda Jamison, Freda Lawrence, Annabelle Burton and Hilda Watson hobbled across the lawn toward her. "What are you all doing out here?" She glanced warily at the aged car in the driveway. "And who drove?"

"Freda drove." Wanda grinned. "She only sideswiped two stop signs getting here."

"I did not," Freda huffed out. "You know what a joker that woman is."

What Erika knew for certain was that the four older women, who had cared for her while Aunt Frannie was busy getting the café on its financial feet, were characters extraordinaire—which made her ask, "What were you discussing with Judd?"

"Can't we say hello to the war hero who moved back to Moon Valley?" Hilda said innocently.

Erika had seen that mock innocent look too many times not to recognize it for what it was.

"He grew up to be quite a looker, didn't he?" Hilda added. "If I were fifty years younger—"

The Harlequin Reader Service® — Here's how it works:

Accepting your 2 free books and gift places you under no obligation to buy anything. You may keep the books and gift and return the shipping statement marked "cancel." If you do not cancel, about a month later we'll send you 4 additional books and bill you just $4.24 each in the U.S., or $4.99 each in Canada, plus 25¢ shipping & handling per book and applicable taxes if any.* That's the complete price and — compared to cover prices of $4.99 each in the U.S. and $5.99 each in Canada — it's quite a bargain! You may cancel at any time, but if you choose to continue, every month we'll send you 4 more books, which you may either purchase at the discount price or return to us and cancel your subscription. *Terms and prices subject to change without notice. Sales tax applicable in N.Y. Canadian residents will be charged applicable provincial taxes and GST. Credit or debit balances in a customer's account(s) may be offset by any other outstanding balance owed by or to the customer.

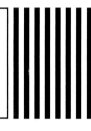

NO POSTAGE
NECESSARY
IF MAILED
IN THE
UNITED STATES

BUSINESS REPLY MAIL

FIRST-CLASS MAIL   PERMIT NO. 717-003   BUFFALO, NY

POSTAGE WILL BE PAID BY ADDRESSEE

HARLEQUIN READER SERVICE
3010 WALDEN AVE
PO BOX 1867
BUFFALO NY 14240-9952

GET FREE BOOKS and a FREE GIFT WHEN YOU PLAY THE...

SLOT MACHINE GAME!

Just scratch off the silver box with a coin. Then check below to see the gifts you get!

YES! I have scratched off the silver box. Please send me the 2 free Harlequin American Romance® books and gift for which I qualify. I understand I am under no obligation to purchase any books, as explained on the back of this card.

354 HDL D36C   154 HDL D36S

FIRST NAME   LAST NAME

ADDRESS

APT.#   CITY

STATE/PROV.   ZIP/POSTAL CODE

7	7	7	**Worth TWO FREE BOOKS plus a BONUS Mystery Gift!**
🍒	🍒	🍒	**Worth TWO FREE BOOKS!**
♣	♣	♣	**Worth ONE FREE BOOK!**
🔔	🔔	🍒	**TRY AGAIN!**

www.eHarlequin.com

(H-AR-02/05)

DETACH AND MAIL CARD TODAY!

"You're not, so act your age," Wanda interrupted as she hobbled up the steps.

Erika narrowed her gaze on the foursome. "Okay, which one of you is going to tell me what was *really* going on out there with Judd?"

"We were setting him straight, right off," Wanda replied. "He might as well know what's what, right from the get-go."

"Looks like that boy fixed this place up nice enough," Freda observed as she halted to pan the living room. "I was afraid it would be a rat hole by now. Most men can't keep house worth a darn."

"Judd hired Thelma Pruitt to keep the place spick-and-span, but he was doing a pretty good job of it beforehand. He's ex-military," Erika reminded them. "Everything has its place…and stays there."

"Just so he stays in his place while you're shacking up with him," Hilda said.

"We are not shacking up!" Erika burst out. "He's been a perfect gentleman."

"Ain't no such thing," Annabelle declared. "They all have hormones and you just never know when they're gonna kick in. It's usually at inappropriate moments, so you keep your guard up, girl."

Erika nodded dutifully, then returned to the kitchen to make coleslaw and potato salad. The foursome tramped off to tour the first floor of the house. Erika wasn't sure what the search party expected to find, but twenty minutes later they came to the kitchen door to announce they were leaving.

"We talked it over privately and decided you should marry him," Hilda said as she leaned heavily on her walker.

"Luckily, he's had his basic training in the army so it

shouldn't take him long to figure out his rank and file in the matrimonial pecking order," Wanda added.

"We aren't getting married," Erika protested. "We're just seeing each other temporarily."

"He looks like decent husband material to me," Annabelle said. "Strong, robust and he did come riding to your rescue, from what Frannie told us."

"You coming to visit on Monday, as usual?" Freda questioned abruptly.

Erika nodded. "First of the month. I'll bring the food and the pinochle cards. Anything else?"

"Yes, bring along your boyfriend," Wanda insisted.

Erika shrugged evasively. "I'll see what Judd has going."

Erika held open the door for the foursome. Amused, she watched Judd glance toward the house, then stride off, under the pretense of feeding his horses. It seemed he didn't want to be in plain sight, in case the foursome decided to surround him again.

Smart man. He knew when to cut and run.

JUDD DIDN'T SEE much of Erika the rest of the morning. He tried to stay out of her way and kept busy tending his ranch duties. By noon he had the place to himself. Erika had called David Shore for permission to stop by the café to pick up last-minute supplies, then she borrowed Judd's truck to run into town.

Alone for the first time in two days, Judd glanced across the pasture to see his livestock grazing in the distance. It was peaceful—and a little too quiet. Strange how quickly he had adapted to having Erika underfoot. When she wasn't popping out to the ranch at unexpected moments or taking over his house he felt…well…lost.

Determined to get something accomplished while he had the place to himself, Judd rolled the riding lawn mower from the shed, then set to work draining the oil and whisking off the dust that had collected while the machine was out of service. When the engine rumbled to life, coughing and sputtering from lack of use, Judd adjusted the choke, then took the mower for a trial run to trim the grass along the fence row.

When Erika drove up he cut the engine and glanced at his watch. She waved to him as she strode over to check the meat in the smoker. Drawn to her by some emotion he couldn't name—or was afraid to because of what he might discover about his feelings for her—Judd halted beside her.

"Everything going okay?" he asked, and got distracted by watching the sun glinting off her shiny, highlighted hair.

"Pretty much on schedule," she replied as she tested the meat. Then she adjusted the vent so the beef wouldn't overcook. "Sorry to invade your space. I stayed away as long as I could."

"I told you that you could come and go as you pleased." He reached out to brush a fleck of straw from her shoulder, his hand lingering longer than necessary.

She peered solemnly at him. "Judd, we need to talk."

"Oh? What about?"

He told himself to concentrate on conversation before he stepped over the line the way he had last night when he impulsively walked up and kissed her. Again, right this very minute, he had a real hankering to take those dewy lips beneath his and help himself to another tantalizing taste of her.

She motioned for him to follow her. "Come up to the house and I'll fix us a bite to eat."

He watched the hypnotic sway of her denim-clad hips as she surged ahead of him. Judd shook his head to dislodge the arousing thoughts that leapt to mind. Unfortunately, the more time he spent with Erika the more difficult it became to curb these betraying needs that assailed him.

Once inside, Erika rearranged the gelatin salads and desserts in the fridge to locate sandwich meat. Judd grabbed the bread, then poured two glasses of tea.

"So, what's up?" he asked impatiently.

"It's all over town already that we are seeing each other socially, thanks to Juanita Barlow and her Texas-size mouth," she reported.

Judd shrugged nonchalantly as he took a seat at the table. "That was the whole idea."

She frowned. "I'm not sure how this is going to work. Sure, I'll be in and out of your house for the next couple of days, and gossip has us doing all sorts of…" She hesitated then said hurriedly, "Intimate things together."

A vivid image popped to mind. Boy, was that happening a lot lately. He had lost his ability to remain distant and detached, thanks to this X-rated fantasy that hounded him.

"When I return to my apartment and we aren't seeing each other very often, people are going to be asking more questions," she continued. "This charade is going to require one fib after another. Maybe your former line of work demanded a cover and a few white lies, but I'm not good at it." She eyed him curiously. "What *exactly* was your job in the military?"

He smiled. "Sorry, that's extremely classified. But I can tell you that in the nameless places I went, the nameless contacts I made didn't recognize the name Foster."

Exasperated, she stared at him. "Great, you can juggle

lies and false assumptions and keep them straight. I'm not sure I can. I'm a terrible liar, always have been. I couldn't even pretend to be sick so I could play hooky from school without feeling guilty. Aunt Frannie saw through me every blessed time."

Judd grimaced. "I guess I didn't think it through when I told Juanita that we were an item. She was pawing at me and I needed an excuse to persuade her to keep her hands to herself."

Erika snickered as she joined him at the table. "Better get used to that. We could claim to be engaged and it wouldn't discourage Juanita. Chasing men is her favorite pastime. But I'm not sure how I'm supposed to act, now that we are *supposedly* a couple."

Judd chuckled at her expression. She looked so adorable with that wide-eyed innocent stare, her lush lips parted and that lopsided ponytail forming a golden fountain on the side of her head. He was magnetically drawn to her—and he couldn't help himself.

"You're supposed to act like this."

He kissed her. Right on those soft, dewy lips—and he nearly drowned in the sensations that instantly flooded over him.

"And this…" He curled his hand around the back of her neck, drawing her closer, absorbing her alluring scent.

Judd let go of his restraint and kissed her for all he was worth because that's what he craved—a deep, devouring taste of her. He didn't have to *pretend* to be involved in the kiss. He *was*—mentally, physically and emotionally.

Yep, he could most definitely get used to having Erika underfoot and kissing her anytime he wanted to. It worked for him. He wondered if it worked for her, too.

Judd didn't withdraw until he had to come up for air. He watched Erika's thick lashes flutter up and noted the bewildered expression on her face. He decided he liked seeing her confused and disoriented. It kept that alert mind of hers from leaping a few mental steps ahead of him.

"We'll do that in public a few times," he said, his voice raspy with the aftereffects of their kiss. "In front of Juanita-the-diva to be specific. Maybe she'll take the hint when she sees how infatuated I am with you."

She blinked twice. She opened her mouth, then clamped her lips shut. It was the first time Judd recalled seeing her speechless. It made him feel exceptionally good about himself because most of the time *she* had *him* baffled.

Wordlessly, Erika picked up her sandwich and took a bite. Judd did likewise. He wished she would say something. A noncommunicating Erika Dunn was totally out of character.

Two minutes later she looked over at him and said, "If you're going to do that in public, you need to warn me first."

"Why? So you can act like you like it?"

She replaced her half-eaten sandwich on her plate and said, "No, because I might forget it's an act and do this…"

Judd melted on his chair when she cupped her hands on the sides of his face and kissed him senseless. He wasn't sure what her point was supposed to be, but he was all in favor when she took the initiative.

When she drew back he tried to figure out what she was thinking and what she was feeling. Unfortunately, his brain had malfunctioned in midkiss. He just stared at her tempting mouth and wanted more. A whole lot more.

"Well?" She peered curiously at him.

"Well, what?" Had he missed part of the conversation during a mental bleep?

"Will *you* be able to handle that in public?"

Judd tamped down the stirring of desire, picked up his sandwich and said, "No problem."

Erika cast him a sidelong glance and asked herself what had just happened between them. It dawned on her that she had subconsciously taken Frannie's advice to grab for the gusto. She had actually come on to Judd after he came on to her. *Her.* Imagine that. She hadn't even felt self-conscious when she grabbed him and practically kissed off those sensuous lips of his. She had felt empowered after he had kissed her first, as if he had given her the green light to be spontaneous and impulsive.

Ah, she would give most anything if this make-believe courtship progressed into a real-live romance.

Careful, Riki, came the warning voice in her head. *Don't make more of this than what it actually is. This is just a ploy to discourage Juanita from hounding Judd.*

When Judd headed down the hall to shower and change for the Little League ball game, Erika spiffed up the kitchen and caught herself wondering what it would be like to live in this wonderful old house on this ranch just outside of town.

She could walk to work at the refurbished barn that she turned into a roomy restaurant….

She squelched the whimsical thought. *Right, like that would ever happen.* She would never actually be playing house with Judd Foster, so there was no sense speculating on what it would be like to have him as her own. For sure, it felt too natural and necessary already.

"Just enjoy it while you can," Erika reminded herself

sensibly. "You're doing him a favor, just as he is doing you a favor by letting you stay here. This won't last. If you get too comfortable and too attached you will find yourself on a collision course with heartbreak. So watch your step!"

It was good advice, Erika mused as she set out the food for the catered parties. But the long-held fantasy kept tripping her up. Maybe it would be worth the heartache to savor whatever amount of time she was allowed to spend with Judd. He'd had the starring role in her dreams since childhood. Better to have loved and lost, yadda, yadda.

There and then, Erika decided this was going to be a no-holds-barred charade. She wanted it all while opportunity was staring her in the face. The friendship, the companionship. And the passion. For as long as it lasted. She wanted to experience, firsthand, what she had read about in books and seen in movies.

Starting tonight.

Well, maybe.

If she could work up the nerve to take the initiative with Judd.

The rap at the door jolted her back to the present. Erika wondered how long it would be before the pup she had given to Judd would start barking to announce the arrival of guests. After the robbery she felt the need to be prepared for surprises—pleasant or otherwise.

Luckily, the two women standing on the porch had only arrived to lend assistance. Erika handed off several desserts and salads to the volunteers that were headed to the respective parties this evening. Thankfully, she wouldn't have to make so many trips in Judd's truck while delivering the meals.

When the two volunteers left, Erika hurried into the

spare bathroom to apply a thin coat of makeup and rear-range her off-center ponytail.

"Ready to rock and roll?" Judd asked as he poked his head in the doorway. "There will be fifteen boys bouncing around like pinballs at the park, anxious to get the game underway. We need to hit the road."

He smelled fresh and clean and his cologne tempted her closer, but Erika held her ground. Later tonight. She was going to try her hand at seduction tonight.

"I'm ready," she said as they carried boxes of food to the pickup. All the while she admired his masculine phy-sique and told herself that she was going to see a lot more of it later.

Maybe...

Chapter Nine

Judd was dismayed to note that Juanita Barlow had showed up for the game and had taken a front-row seat near the dugout. The woman appeared to be serious about running him to ground and breaking up the supposed courtship between Erika and him. Jeez, no wonder that vamp had already been through two husbands by the ripe young age of twenty-nine.

Every time Judd glanced in Juanita's general direction she waved and flashed him a sultry smile. He kept checking his watch, wishing Erika would show up to run interference. He would put her right beside him on the dugout bench, he decided. Everyone in the grandstands would realize they were a couple.

"Coach?"

Judd started, then glanced sideways to see Matt Vaughn peering at him. "You're supposed to be on first base, remember? That's your position."

The kid bobbed his head, then shifted from one foot to the other. "But I gotta go to the bathroom. I can't wait."

Judd came to his feet and signaled to the home plate umpire for time out. "Make a run for it," Judd murmured to Matt. "And take this with you."

Grabbing his discarded mitt, Matt scurried off. Judd made a big production of wandering out to the mound and calling in the rest of the team.

"What's wrong, coach?" the dark-haired shortstop asked. "Is Matt sick or something?"

"Naw, he just needed a bathroom break. We'll act like we're discussing defense strategy until he gets back."

The boys huddled around him.

"While we're here, let's remember our fundamentals," Judd suggested. "Remember to get your glove on the grass to field a ball. The play is going to be at first base if there's a hit. If you can't handle the grounder that comes to you, don't throw the ball. The runner might take an extra base."

"What if it's a fly ball?" the third baseman asked.

So far, no one had been able to catch a fly ball, but Judd didn't remind them of that. He grinned and said, "Go ahead and catch it and then we won't have to worry about where to throw it."

When Matt jogged to first base, Judd sent the team back to the field, then went over to hand the ball to the opposing team's coach who had manned the pitching machine.

"You plan to have these strategy conferences between innings?" the other coach asked teasingly.

Judd nodded and winked at the man who had been an older classmate when he was in school. "Yup, every time these little midgets need a bathroom break. I'm sticking to the very basics with these beginners. Not much baseball strategy going on here."

Chuckling, the other coach nodded in agreement. "Glad to see you aren't taking the game too seriously. But I'm giving you fair warning that some of the other coaches in the league are so eaten up with this stuff that they act like they're coaching in the majors."

Judd had no intention of taking life so seriously again. Well, except for this courtship with Erika. The thought prompted him to glance at Juanita who was decked out in a skimpy outfit better suited for barhopping. It was refreshing to encounter a woman like Erika who didn't advertise her wares—attractive though they were—to every man who wanted to sneak a peek.

And speaking of Erika, where was she? She should have been back from the catered parties by now, shouldn't she? Considering her streak of bad luck he wondered if she'd had trouble with his pickup or if some kind of catering catastrophe had waylaid her.

His concern dissipated when he saw his truck pull into the parking lot. Erika bounded out and headed toward the ball field. Good, he could relax and concentrate on his small-time coaching debut.

Pulling his cap low on his forehead, Judd dropped onto the bench to watch his second baseman bobble the slow-rolling grounder. The ball rolled between the boy's legs and he scurried over to pick it up. Thankfully, the kid didn't try to make a hurried throw to first base, allowing the other runners to circle the bases and score on one wild throw after another.

At least the kid remembered one of the two things Judd had told him. It was one more than he expected from these youngsters.

ERIKA ROUNDED THE CORNER of the dugout—and found herself enveloped in Judd's arms. He kissed her right smack dab on the mouth and said, "Glad you could make it, sweetheart. Everything go okay with the dinners?"

Although Erika felt self-conscious, aware that at least half the baseball fans sitting in the bleachers had witnessed their embrace, she felt sizzling pleasure streaming through her. For the duration of their make-believe courtship, she wouldn't have to conceal her affection for Judd.

And furthermore, if he wanted to call her sweetheart for the rest of her life it would be fine with her. For a while at least, she felt as if she belonged to someone and someone belonged to her. It was an exhilarating feeling.

"There was only a minor glitch. It happened on the way to the parties," she told Judd as he plunked on the bench and drew her down beside him. "A container of baked beans tipped over on the floorboard of your pickup. Fortunately for you, I took the precaution of spreading newspapers on the floor." She squinted at the distant scoreboard. "Good grief! Does it say *twenty-four* runs to *twenty-five* runs? In the top of the fifth? Which one is our team, by the way? Home or visitor?"

"We won the coin toss so we're the home team and we're ahead by one," Judd replied.

For a quarter of an hour Erika watched the game—watched Judd mostly. He looked as if he fit into small-town Texas. He was enthused and involved. The kids seemed to look up to him—and not because he was more than three feet taller than they were.

She was relieved that she had pushed and prodded Judd to take an active part in his hometown. This was excellent therapy for a man who had shut himself off from the world.

When Judd stood up beside her to shout instructions to the catcher, Erika watched the ball whiz past home plate.

"Comedy of errors," he said, grinning. "If you hit a sin-

gle in this league, your chance of stretching it into an in-
the-park home run is pretty much a given."

So it seemed, Erika mused as she watched the runner
round second base and dash to third. His coach, whom
Erika remembered from school, was waving on the runner
with expansive gestures of his arms. To her amusement, she
watched the boy veer away from third base and head directly toward home plate. After all, that was where his
coach was pointing. Fans and other coaches simultaneously began shouting instructions for the kid to reverse
direction to touch third base.

Meanwhile, Judd's catcher finally located the ball near
the backstop and launched it toward third base. The ball
made it halfway, so the runner, watching his coach hop up
and down in excitement, backtracked to third then zipped
toward home to score the tying run.

To Erika's amazement, the two umpires started flapping
their arms when the runner crossed home plate. Erika
wasn't an expert in baseball, but she figured the runner
must have committed a serious error when he veered so far
off the base path. Sure enough, the umpires called him out
and the game was over. Judd's team had barely squeaked
by with a win.

"We're undefeated!" Matt Vaughn shrieked excitedly as
he bounded into the dugout.

"How about that!" Erika enthused as she gave him a
congratulatory pat on the shoulder. "So how many games
has the team played?"

"It's our first!"

Straight-faced, Erika said, "A one-game winning streak.
Very impressive."

When David Shore, decked out in his khaki shorts and

matching team T-shirt, headed toward Matt, the boy leaped into his arms and gave him an excited hug. They had certainly bonded, Erika noticed.

She glanced toward the bleachers to see if Sylvie was watching. Despite what Syl said, Erika decided that she needed to speak privately with Dave. She knew exactly what it felt like to have inadequacy issues with men and she wanted to spare Syl the anguish of not knowing where she really stood with Dave.

If Sylvie's happiness wasn't Dave's first concern, then he wouldn't last long at the Vaughn residence. This, of course, would upset Matt, who seemed to think David Shore hung the moon.

When Erika noticed Juanita Barlow leaning into the backstop, decked out in her painted-on shorts and knit blouse, to nab Judd's attention, she strode over to loop her arm possessively around his waist. Juanita's provocative smile didn't diminish in wattage. She still looked as if she wanted to gobble Judd alive.

"Great game, honey," Erika praised as she pushed up on tiptoe to press a kiss to Judd's cheek. "You're in luck. This is bonus night for the winning coach." She hoped her seductive smile implied Judd was going to get lucky tonight and prompted Juanita to back off.

The smoldering glance Judd directed at her made her toes curl and her pulse accelerate. "You're wearing me out, sugar britches," he said huskily. "But for you, I'm always willing to go extra innings."

When Juanita scowled, turned around and stamped off, Judd chuckled. "You showed up just in time. I was getting propositioned, right here behind home plate. I'm pretty sure I could have scored if I had wanted to."

He hooked his arm around Erika's neck and dropped a quick kiss to her lips. "Thanks for coming to my rescue. You did good."

"My pleasure," Erika murmured as they walked arm-in-arm to the dugout.

She was beginning to wish that Juanita hung in there and didn't give up too easily. Otherwise Judd wouldn't require her assistance and there wouldn't be any excuses for her to kiss and touch him whenever the mood struck her.

"As soon as I gather up the gear, I'll go with you to pick up whatever you left behind at the catered meals," Judd offered. "So don't leave without me. I'll only be a few minutes."

While Judd was occupied, Erika wandered over to speak to Dave. "You and Matt really seem to have hit it off."

A wide smile spread across Dave's face. "He's a great kid. In my line of work, I've seen so many of them go bad that I just want to latch on to that sweet kid and enjoy every minute I can with him."

"Sylvie has done an excellent job of providing for Matt and being both mom and dad." Erika flashed a smile, hoping to diminish the sting in her next comment. "I sure hope Syl doesn't get the idea that you're hanging around her, just to be close to her loveable kid."

David, in the process of pulling the anchors from second base, jerked upright and gaped at her. "Did she tell you that?"

"Didn't have to," Erika hedged. "You were the first place Matt came to celebrate the victory tonight. *Not* to his teammates or his head coach. *Not* to his mom, but to *you*. I think he idolizes you, Dave."

She went very serious on him. "I consider you a good friend, but you need to know that I will tear your heart out if you hurt Sylvie. She's like a sister to me—"

"Hey, Dave, you promised me a snow cone after the game," Matt interrupted as he bounded across the infield like a jackrabbit.

"I remember," Dave replied, giving the boy a fond smile. "Go check with your mom to see if that's okay with her."

When Matt was out of earshot, Dave retrieved the base then stared somberly at Erika. "While you're handing out free advice, let me return the favor. People are already talking about you and Foster. That was quite a little performance the two of you put on tonight and it will fuel more gossip."

Erika couldn't argue with that, so she didn't try.

"I don't know Judd well enough to know how much of a Don Juan he is, but that brunette in the skintight clothes is obviously his for the taking. Looks like you and I both have a problem to resolve," he said.

"If Sylvie is at the top of your priority list, that will be one less problem that concerns me," she replied.

"And Foster better have you at the top of his list," Dave countered. "Otherwise I'm going to have a problem with him."

"I want to see Syl happy and I tried to play Cupid by matching you two together," she confided. "Personally, I think you two are great together. Just don't screw up." She waited a beat then asked, "You *do* like Syl, don't you?"

Dave nodded his sandy-blond head. "Yeah, I do. A lot. Maybe I haven't been clear enough on that. I didn't want to come on too strong too fast." He eyed her pensively. "And maybe you're just what Foster needs. I just hope he's smart enough to realize what a sweetheart you are. I don't want to see you hurt, you know."

When Erika wandered off the field to rejoin Judd he

glanced at her then stared speculatively at Dave. "That looked like a serious conversation. Was the cop warning you away from me? He gave me a little talk at Frannie's house this morning. You know, man-to-man stuff."

Erika flashed him a cheeky grin. "So you've been warned not to break my heart? Good. Nice to know the cop is watching out for me."

"Don't know why you need a cop when you've got a dream team of senior citizens circling like buzzards, waiting to peck me to pieces if I foul up," Judd said as he carried the canvas bags of equipment to his truck.

Erika winced. "I forgot to ask how that interrogation went this morning. They really don't mean any harm," she tried to reassure him.

"Easy for you to say." Judd smirked. "They didn't threaten to do you bodily harm if this courtship goes sour. We may have to run this scheme indefinitely to keep those old hens off my back. Personally, I think the fearsome foursome can pack a mean wallop."

Would an indefinite courtship be so bad? Erika wanted to ask him, but she didn't have the courage. Things would be much easier if Judd would simply fall in love with her during this charade. But, after seeing Juanita throw herself at Judd, Erika decided straightforward wasn't the approach to take with him.

She might have to rethink her planned seduction this evening. If Juanita, the skilled diva that she was, couldn't pull it off, Erika wouldn't have a snowball's chance in Hades.

Chapter Ten

Judd got reacquainted with a few more locals while he helped Erika gather up the empty bowls, dishes and utensils from the two parties. Facing the four-woman firing squad at the retirement center was a little unnerving. They pulled him aside and repeated their threat, just in case he had forgotten what they had told him that morning.

Erika had assured him that they were all bark and no bite, and were her guardian angels. He thought she was being way too lenient and optimistic. *Avenging* angels, maybe. Definitely not *guardian* angels.

In his opinion, the military and intelligence communities had made a serious oversight by not enlisting the services of the "firing squad." Those women had missed their calling, Judd was sure of it.

"Lord, I'm tired." Erika sighed as she slumped on the pickup seat during the drive home. "Another full, rich day." She glanced at him apologetically. "I've really complicated your life, haven't I? I swear this isn't intentional. Tomorrow should be better. Sunday is my downtime day. I'll just chill out and give you all the space you need. Promise."

"No meals catered from my kitchen? No return visits from your hell's angels…oh, excuse me, your *guardian* angels? And what about your would-be big brother, Crime Dog Dave?"

"Nope. You're just stuck with me. I'm sure that will be bad enough for you. Fortunately, your ranch shouldn't be more crowded than one unwanted guest."

Judd drove in silence for ten minutes, and then glanced over to see that Erika had fallen asleep. Her head rested at an uncomfortable-looking angle against the passenger window.

Well, what do you know, he thought, the Energizer bunny did occasionally wind down. She didn't even wake up when he pulled in the driveway.

He climbed from the truck and walked around to lift her sluggish body into his arms, then carried her to the house. She sighed softly, her breath whispering against his neck like a lover's caress. Desire thrummed through him as he shifted her carefully in his arms to unlock the front door.

She awoke momentarily when he set her on the edge of his bed. "We're home already?" she mumbled dazedly.

Home. Judd hadn't thought of anywhere as home for over a dozen years. "Yeah, we are. Go back to sleep. I'll see you in the morning."

"No," she protested. "My turn to take the couch."

When she tried to lever herself to her feet, Judd pressed her to her back, and battled the instinctive urge to follow her down. "Stay put," he insisted.

"Okay, but I owe you." She turned over on her side, still fully clothed, and promptly fell asleep.

Judd closed the drapes, then ambled into the hall. He glanced disconcertedly at the couch and made a face. He couldn't deal with the cramped quarters two consecutive nights. True, he had slept in worse places during his tour of duty, but he was done with that.

Since he had yet to purchase spare beds for the extra rooms upstairs, he decided to make a pallet on the floor in his office. Gathering quilts, he made his nest, then wormed and squirmed to get comfortable.

He would be a lot more comfortable—in more ways than one—if he just cuddled up beside Erika.

First thing Monday morning he was going to buy another bed. Or save his money and just climb in beside Erika.

Whoa, boy! came the voice of conscience—a voice he really was beginning to hate. Charade or not, he was going to have to play it straight with Erika, even though his male body was scowling at him to get up close and very personal with her. He wasn't going to push.

He had reasonably good instincts. Usually. He would know when the time was right. If, indeed, the timing would ever be right for them.

By mutual consent or not at all, Judd told himself as he laced his fingers behind his head and stared up at the ceiling. He listened to the computer's electronic hum and told himself to go to sleep.

Damn, he hoped Juanita Barlow didn't give up and go away too soon. It was nice to have an excuse to stay chummy with Erika, to loop his arm around her when he felt like it and kiss those tempting lips every once in a while.

"You go, Juanita," Judd murmured as he shifted onto his side. Maybe Erika would hang around long enough to actually *like* him instead of perceiving him as one of her charity cases.

Judd hated to admit it, but he was probably the kind of man who took some getting used to. He had been a bachelor, set in his ways, for years on end. According to the four old hens, men had to be trained and whipped into shape to make good boyfriends or husbands. Considering the life he had led in the military, his experiences were worlds apart from Erika's. Could he be the kind of man she really wanted and needed? He certainly didn't perceive himself as much of a catch.

The more he thought about it the more convinced he became that he would be a lousy steady boyfriend or husband. Then there was Erika. She was independent and strong-willed. She had developed her routine of chasing around town, doing her good deeds and playing Cupid when opportunity presented itself. No doubt, she had lived on her own long enough to be pretty set in her ways, too.

So there you go. Maybe a man should just stick to hot, sweaty sex and avoid emotional complications, he thought as he rolled to his back and stared at the underwater screensaver on the computer monitor. The thought brought Juanita Barlow to mind and Judd grimaced. He didn't want to become that aggressive brunette's between-meal appetizer until she landed her third husband. If sex didn't mean something...

His eyes shot wide open. What the hell was he saying?

If he let himself care too much and things didn't work out with Erika he would be back to square one. Judd scowled ferociously at himself.

Having Erika planted right in the middle of his life, on his ranch, was fouling up his thought processes. He had returned to his hometown to revitalize the family farm. He had come home to be alone, to grieve, to decompress after years in the elite, demanding branch of the military. Now he was an average Joe, a small-time baseball coach and the employer of the hardship cases Erika had foisted off on him.

For a man who had once been very much in control, he had definitely lost control.

Worse, he wasn't even sure who he was these days, due in part to Erika's philosophy that if Mohammed wouldn't come to the mountain then she'd bring the mountain to Mohammed. Since he hadn't mingled with folks in his hometown Erika had filled his ranch with hired help so he wouldn't be alone.

He had to admit that he enjoyed all the activity. But mostly he enjoyed kissing and touching Erika every chance he got. Now he wanted her in the worst way.

The thought got him all stirred up again. He shifted uncomfortably on his pallet. There was nothing wrong with his sex drive, he mused. Other than the fact that it had been stuck in neutral far too long. Now he was raring to go and the woman he wanted was sleeping in his bed while he was sprawled out on the floor. What was wrong with this picture?

Sighing in frustration he flounced on his bedroll. As he expected, he had to count several flocks of sheep before he finally drifted off.

WHEN THE PHONE RANG early the next morning, Erika groped to locate it on the nightstand. It took her a moment to orient herself and remember that she wasn't at her own apartment. Judd's phone was on the other side of the bed.

Rolling sideways, she snatched up the receiver. "Hello?" she mumbled as she raked her hair from her face, then kerplopped back on the pillow.

"Riki? Did I wake you up? Sorry. You're usually up and moving by this time of day," Aunt Frannie said too cheerily.

"It's been a long, nerve-wracking few days," she replied with a drowsy sigh.

"Well, I had to call so you would be the first to know that Murph and I have decided to get married."

Married? Her groggy mind stalled out. Getting married already?

Erika discarded the wayward thought and frowned as she tried to gather her thoughts. "I'm happy for you. Really. I like Murph and he's been good for you. But isn't it a little soon to be talking marriage? You and Murph have only been hanging out together for a couple of months."

"A little longer than that, actually. But it's June," Frannie said, as if that explained everything.

It didn't, not to Erika's satisfaction. "What has June got to do with anything?"

"Well, we always stock up at Blue Moon Café to cater weddings and rehearsal dinners so we can plan our celebration without much expense or extra effort," Frannie said pragmatically.

That was Frannie. Practical to a fault…until she had suddenly decided to plunge, headfirst, into wedlock. But that was also like Frannie, she realized. When Frannie made up her mind, she didn't hesitate, just plowed forward, full steam ahead.

"Murph seems like a nice guy, but what do we really know about him?" Erika questioned. "Is he divorced with children? Am I getting a new daddy and stepbrothers and sisters?"

"Widowed," Frannie reported. "And yes, you'll be getting two big brothers."

"Wonderful." She glanced up to see Judd propped against the doorjamb, looking adorably rumpled with his raven hair standing on end and a five o'clock shadow rimming his jaw. He was staring curiously at her so she put her hand over the receiver and said, "It's Aunt Frannie."

Judd frowned in concern. "More problems with the café or your apartment?"

"No, but she has decided to marry Murph. This month. We're the first to know."

"Good for them." Judd pushed away from the doorjamb. "Tell them congrats for me while I put on the coffee."

Judd had taken the news in stride, but Erika was having a little difficulty adjusting to the idea because she and Frannie had been an inseparable team for years and everything was about to change drastically. "Aunt Frannie, I know you said it was time to grab for the gusto and I'm fine with that, but I think you're rushing this a bit."

"I'm fifty-five and he's sixty," Frannie replied. "We're in the October of our years."

"What is this preoccupation with the months of the year?" Erika asked, befuddled.

Frannie ignored the question and said, "This is our good news. I'll let you talk to Murph about the other stuff."

Erika's hand clenched around the phone in wary anticipation. Now what had gone wrong?

"Hi, Riki. Murph here. Just wanted to update you on the stolen IDs and credit card."

His voice sounded serious. Erika gulped.

"The thieves couldn't use your credit card, but they racked up several hundred dollars in fuel, motel rooms and supplies. They seem to be spending café profits as fast as they can. They have apparently headed west through Texas, New Mexico and Arizona. Your car has been spotted several times, but the men are still on the run. At least now the police have some idea where to search for them."

The news left Erika feeling outraged and helpless. If she had to pay for those criminals' cross-country joy ride it was going to put a serious dent in her savings account—if there was anything left by the time she compensated for the loss at Blue Moon Café. Her dream of purchasing Judd's old barn and paying for the remodeling was headed straight down the toilet.

"However," Murph continued, "I did freeze your bank accounts so the thieves can't touch it. What about your car insurance?"

Erika gnashed her teeth. "I was only carrying liability. Looks like I'll have to buy a bicycle with a basket strapped to the front of it to get around town."

She looked up when she saw Judd entering the room, carrying two coffee mugs. "Thanks for the help and the report, Murph. I really appreciate it. And congrats on your upcoming wedding."

"I'll take good care of Francine," Murph said very sincerely.

"You better," Erika threatened—after Murph hung up.

"Something tells me that you're upset," Judd said as he sank down on the edge of the bed.

"Why should I be upset?" Erika said, and scowled. "I've lost my transportation indefinitely because I didn't have the right insurance coverage. The thieves have been spending café money fast and furiously. And Frannie wants to get married immediately and I'm inheriting two big brothers that might not be thrilled to have me as their new sister…"

Judd handed her a mug. "Drink this. Life won't seem so depressing once you're fully awake and have decided on your plan of action."

"You mean this is just a nightmare, not reality?" She smirked. "*I wish.* I didn't need for Aunt Frannie to spring this hasty wedding on me while I'm in the middle of two emotional crises."

Judd frowned. "Two? What else is bugging you besides the fallout from the robbery?"

Erika averted her gaze and sipped her coffee. It wasn't the best coffee she had ever tasted, but it was the first time in years that someone had made it for *her*.

"What gives?" Judd prodded when she avoided his question. "What is the second crisis?" When she didn't respond he got right in her face and demanded, *"Tell me."*

"You are." The words burst out involuntarily and just kept on coming. "I wanted to have a flaming, rock-my-world affair with you, but you don't seem that interested and I don't know how to seduce you, damn it. Obviously the direct approach that Juanita is using doesn't appeal to you and I—"

When she finally got control of her runaway tongue her face went up in flames. Apparently Frannie and Murph's phone call had triggered too many emotions and set her off.

Good gad, had she really said all that stuff to Judd? She wished she *were* living a nightmare so she could wake up and discover the past few days had been a bad dream. Well, except for staying with Judd. She didn't want to give that up.

"What did you just say?" Judd stared intently at her.

"Here, hold this." Erika shoved the mug at him, then buried her head under the pillow. "Don't pay any attention to what I said. I am totally deranged."

Judd pulled away the pillow. An amused smile quirked his lips. "Come again? I didn't catch that muffled comment."

"I said I've finally flipped out and have no idea what I'm saying."

Judd chuckled at her cornered expression and the wild rush of color that pulsed in her cheeks. "So let's have a flaming, rock-the-world affair. I was trying not to act interested because I didn't think you were interested. Since we have a day off, we have time," he added with an all-in-favor grin. Then his brows furrowed into a suspicious frown. "Or is this about seducing me out of my cedar barn?"

"No. Your barn is the very last thing on my mind at the moment. It's—" Erika rolled off the opposite side of the bed and headed for the bathroom, lickety-split. "I'm going to shower so I can jump-start my brain."

"Fine, we'll discuss the details of the flaming affair after you dry off," Judd teased unmercifully.

She shot him a dour glance, then slammed the bathroom door.

Judd felt as if a burden had been lifted from his mind. It was a relief to know that Erika, too, had contemplated the possibility of taking their relationship to an intimate level. For certain, he had been doing some serious fantasizing lately.

It would have to be just sex, of course, he reminded himself. After losing Steve, Judd had made a pact not to let anyone else close enough to risk enduring that anguish again. There had to be ground rules. No permanent commitment. No chance of getting so attached that he wouldn't know what to do with himself if Erika got fed up with him and left. They had to keep it simple and uncomplicated.

But he was definitely long overdue for some heady, heart-pumping sex.

The erotic thoughts and images that sprang to mind made him hard and needy in three seconds flat. He could easily visualize Erika naked in the shower. Both of them naked in the shower. There would be several minutes of visual stimulation. And touching. He wanted there to be a lot of touching, too.

Judd was on his feet, stripping off his clothes as he crossed the room. He had been fighting this lusty attraction for quite some time now.

He was done fighting temptation.

When he eased open the door, stark-bone naked, he saw the vague outline of Erika's profile through the frosted glass of the shower door. Lust and anticipation delivered a staggering blow.

No more pretenses, he told himself. No more distancing himself from what he wanted—badly. This might be a one-day affair, but it was going to be a doozy.

When Judd opened the shower door and stepped inside, Erika's jaw dropped open and she stared at the evidence of his arousal. She savored the unhindered sight of his lean, muscular physique, but the jolt of embarrassment that bombarded her nearly knocked her legs out from under her. Her wild gaze flew back to his face to note that he was looking his fill at her. Gasping for breath, she tried to cover herself, then spun to face the wall.

"What are you doing?" Her voice hit a shrill pitch.

"It's obvious, isn't it?" he said as he closed the door behind him.

She glanced over her shoulder, watching him stare at her back, her rump and her legs. Her wide-eyed gaze devoured him before she came back to her senses and whipped her wet head around to huddle beneath the spray of water.

Awkwardness and self-consciousness buffeted her to such extremes that she suffered a head rush. "I've n-never showered with a m-man before," she got out—barely.

"Well, this is how it's done," he said, chuckling.

Judd slid his arms around her trim waist and gently drew her rigid body against his. With the water pulsating around them and a cloud of steam engulfing them, Judd nuzzled his cheek against the curve of her neck.

"Relax," he whispered. "Surely you know by now that I would never hurt you. We're just going to get to know each other better."

His hand drifted from her waist to the enticing flare of her hips. He felt her tremble against him, heard her breath catch. Fascinated by the pleasure he derived from caressing her, he retraced the leisurely path, then brushed his thumb against the under swell of her breast.

And suddenly, she turned in his arms, hooked her hands behind his neck and kissed him with such ardent passion that he staggered on his feet. His hands were all over her, mapping every luscious curve and swell, and her hands were all over him—except in the place where he wanted her to touch him most.

Judd knew already that Erika was vibrant and energetic, but he hadn't expected her eager, uninhibited response to set off so many frantic sensations inside him. She was driving him crazy, but he wanted to slow down, to explore her one caress at a time. Why that seemed crucial he couldn't say for sure, but that's what he wanted.

Unfortunately, she was fueling his desire to such extremes that he wanted to devour her. Here. Now. This very minute.

Wasn't it just last night that he had made a vow to get control of his life? Well, so much for that noble idea. Right now he was about as *out* of control as a man could get. And suddenly he could have cared less. His world had shrunk to the size of this shower stall and his senses were overloaded with pleasure. He couldn't think, just *respond* wildly to this incredibly alluring woman who had come alive in his arms.

He kissed her feverishly, demandingly, possessively and she reciprocated. Another blast of desire seared him as he clutched her slippery body tightly against him, letting her feel what she was doing to him.

Another minute of this and it was going to be all over but the shouting, he realized as he came up for air. That would be fine. Great in fact. But he also found himself wanting all the space he needed to roll and tumble all over his king-size bed with Erika in his arms.

The thought prompted him to shut off the faucets. He clasped her hand in his and led her, dripping wet, to the un-made bed. When he tugged playfully on her hand, she fell off balance and they tumbled together in a tangle of arms and legs.

"Well, that takes care of my dilemma about how to se-duce you," she said with a laugh.

"All you had to do was ask," he assured her, grinning rakishly. "We've already wasted two days. Since when have you held back in telling me what you wanted?"

Her smile faded as he wedged his knee suggestively be-tween her legs and positioned himself above her. She started to say something—and must have thought better of it because she clamped her mouth shut. When she peered up at him with those enormous blue eyes another jolt of lust riveted him.

"What?" he asked, his voice strained, his body tightening with need. "We've already discovered that we can tell each other anything. Don't hold out on me now, sweetheart."

She hesitated briefly, looped her arms over his shoul-ders, took a deep breath that diverted his attention to her full breasts and said, "I haven't done this before."

He nodded in understanding—or so he thought. "I

know. The shower thing. I sort of started off backwards."
He chuckled. "That's supposed to come after the wild,
sweaty sex. We'll follow normal procedure next time."

"No," she murmured, looking really self-conscious and
nervous now. "I mean I haven't done *it* before." She finally
met his stunned gaze. "And I wish you would hear what
I'm saying so I don't have to repeat it again."

His smile evaporated. He was poised above her like a
muscled warrior and his eyes narrowed in confusion. He
stared at her as if he had never seen her before. Or maybe
like she was some endangered species. Whatever the case,
he didn't look quite as eager as he had moments before,
Erika noted.

Well, too bad. Erika had been fantasizing about this moment with him for years on end. But never in her secret
dreams had she envisioned him gaping at her in stunned astonishment. Blast it, she wished she had kept her trap shut.

"You are kidding," he said eventually.

Erika shook her head. "You've seen what my work
schedule is like. When would I have had time for an affair?" When he tried to shift sideways, Erika tightened her
hold on his broad shoulders. "I want this. With you. I've
waited a long time to find out what all the fuss is about. So
don't ruin my day, because it has been a really bad week
already."

"Why me?" he asked on a strangled breath. "Why now?"

He looked so adorable and bemused that she couldn't
help but grin at him. "Because you're here and it's my day
off," she said teasingly. "Perfect timing." She drew his
head steadily toward hers, until his sensuous lips were
only a breath away. "I really like you a lot. And that great
body of yours feels wonderful when I'm snuggled against

you. I'm asking this one last favor before I pack up and leave you alone. Is that enough reason?"

He studied her intently. "You're absolutely sure about this?"

She nodded very deliberately. "I'm sure."

Judd was still reeling from the realization that Erika hadn't been intimate with a man. She wanted him to be the first and she wanted it to be now? Well, who was he to argue with a woman who obviously knew her own mind?

He was all in favor—couldn't deny that—but he was definitely going to use another approach. Just doing it for the sake of appeasing an elemental need with Erika seemed inappropriate. Of course, he had already considered that thought before he discovered she was a virgin.

That fact still threw him for a loop.

Judd stared down at her and made a silent pact that he was going to take his time with her. He would make it good for her. He would be seriously disappointed in himself if he didn't.

"Judd?" She peered uncertainly at him, her soft lips so close, yet unbearably far away. "I really do want you."

He caved in immediately. He brushed his lips over hers as he shifted to stretch out beside her. Then he made a slow study of her silky body. He caressed her gently, and took immense pleasure in arousing her and watching her arch into his hand. She was like silk and satin, and memorizing the feel of her shapely body by touch totally fascinated him.

Truth was, he had never taken quite so much time with a woman, never had been this mentally, physically and emotionally involved before. But passion was new to her and he wanted to make the moment extra special. If what happened next between them wasn't as good as her speculations, then he was going to feel as if he had let her down.

That was not acceptable.

After he had brought her body to life with the touch of his hand, she reached impatiently for him. "I'm not finished yet," he murmured huskily.

"You should be," she rasped. "I ache all over. Now is a very good time."

He chuckled, trying to remember the last time he had laughed and loved simultaneously—and came up with *never*. Not even once. Being with Erika made passion new and intriguing. This wasn't just the scratch-an-itch-during-a-weekend-furlough fling that he was accustomed to.

"I'm doing this my way," he said as he leaned over to brush his lips against the column of her neck, and noted her pulse was thundering in triple time. "That was just phase one of do-it-up-right, knock-your-socks-off sex… And this is phase two."

"Ah…" Erika's breath came out in a wobbly rush when Judd's lips skimmed over her shoulder. Then he flicked his tongue against her nipple. "This is going to drive me crazy. Guaranteed."

Sure enough. Heretofore unexperienced sensations surged through her body, leaving her quivering and burning like a forest fire. He suckled her breast, then glided his hot mouth to the other aching peak. His hands were moving everywhere, sensitizing her with feather-light caresses that made her skin prickle with heat. And when those maddening kisses drifted over her rib cage and descended down her belly, fiery anticipation seared her all the way to the core.

So this is what it felt like to be on fire with desire, Erika thought in breathless awe. She hadn't expected such dedicated patience from Judd. But then, she was dealing with a former military specialist who had obviously learned the importance of being thorough and deliberate.

And man, oh, man, was he thorough and deliberate! He could have had his own satisfaction minutes ago. She was more than ready to end the suspense. But now, he was embellishing her secret fantasy, giving her what she hadn't even known she wanted and liked.

"Oh—" Her voice deserted her when his lips skimmed her inner thigh. She lost the ability to think when he flicked at her with his tongue. Wild, burning sensations assailed her like a barrage of blazing bullets. He caressed her intimately with his moist tongue and fingertips and the world went out of focus momentarily.

Erika struggled to draw breath. She was desperate to draw him closer so he could make this inexpressible empty ache go away. Sensations mushroomed until she shook with urgency combined with immeasurable pleasure. She was going out of her mind while he touched her intimately, stroked her until she wanted to scream and curse him for prolonging this erotic torture.

She swore she was dying, one fiery sensation at a time, and he was letting it happen. She swore she was hyperventilating and was about to pass out. She did not want to miss this milestone in her life by being oblivious. This was the moment in time when her fantasy finally connected with reality. She darn sure wanted to be conscious to enjoy phase three—and she wanted him to hurry up about it!

"Now. Please," she panted as she clutched at his forearm, knowing she was probably going to leave claw marks while she was clinging to him in wild desperation.

Judd felt the first wave of her climax buffet her and he swore inventively when he remembered the protection he kept in his wallet was in the hip pocket of his jeans, which were halfway across the room. She was so ready and eager for him that her nails were digging into his triceps like spikes. Not that he cared. He was so hot and hungry for her that his entire body thrummed in rhythm with his accelerated pulse and he was feeling no other pain except throbbing desire.

"Where are you going?" she wheezed when he rolled away.

"Not far. Hold that thought. I'll be right back."

Like a shot, he darted across the room and dropped to his knees to fish out his wallet. He hadn't checked his supply of condoms lately. Hadn't needed one. If he was fresh out he was going to kill himself. He figured he would die of sexual deprivation shortly anyway.

He was mightily relieved to find one foil packet. He hurriedly donned protection then joined her in bed.

Her vivid blue eyes were enormous in her flushed face as she stared at his erection. Then she lifted her gaze to meet his smile. Judd didn't remember wanting anyone or anything as much as he wanted to sink into her sultry softness and appease this indescribable need that hammered at him. But he reminded himself to be gentle—or as gentle as he could be when frantic impatience was making its demands known—and felt.

"Phase three," he whispered as he braced himself above her. He nudged her legs farther apart with his knee and grinned seductively. "The grand finale…"

When she reached out to enfold him in her hand and guide him exactly to her, his voice dried up. Need exploded through him like a nuclear blast. Judd instinctively surged forward, feeling her hot and tight around him.

She planted her feet beside his knees and arched into him—and he really lost it. Wild desire took control of his mind and body, sending him plunging deeper. And deeper. With one hand planted beside her head, he used the other hand to guide her legs around his waist, and then up to his shoulders.

She stared unblinkingly at him as he moved within her, and he knew she could see the sensations building inside him by the expression on his face. Her open honesty got to him. She made this moment as intimate as it could possibly get by watching *him* while he watched *her* slide into the depths of breathtaking passion, then soar to the dizzying heights of ecstasy like a phoenix rising from the ashes.

Judd felt the second wave of spasms grip her body, saw her luminous eyes widen and her mouth form a silent O as she tumbled over the edge—and took him with her on a free fall that was like nothing he had ever experienced.

He half collapsed upon her as his body shuddered in release. He clutched her tightly in his arms, feeling her soft and trembly beneath him. The world whirled like a pinwheel while he savored the amazing feeling of being buried so deeply inside her that they were one entity sharing the same ragged breath.

"Well," she said a long moment later. "That takes care of breakfast. How long do we have to wait for lunch?"

Somehow Judd found the energy to raise his head— which was amazing because he swore he didn't have an ounce of strength left. He grinned down into her impish smile. "I should have known that you, being a chef, marked the passage of time with the scheduling of meals."

"It's what I do," she replied as she reached up to trail her forefinger over his brows, the bridge of his nose, his lips. "Finish up one meal and prepare for the next." Her mouth quirked and her eyes twinkled mischievously. "Best sample platter I ever had."

Judd chuckled. Best *time* he'd ever had. Being with her like this gave him a warm, fuzzy feeling from the top of his head to the soles of his feet—and all parts in between.

"You *are* serving lunch, aren't you?" she asked hopefully. "I only have one day off, you know. This sex-fantasy cruise darn well better come with a midnight buffet, too."

This playful side of her personality intrigued him. He could get used to being with her like this on a regular basis. "If you want all the bells and whistles I'm going to have to make a run into town to restock." He grinned scampishly. "No ports of call to scuba dive without wet suits."

She snickered at his comment. "Well, shoot. I had visions of spending the day right here. No shore leave for either of us."

"I'll set a land speed record getting back here," he promised as he eased away.

Erika pulled him back to her. "One more thing before you go."

And then she kissed him until his eyes crossed and desire made him hard and aching again.

"Now, *you* hold that thought," she murmured provocatively.

Judd dressed in record time. He cast one last longing glance at Erika who had modestly drawn the sheet over her luscious body and smiled at him in promise.

He was out the door, jogging to his pickup in nothing flat. The rational side of his mind kept whispering that he didn't want to involve himself in a relationship that might end unpleasantly somewhere down the line. Nothing was permanent, after all. He had learned that the hard way time and again during his previous profession.

Oh, what the hell, he decided as he whizzed into town— and hoped the local cops—especially Dave!—weren't out in full force. He wanted Erika and she wanted him. No one was going to get hurt because they would set up the ground rules—as soon as he got back.

Chapter Eleven

After Judd left, Erika flung back the sheet and headed for the shower, wearing the kind of smile on her face that she had never worn before. Judd had caught her completely off guard after she had stepped into the shower, but she had overcome her embarrassment and seized the moment.

It had been even more amazing than her expectations. She had been in love with the dream for years, but if Judd hadn't come after her, she doubted she would have worked up the courage to make the first move. Telling him what she wanted had been difficult, because if he turned her down she didn't think she would ever have been able to face him again.

Considering that he had turned down *Juanita* previously, Erika had known there was a very real possibility that he might turn her down, too.

Thank goodness he hadn't. She wouldn't have wanted to miss the passion they had shared for that moment out of time.

Sweet, incredible memories cascaded over her as she stood beneath the shower spray. She smiled. Cinderella had been granted her magical night at the ball, but Erika was going to enjoy a full day with her Prince Charming. Maybe she had only a one-day honeymoon—without the traditional wedding—but she was going to make the most of her time with Judd to compensate for all the years that her dream had shimmered beyond her reach.

Guilt stabbed at her momentarily when she remembered that the old-fashioned values she had grown up with didn't include wild, wanton trysts without some kind of permanent commitment. Willfully, Erika flung aside the niggling thoughts and told herself that in order to share intimacy with Judd Foster she couldn't permit herself to expect more than the moment.

He didn't seem to have much interest in a wife or family. Heavens, she'd had to keep after him, just to get him to accept the makeshift family she had delivered to his doorstep.

Erika would not let herself harbor any illusions about happily ever after. She refused to allow herself to think past the moment. She was going to live in the now and count her lucky stars that she had one day with Judd. This was no time to get greedy, she lectured herself.

Wrapping up in a towel, she padded into the kitchen to whip up omelets and ham. She smiled mischievously as she carried the plates and silverware back to the bedroom. She fully intended to feed Judd lunch. Then make a meal of him.

Erika was ready and waiting when Judd returned with his sack of supplies. He halted in the doorway, grinned then peeled off his shirt. "Don't start without me," he teased on his way to the shower.

He was back in a flash, walking toward her, gloriously naked. Muscles rippled. Dark eyes fixed on her.

Erika caught herself wondering what it would feel like to be the focus of his intent attention for, oh, say, the next fifty years.

Hey, one day at a time, remember? she told herself.

She whittled off a forkful of omelet and offered it to him after he settled in beside her. He reciprocated by offering her a bite of ham from his plate. When Erika purposely dropped a piece of omelet on his chest, she leaned over to nibble at it.

"That will get you in trouble," he said, his voice dropping an octave.

He stopped talking altogether when she glided her hand down his washboard belly. Desire and feminine curiosity overwhelmed her as she folded her hand around his hard flesh. She wanted to arouse him as thoroughly as he had aroused her. She wanted to know him by touch, by heart. As she stroked him with her fingertips, she spread a row of kisses across his abdomen, then traced his rigid length with the tip of her tongue.

Judd clenched his fingers in her hair and groaned her name when she kissed and caressed him intimately.

His response made her feel empowered, encouraged her to fulfill her own fantasy of making Judd want her to the point of mindless desperation. When she took him into her mouth and suckled him she heard him hiss out his breath, felt his muscular body shudder.

She might not have his heart, but she was sure that she had his body's undivided attention. And that was enough because she was living and reveling in the moment. Period.

Judd clenched his jaw and bit back a howl of pleasure when Erika brought him ever closer to the crumbling edge of self-restraint. "You're killing me," he groaned, then gasped and made a frantic grab for control.

The sensations she aroused in him were so intense and demanding that Judd clutched her arm and pulled her up his body. He settled her on top of him, then curled his hand around her neck to bring her mouth down on his. Tasting his own desire for her on her lips sent his thoughts spinning like a cyclone. He needed to be inside her again. Now. He was going to come apart at the seams if he wasn't.

He opened his eyes to see her smiling smugly at him. The wicked woman. She knew exactly how desperate he was for her. Well, turnabout was fair play, he supposed. He had reduced her to begging that first time and he had felt pretty smug about that, too.

He flashed her an okay-you-win grin and grabbed a foil packet from the nightstand. A moment later he brought her hips down onto his and drove himself deeply into her. The pleasure of feeling her holding him so intimately made him moan aloud.

"Happy now?" she teased as she rocked above him.

"Ecstatic." He brushed his thumbs over the peaks of her breasts, then skimmed his hands downward to guide her hips against his. A slow, hot burn went through his body and he shut his eyes to savor the incredible pleasure.

"Whatever you need. Whatever you want," she whispered as she bent to kiss him.

Her breasts skimmed his chest, her lips melted upon his and he whispered back, "All I want and need is you."

They moved as one, as if they had been lovers for months, not hours. Judd felt himself rushing toward completion—out of control again. But he wanted Erika right there with him, every step of the way, because her pleasure had become a priority. Giving less than all of himself to her, for her, had become tantamount to him.

When she reared back, riding him, moving with the motion he'd set he looked up to see her silky hair tumbling over her shoulders and her blue eyes shimmering with desire and pleasure. Judd swore he had never seen anyone so radiantly lovely and alive. And what she made him feel, while they were locked together in the throes of passion, defied words.

He had never felt so intimate with or connected to a woman. Until now. But all sorts of emotions converged on him when he was with Erika. What he was feeling for her was dangerous and a little unnerving, but there you had it. Wondrously unique. Incredibly special.

His thoughts scattered in four different directions when the dam of self-restraint broke loose. He clutched her frantically to him as wild sensations sent him into a mindless spin. He felt Erika let go of every inhibition and cling desperately to him as they catapulted over the edge of oblivion and plunged into an undercurrent of pulse-pounding, mind-boggling pleasure.

In the aftermath of unbelievable passion, he wrapped her securely in his arms and nuzzled against her shoulder. A sigh escaped his lips as his energy and strength flowed out like the tide.

Definitely rock-the-world quality sex, he mused as he battled to bring his breathing under control.

Once his head cleared—which seemed to take the longest time—he glanced sideways to see upturned omelets and plates strewn on the bed. This was not good, he decided. It was bad enough that he wouldn't be able to crawl into his own bed without picturing the two of them hot and wild for each other. Worse, he wouldn't be able to sit down to a meal without remembering Sunday brunch with Erika.

With a sigh, he closed his eyes to compensate for tossing and turning on his pallet for several hours the previous night. She had worn him out completely and he needed a nap. The ranch chores could wait. The world would have to be put on hold because Judd was too content where he lay.

Life just didn't get any better than this, he decided before he fell asleep.

WHILE JUDD WAS DOZING, Erika inched away, then tiptoed over to grab some clothes. She walked naked into the hall, dressing as she went. She entered the kitchen to get a drink—and lunged for the phone the instant it rang, hoping the sound hadn't disturbed Judd.

"Hello?"

"I am really mad at you. I just called to tell you that I'm not speaking to you for a while."

Erika frowned. "Sylvie? What's wrong?"

"You know what's wrong. I saw you out at second base with Dave last night. You had a talk with him, didn't you? I told you not to!"

Erika pulled the phone away from her ear when Sylvie yelled at her. "Okay, I did talk to Dave, but I didn't tell him how you felt about his affection for Matt. I just made it sound like I was making an observation and that he and Matt seemed close. I asked him if you felt left out."

Sylvie groaned. "Same difference. It makes me sound pathetic. I still don't know what to think about what Dave said."

"What did Dave say?" Erika prodded.

"After we put Matt to bed last night Dave and I… Well, never mind about that. Afterward he told me that he was falling in love with me."

Erika chuckled. "And this upsets you *why?*"

"Because I don't know if he said it because he thought

it was what I wanted to hear, after your talk with him, or if he really meant it."

"I could ask. Discreetly, of course," Erika offered.

"No!" Sylvie erupted. "You've done enough damage. And if that whole fiasco wasn't enough to make me nuts, Richard showed up in his usual condition while Dave was here."

Erika tried to put a positive slant on that. "That's good. Richard needs to know that he can't keep showing up at any time of the night. And Dave needs to see, firsthand, what you've been dealing with for three years."

"It didn't work out that well," Sylvie muttered. "Richard got all huffy and when he staggered back to his car and tried to drive off Dave arrested him for DWI. How am I supposed to tell Matt that the man he idolizes arrested his real father and is urging me to get a restraining order? I am trying to get past Richard, but Matt isn't. He still holds the hope that his father will be a part of his life.

"And by the way, this is the last straw," Sylvie declared. "No more men disrupting my life. I've had it with all of them. They complicate everything."

Erika glanced up to see Judd striding into the kitchen, then she said, "No, they don't."

"Mark my words, girlfriend, they do." She sighed audibly. "I'm done venting now. I'm going to eat a quart of double fudge ice cream and hope it makes me feel better."

"I'll be right over to talk you down from your emotional cliff," Erika insisted.

"No, you have enough to deal with right now. And here I am unloading on you," she added with a self-deprecating groan.

"I'm on my way," Erika said, then hung up before Sylvie objected. She turned to Judd. "May I borrow your truck?"

"Sure. What's up?"

"Sylvie is having a crisis and she needs me."

Judd grinned at her. "Okay, but your shirt is on inside out. You might want to fix that before you go."

Erika glanced down to note the shoulder and side seams were showing. Modesty prevented her from peeling off the knit shirt in front of Judd. Crazy, wasn't it? Earlier they had been as close and intimate as two people could get and now she was feeling uncomfortable about undressing in front of him.

Just went to show you that moments of wild passion wreaked havoc with your usual perspectives.

"So, what's Sylvie upset about?" Judd questioned as she turned her back to rearrange her shirt.

"Her ex-husband, Richard, showed up last night, four sheets to the wind, while Dave was there. Richard refuses to acknowledge the fact that Sylvie isn't his wife anymore. Knowing Richard, he was being jealous and demanding."

Erika turned to face Judd. "Richard is the type who likes to drink and carouse. He didn't even bother to show up when Syl went into premature labor. I was the one who was there to hold her hand and help with Matt because Richard was so unreliable. I was also there for moral support during the divorce and to reassure her that all men weren't pond scum."

"Richard Vaughn." Judd frowned pensively. "Seems like I remember him vaguely from high school. He was three or four years younger, right?"

Erika nodded. "That's the one. His family had money to throw at him. Richard was spoiled rotten and self-indulgent. He never grew up, even after he became a father.

"Last night he really got ticked off when Dave arrested him for drinking and driving," she informed him.

Judd grimaced. "Doesn't make for amicable relations."

"Gotta go, Tex." She drew his head to hers to deliver a quick kiss, then dashed off.

She was going to help a friend in need, but she was anxious to return to Judd and cherish their last day together—and their night. This might be all she had of her secret dream and she didn't want to waste a moment of it. If it hadn't been her best friend who needed moral support, Erika wouldn't have left the ranch until Judd got tired of her and shooed her on her way.

ERIKA PULLED INTO Sylvie's driveway, surprised that Matt wasn't outside playing stickball with the neighborhood kids. When Syl answered the door, Erika craned her neck to glance into the living room. Matt wasn't planted in front of the TV, either.

"Where's Matt?" Erika asked as she breezed inside.

"My mother picked him up after Sunday school because she hasn't seen him in a week," Sylvie replied. "I finished off the ice cream and now I'm a ball of nervous energy. Let's go clean up your apartment or something. Dave said the cops are finished investigating and Francine gave you the keys to the new locks last night. I haven't even seen the disaster zone yet."

Before Erika could suggest some sort of distracting entertainment, Sylvie grabbed her purse and shot through the door. "I'll drive. You don't have a license right now. Good thing you know a cop who will overlook the infraction."

Erika fastened her seat belt and held on when Syl whipped from the driveway, then sped off. "You ingested way too much chocolate. You need to calm down."

"Do I? I would rather just hit something to relieve my frustration."

"I would rather you didn't hit something with your car while I'm in it," Erika put in. "I've had a traumatic weekend, you know."

Sylvie took a deep breath and expelled it in an audible rush. Then she relaxed behind the wheel. "Enough about my problems. So, what is going on with you and Judd?"

Erika was uncomfortable discussing what had been going on between them. "We're getting along fine," she hedged. "I'll go back to my apartment in the morning."

When Sylvie stopped in the parking lot, an uneasy sensation rolled through Erika. She had been able to distance herself from the thought of having those thugs invade her personal space while she was staying at Judd's ranch. Now she had to deal with knowing they had rummaged through her belongings. Had to deal with putting her home back together and moving back to her own place.

Her world had seemed safe and secure…and perfect while she was with Judd. It had been a fairy tale come true, but she had to return to reality, she reminded herself sensibly.

"Oh, my God!" Sylvie howled when she got her first look at the ransacked apartment. "What a mess!"

Erika was aware that Sylvie was presently in an emotional tailspin because of Dave and Richard, but hearing her rant in outrage did nothing for Erika's mood. She was definitely going to have to clean everything to erase those thieves' presence—and it needed to be soon or she couldn't reclaim her home.

"Surely you don't plan to stay here until you've had time to replace the items that were taken," Sylvie said as she swooped down to upright the coffee table. "You can stay with me. I could use a buffer right now."

Erika thought it over while she scooped up the candles

and magazines and returned them to their place on the end table. "I'll be fine here, as soon as I clean and disinfect. I'm not around much anyway. This week I have a wedding rehearsal dinner at the café and several deliveries to make for business lunches." She shot Sylvie a pointed glance. "Besides, you need to deal with your feelings for Dave and you know it. I will only be in the way of that at your house."

Sylvie huffed out a breath as she veered into the cubbyhole kitchen to restock the cabinets. "Maybe I should break it off with Dave and stick to my original plan of raising Matt alone."

Erika smiled dryly. "Or maybe you should latch on to the best thing that has happened to you and follow Aunt Frannie's theory of seizing the moment. She called this morning to tell me that she and Murph are getting married right away."

Wide-eyed, Sylvie lurched around. "Are they really? Just poof! Married after what? A month of dating?"

"Three months, according to Aunt Frannie."

"After all those years of raising you alone, she finally decided to make time for herself, huh? Well, isn't that something? Good for her. It's past time."

Erika still had reservations, but maybe that was because she and Frannie had been a team for years. Maybe she was being selfish, knowing she just couldn't pop in on Frannie whenever she felt like it anymore.

Erika was going to be the odd man out—again.

She studied Sylvie, still young and attractive and active and realized how much Frannie had sacrificed to provide a home and family support for Erika. The thought of Sylvie following the same lonely path as Frannie broke her heart.

"You should marry Dave," Erika said decisively. "When I think of all Frannie gave up for me, it doesn't seem fair. I don't want you to do the same thing. As an added bonus, Dave adores Matt and wants to be an integral part of his life."

Sylvie tensed, then wrung her hands nervously. "I just don't know. I'm afraid to make another mistake."

Erika rolled her eyes. "For Pete's sake, Syl, surely you can see that Dave cares about you and shows all the signs of being ready for a commitment. He told me last night that he's seen so many kids go wrong that he just wants to enjoy Matt and have a positive influence on his life. And yours, too."

"That is *sooo* sweet." Sylvie's eyes filled with tears. Then she covered her face and sobbed. "I didn't realize how much Dave probably needs a sense of normalcy to anchor him while he's dealing with the ugly side of society."

Erika walked over to give Sylvie a supportive hug—as she had so often while her best friend rode an emotional roller-coaster, compliments of her ex. "You have given Richard one chance after another, hoping he will become reliable and responsible where Matt is concerned. He has shown up unexpectedly too many times, trying to persuade you to take him back and promising to change his ways. You've got to convince him that you are never going to take him back so you can get on with your life."

"I know," Sylvie mumbled. "I've tried to be firm with him, but he always upsets me. I have Matt's feelings to consider and that makes it more complicated. I don't know how to handle it."

Erika glanced over her shoulder when she heard the neighborhood dogs barking up a storm. Her first thought was that the robbers had returned, but she reminded herself that they had crossed the state line and headed west.

"I just need time to figure this out with Dave." Sylvie drew in a restorative breath and tried to pull herself together.

Although Erika knew she was going to sacrifice precious private time with Judd, she decided to give Sylvie what she needed. "Why don't I pick up Matt from his grandma's and take him with me to Judd's ranch? Then you and Dave can sit down and sort everything out and figure out how to deal with Richard's constant intrusion."

When Sylvie nodded and wiped her eyes, Erika gave her another reassuring hug. "Good. That's settled and out of the way. Now let's put this place in order so I can pick up Matt. Maybe we can work in a horseback ride before dark. That should make Matt's day."

Together they cleaned the kitchen counters, the living room and bedroom. Erika promised herself that she would take time tomorrow evening to disinfect every nook and cranny.

"Thanks, Riki," Sylvie said as they surveyed the restored apartment. "You have always been there to talk me through my inadequacies and insecurities and prod me into dealing with them." She shook her blond head and laughed ruefully. "At school, I confront situations head-on before they escalate, but when it comes to my private life I keep dragging my feet and hoping things will work out by themselves."

"That's because Richard messed with your head and your heart," Erika insisted. "He will continue to control you until you take charge. Maybe you should consult Dave about how to approach Matt with his father's problems. He might be a wealth of helpful information."

"I will." Sylvie headed out the door. "No more enabling Richard to misbehave. I am definitely done with that," she added with firm conviction.

Erika sat on the passenger seat during the drive and

sighed in relief. She had watched Sylvie cut herself off from men for three years because Richard was like an albatross around her neck. It was high time that Richard learned to play by *Sylvie's* rules.

What Sylvie needed was a capable, caring man like Dave around to *enforce* those rules.

As for herself, she'd had her day in the sun, her fantasy weekend in Never-Never Land. Well, part of one anyway. What she had shared with Judd was more than she had dared to hope for. She wished she could stay at his big, wonderful house indefinitely. Permanently. She wished she could laugh with him, love with him and spend her life trying to make him as happy as he made her.

It was just a whimsical dream, of course, but it really was a nice thought.

Unfortunately, the three little words she longed to hear Judd whisper to her would never come. He didn't want permanent commitment, especially while he was struggling to deal with the loss of his friend and trying to acclimate himself into civilian life. Her only lure for him was that she had been accessible and convenient and he'd had no complaints about a short-term fling.

Boy, that was a depressing thought. Erika shifted uncomfortably on the car seat. Then she reminded herself that she had asked for this. She'd also had her eyes wide open going in so it was too late to whine about her decision.

Be careful what you wish for because you might get it.

"Too bad no one guaranteed that you get to keep what you wish for," she said under her breath.

"What did you say?" Sylvie asked, cutting her a quizzical glance as she pulled into the driveway.

"Nothing. Just thinking out loud." She manufactured a

bright smile as she dug into her pocket to retrieve the keys to the borrowed pickup. "Go call Dave and invite him over for supper so you can hash this out. I'll pick up Matt from your mom's house and have him home shortly after dark."

Silently cheering Sylvie on, Erika watched her friend march resolutely up the front steps and disappear into the house. Keeping her fingers crossed that everything worked out satisfactorily, Erika went to get Matt.

JUDD FROWNED CURIOUSLY when Erika returned long after he expected her. He noticed Matt was riding shotgun and wondered what crusade the local do-gooder was on this time. He also wondered if this was Erika's subtle way of telling him that she wanted their one-day fling to come to an end prematurely because she'd had enough of him.

What changed her mind? he wondered. Was she having misgivings after the fog of passion cleared up? Too bad he hadn't spent enough time around women to understand them. He was definitely at a disadvantage here.

"Coach!" Matt bounded from the pickup and darted across the lawn. "Riki said we could go horseback riding while I'm here. She said Old Nell was the perfect mount for me. Can we go? I've never been on a horse before."

Judd chuckled at the kid's enthusiasm for life. Had he ever been that exuberant? Yes, he recalled. He had felt pretty alive and happy this morning. With Erika.

He cut her a quick glance, noting the pleading expression on her face. Hell, what was there about this woman that always got to him? She kept pushing him around, getting him to do things he hadn't planned on doing with his personal life. And he just kept letting her get away with it. Why was that?

"Where are the horses?" Matt surveyed the grazing cattle. "Are we riding the cattle? Can you put saddles on them, too?"

"Easy, pardner," Judd drawled. "Have a little patience and we'll bring the horses from their stalls and saddle up."

Matt whooped with excited anticipation and bounded toward the metal barn.

"I hope you don't mind," Erika said after the boy was out of earshot. "Dave and Syl need some quality time to work things out."

"Catch me up. What things?"

"Like, is this relationship going somewhere? Do you want to take the next step? How will it affect Matt?" she replied.

"Sounds complicated," Judd said as he watched Matt climb up the rails to sit atop the fence.

"It is." Erika ambled toward the barn. "I told you about obnoxious Richard. His only contribution in life is siring an adorable kid who wants a dad like most of his friends have. Now Richard is probably really steamed because he had to spend the night in jail. He'll likely show up to take his frustration out on Sylvie. I hope Dave is there if he comes calling again."

"How big a problem do you think Richard will be for Dave and Sylvie?" he questioned.

"Depends on how much booze Richard consumes," she murmured. "Matt was asleep during last night's fiasco. Dave and Sylvie have to figure out *if* they should tell him or *how* to tell him. I'm sure the decision will have to be weighed carefully and it won't be easy."

"Then we'll show the kid a good time before he has to deal with problems kids shouldn't have to face," Judd decided as he quickened his step. "The meteorologists are forecasting thunderstorms for this evening so we better get a move on. Sure would hate for it to rain on the kid's parade."

He halted when Erika latched on to his arm. The smile she bestowed on him had to measure at least fifteen hundred watts. When she pushed up on tiptoe to give him a loud, smacking kiss, he decided she hadn't gotten tired of him yet. That was heartening.

"What was that for?"

"Because you're my hero, helping me out in a pinch—and you're saving the day for Matt."

Judd hooked his arm around her waist, feeling as if everything was right with his world again. "Don't wanna be your hero, sugar britches," he murmured huskily. "I'd rather be your lover."

"You're both," she whispered. "I—"

Whatever she intended to say—and judging by the expression in those luminous blue eyes, it was important—was overridden by Matt's impatient voice. The moment was lost.

"Are you guys coming or not? Where's the saddles? I don't have cowboy boots. Is that okay?" He glanced skyward. "Do those clouds mean it's gonna rain? We need to go right now, don't we?"

Judd chuckled in amusement and strode forward. "Pushy kid. He's spent way too much time around his honorary aunt."

Erika pulled a face as she hurried after him. "Thank you so much for the insult. By the way, I don't know how to ride."

"You didn't know how to have wild, rock-your-world—"

Erika clamped her hand over his mouth and her face

turned crimson red. "Do not finish that sentence, hotshot. There's a kid with rabbit ears present." She stared at him with mock severity. "I will deal with you later for that wisecrack."

"I'll be looking forward to it," he guaranteed with a rakish grin, and then turned his attention to Matt.

ERIKA SAT on horseback and marveled at Judd's natural ability to relate to Matt. It made her yearn for a child of her own—and a husband who was as playful and patient as Judd.

You're really torturing yourself today, aren't you? This is a great picture, but it's not going to happen. The image of what she was missing struck another heart-wrenching blow as she listened to Matt chatter incessantly and watched Judd sit a horse with such experienced ease.

Erika had been in love with Judd for years, in love with the image of the handsome hero who had rescued her from emotional turmoil and restored her shattered pride. But she had definitely fallen in love with the man himself, not just the picture that had occupied her dreams for sixteen years.

Endearing qualities and exasperating flaws alike, Judd Foster was the man she wanted to spend her life with. She didn't want to *pretend* to be a couple to counter Juanita's advances. She wanted this to be real and everlasting.

You want the whole fairy tale, but you aren't going to get it. Accept that. Quit sitting here feeling sorry for yourself, she chastised. *You're staring at panoramic scenery and admiring a ruggedly handsome rancher. Not to mention spending time with a little boy who is in cowboy heaven. Enjoy this while you can.*

After her pep talk, Erika drew in a deep breath of clean

country air. This was her last night of leisure this week. No sense in spoiling the last few precious hours by sulking.

THREE HOURS LATER, they returned to the barn to unsaddle and feed the horses. While Matt talked Judd's leg off and a thunderstorm grumbled in the distance, Erika headed to the house to throw together a meal.

Her heart melted down her ribs when Judd entered the kitchen, carrying Matt on his shoulders. She had missed out on this by not having a father, she mused. Heck, she didn't even know who her father was. She had missed out on a lot by not being part of a normal family. She wished for a better childhood for Matt.

She sincerely hoped things worked out between Sylvie and Dave. And Matt. Having a home and family was something she had longed for. If nothing else, she could enjoy watching Sylvie find the happiness *she* deserved—the kind that continued to elude Erika.

"This is a great kid," Judd said after he sent Matt off to wash up for supper. "I'm surprised you didn't give me one of these little tykes, too, while you were delivering my ready-made family."

"Maybe you should rent one. Make sure it isn't just a whim," she suggested as she put supper on the table. "According to Syl, little squirts require a lot of time, patience and commitment."

"Right. During the week I'm already tripping over the pets and employees you handpicked for me. A six-year-old boy might be a bit too much."

She smiled when she heard Matt romping down the hall. "I'm sure Matt will have another million questions for you, in between bites of supper."

"Bring on the grub!" Matt bellowed as he burst into the kitchen. "I'm starving. Is there dessert? Mom always lets me have dessert."

"She does not," Erika contradicted. "Nice try, kid."

While Matt chowed down, Judd tugged on her shirt-sleeve to nab her attention. "I'll take my dessert later."

Erika dropped the serving spoon and it clattered on the table. Judd's dark, smoldering gaze focused intently on her. Desire surged through her body, triggering memories of the intimacy they had shared and leaving her to burn. Her face flushed with color and she looked away because the heat in his eyes kept pulsing through her.

She wasn't used to dealing with this sexy, rakish side of his personality and it rattled her. But she liked it—a lot. Ah, how easy it would be to get used to having Judd come on to her like this for the rest of her life.

Snap out of it, you fool! He is never going to ask you to make this permanent, came that sensible voice in her head.

Erika was really beginning to despise that voice.

Chapter Twelve

By the time Erika was ready to take Matt home the wind had changed direction and a cool breeze whipped around her. Judd followed Matt and her outside and stared pensively toward the threatening sky.

"I better move those two young cows into the barn," Judd said. "According to Ivan, abrupt changes in temperature and weather can send cows into labor. They might as well have a dry place to bring their first calves into the world."

When Judd strode off, Matt bounded along beside Erika. "Can we stay and see if Judd gets new calves?"

Erika shook her head. "Sorry, champ, I told your mom that I would have you home about dark." When his hopeful expression crumpled, she added, "Dave should be at your house by now. He will be anxious to hear about your adventures on the ranch."

The distraction worked superbly, Erika noted. Matt shot toward the pickup, ready to head home to fill in Dave and his mom on his horseback ride along the river.

The sky opened up before Erika reached Sylvie's house. Clutching Matt's hand, Erika made a mad dash for the front porch. She noticed how Dave went down on one knee to meet Matt at his level when he flew across the room—and into his arms.

Erika cast Sylvie a discreet glance to gauge her reaction to the reception Dave received. She was all smiles rather than wary concern. Erika took that as a good sign. Surely that implied Sylvie had been reassured of Dave's feelings after their heart-to-heart talk.

"Come on back to the bathroom, Rik, and I'll get you and Matt a towel to dry off," Syl requested.

Erika followed her down the hall. "So…is everything okay between you and Dave?"

Smiling, Sylvie nodded her curly blond head. "Better than okay, actually. He asked me to marry him and I said yes."

Erika's eyes nearly popped from their sockets. "That's wonderful news. When's the big day?"

"The sooner the better," she replied as she handed over the towel. "Definitely before school starts so we can all three adjust to the new arrangement. We're thinking the end of June."

Two more weddings in June, she thought, her mind whirling. The next few weeks were going to be chock-full of arrangements.

"You'll be my maid of honor, of course," Sylvie insisted.

Always the bridesmaid and never the bride. Oh well, what else was new? At least part of her fantasy had come true this weekend. She was grateful for that.

"Oh, Rik, I'm so happy. And relieved!" Sylvie gushed as she lurched forward to hug the stuffing out of her. "He said he loves me like crazy and I believe him. And I'm crazy about him, too. I was just afraid to let him know for fear I would get hurt again. Maybe I can get on with my life now. Maybe Richard will finally realize I'm never going to take him back. It's the closure we both need."

Cupid and the Cowboy

Erika nodded in agreement as she stepped back to towel-dry her hair. "I'm really happy for you, Syl. Whatever you need, whatever I can do to help with the wedding, I'm there for you."

Sylvie smiled affectionately. "You always have been there for me, Rik. I probably haven't told you often enough how much I appreciate having a loyal friend like you, but I do."

"Hey, Mom!" Matt called out as he bounded down the hall. "Dave wants to marry us! He asked if that would be okay with me and I said yes!"

Erika chuckled in amusement when Matt threw his arms around his mother's waist and hugged her close. She glanced over her shoulder to see Dave leaning against the doorjamb, smiling adoringly at Sylvie and Matt. Apparently Dave was about to get what he had always wanted, too. A family that was nuts about him. A place he could go when the frustrations and torments of his difficult job began to wear on him.

There was no doubt in Erika's mind that Dave cared very deeply and devotedly for Sylvie and Matt. It was written all over his face, glowing in his smile.

"Officer Shore, you got yourself one heck of a prize," Erika murmured as she brushed past him. "Make sure you treat 'em right or you'll have to answer to me."

"Not to worry on that count." Dave, still grinning from ear to ear, pressed a kiss to Erika's cheek. "I have you to thank for introducing me to my future happiness."

Erika swallowed a sentimental lump as she watched the soon-to-be family offer each other a group hug. She wondered fleetingly if all crucial decisions and conversations took place in the smallest room of the house. Probably, she decided.

"Well, my work here is done," Erika teased. "I better hit the road before the storm gets worse."

She hotfooted it off the front porch to face another soaking before she could yank open the door and launch herself into the pickup. She stabbed the key into the ignition and sat there for a moment, feeling happy yet envious that her best friend was wanted and loved and that Dave was going to be the husband and father that Richard Vaughn had never been.

If she was partially responsible for two wonderful, well-deserving friends finding each other then she was extremely satisfied. Playing Cupid was the next best thing to finding happiness herself.

If only Judd felt half the affection she felt for him…

Erika stifled the thought as she shifted the pickup into reverse and backed onto the street. She had one full evening left with Judd and she was going to make the most of it.

She eased down on the brake in the intersection, then frowned worriedly when she noticed a rain-drenched silhouette waving wildly to her. The man stood beyond the beam of her headlights so she couldn't tell who he was. More than likely one of Sylvie's neighbors had had car trouble and needed a lift home. Having made two wild dashes in the rain, Erika pitied anyone who was afoot tonight.

The shadowy figure dashed toward the passenger side of the truck. A sense of unease, triggered by her frightening ordeal at the café, shivered down her spine. Curse those two thieves for destroying her faith in the good of humanity. She was not going to let that bad experience define her interaction with friends and acquaintances. Willfully, Erika shoved aside the wary thought and unlocked the doors.

When the door whipped open and the dome light flicked on, Erika was startled to see a drenched Richard Vaughn.

She winced when she spied the pistol that he jerked from his coat pocket and pointed directly at her. She could tell by the glassy look in his eyes that he had gone on a binge after being released from jail.

"Drive," Richard growled, then bounded onto the seat. "To your place. You think you're the guru of relationships, so you can prove it. You messed up everything between Sylvie and me and now you're going to fix it."

Erika gulped hard and clamped her shaking hands around the steering wheel. Now was not a good time for her to recall that adage about no good deeds going unpunished. Richard was going to make her pay for seeing that Dave and Sylvie got together.

"Richard, let me take you home so you can calm down," she offered in a nonconfrontational voice.

"No. I'm not going to calm down or go home until you undo what you've done," he muttered bitterly. "I came by Sylvie's place this afternoon to get things worked out with her, but you showed up to interfere, as usual. So I followed the two of you over to your apartment. I was standing outside the window while you convinced Sylvie to forget about me and marry that damn cop!"

Erika winced when his voice hit a loud pitch. As she veered left to drive to her apartment, she remembered hearing the neighbors' dogs barking to beat the band and wondered if someone was prowling around outside. Sure enough. Richard had eavesdropped on her conversation with Sylvie and it had made him furious.

"You never did like me. Not that I'm too crazy about you, either." Richard scowled. "You always meddled in our affairs and tried to turn Sylvie against me. It's *your* fault our marriage failed!"

"No," she contradicted, trying to keep her voice even. But it was difficult when Richard glared hatefully at her while holding her at gunpoint. "You were never there for Sylvie or Matt when they needed you most. If you want Sylvie back you're going to have to make some major changes."

"I'm getting her back, all right," Richard said slurrishly. "You talked her into marrying that cop and now you're gonna talk her out of it. Then I'm gonna tell her how it's gonna be between us again and you're gonna keep your damn nose out of it, *for once.*"

Erika spared Richard a discreet glance as she pulled into the parking lot and stopped several doors down from her apartment. If she got a running start, she might be able to lock the door before Richard could overtake her. But no matter what else happened, she was absolutely *not* calling Sylvie to come over. She would *not* endanger her best friend's life and future happiness!

JUDD PULLED HIS CAP LOW on his forehead, then hightailed it from the barn to the house. He had penned up both young cows in the stalls and had checked them over carefully. By morning he predicted that he would have two new additions to his Black Angus herd. In the meantime he and Erika were going to make the most of their last night together.

A wry smile quirked his lips as he peeled off his wet clothes on his way to the shower. He wanted to make this a night to remember for Erika because... Well, because...when he was with her he was happy. He felt at peace with himself, content. Knowing she intended to return to her own apartment and to her job in the morning left him feeling restless and dissatisfied.

Exactly when had that happened? he asked himself as he stood beneath the shower spray. Obviously it had happened sometime after that first afternoon when she had barged into his home, bearing platters of tempting meals and flinging open the drapes to bring sunlight into his dreary world. Now she was on his mind constantly and the mere anticipation of their upcoming night together made him hard and needy.

She had turned his life upside down and burrowed into his heart—even when he had fought to keep his emotional distance from her. Mission impossible. He might as well face the fact that he was hooked on her and that he felt lost and empty when she wasn't around to brighten up his days.

Wrapping a towel around his waist, he padded back to his room to grab clean clothes. He checked his watch. Erika had been gone an hour and a half. He wondered what was taking her so long to return from town. It was a real downpour out there tonight. He would feel much better when she was back here with him.

He wondered if she would take offense if she knew he was fretting over her. She was a strong-minded and independent woman and she was accustomed to taking care of herself. Would she think he was overly possessive if he called Sylvie to see why Erika was running late? Most likely.

"Well, tough," Judd said as he reached for the phone. Erika had run into a streak of bad luck this weekend. Just to be on the safe side, he was going to check on her.

Sylvie answered on the second ring. "Hello?"

"Sylvie, this is Judd. Can I talk to Erika for a minute?" He needed an excuse—fast. "I was going to ask her to pick up a few things for me at the convenience store on her way home."

That sounded reasonable, didn't it? Yeah, he would ask her to buy whipped cream, he decided wickedly. That would give her a strong indication of what he planned to do with it when she got home.

"She's not back yet?" Sylvia questioned in concern. "She was only here about twenty minutes. I told her that Dave and I decided to get married and she took off so the three of us could make our plans."

"Married?" Judd croaked. "Already?"

"Well, when you know, you just know," Sylvie declared, a smile in her voice. "When Rik gets there, give her a hug and kiss to thank her for getting Dave and me together. Cupid has struck again."

Judd congratulated the happy couple, then hung up. Married? Matt would be thrilled to have Dave around permanently. And from what Erika had told him about Richard, Sylvie deserved a kind, caring, reliable man to help her overcome her disappointment and disillusionment with her ex.

Wheeling around, Judd headed to the living room to stare out into the rainy darkness. Any moment now Erika would pull into the driveway, he convinced himself.

He checked his watch again. Okay…so where the hell was she? he thought with an impatient sigh.

ERIKA SWITCHED OFF the headlights and watched Richard from the corner of her eye. It was now or never, she convinced herself. She reached into the pocket of her jeans to retrieve her spare apartment key. It was going to take a few crucial moments to unlock the door, so she needed to be several steps ahead of Richard. Considering the condition he was in, she was counting on his reflexes being as sluggish as his voice.

Shouldering open the door, Erika bounded out and took off at a dead run, knowing Richard had to climb down and dash around the hood of the truck to catch up with her.

"Damn it!" Richard sneered as she rushed off.

He lurched from the truck, stumbled, then righted himself by bracing his free hand on the hood. Pushing himself away, he pointed the pistol at her and charged through the downpour.

Erika crammed the key into the lock, then gave the knob a quick twist. She spared Richard another glance before she plunged into her apartment. Unfortunately, she couldn't shut and lock the door before he plowed into it.

Pain exploded in her head when the door slammed against her temple. Richard's forceful entrance sent her staggering backwards. She tripped over the arm of the sofa and landed in a dazed sprawl.

Keeping the handgun trained on her, Richard slammed and locked the door behind him. "Try something like that again and you're gonna get yourself shot," he snarled in between seesaw breaths. "Now get Sylvie on the phone right now and tell her to come over here, pronto. And tell her not to bring that damn cop with her. If she does, I'll shoot him. No cop. I just want to talk to her alone. Got it, Riki?"

"Got it." Erika rubbed her aching head as she rolled from the sofa. Reluctantly she walked over to pick up the phone. "You better show a little patience," she cautioned Richard. "It will take a while for Sylvie to get here. The streets are probably starting to flood from all this rain. In the meantime, you should rehearse what you intend to say to her. And it better be good. You have some apologizing to do."

"Since this is your fault in the first place, you're the

last person I plan to take advice from," he said bitterly. "I know exactly what to say to Sylvie. The same thing I've told her for the past three years. This time she is going to listen. We were meant to be together and my kid needs me."

Matt needed Richard's empty promises like Erika needed a hole in the head. Bad analogy, she thought, grimacing, as she stared at the speaking end of his pistol.

"She won't buy into that," Erika warned. "You have been telling her the same thing for too long. You break as many promises as you make. And worse, you never show up to take Matt when you say you will. You have to make an effort to be reliable and to be there for her and Matt for a change."

Richard's face puckered in a sneer. "Clam up. I told you I don't want your advice or your interference. If not for you, Sylvie would never have divorced me. You're going to fix the mess you've made of everything! Make that damn call. *Now!*"

Erika stared at Richard, then at the handgun aimed at her chest. She wasn't as terrified as she had been when she was robbed at gunpoint. She should be. Richard was bristling with hostility and he wasn't thinking rationally at the moment. It wouldn't take much to set him off.

Plus, he had been outraged and insulted when Dave arrested him and made him spend the night in jail. Now Richard was striking back to get even by taking Sylvie away from Dave. There was no telling what might happen if Sylvie showed up and told Richard that it was over. For good.

"Quit stalling, damn it," Richard snapped when Erika tarried too long in thought. "Make the call."

Erika sucked in a cathartic breath to calm her nerves. It

didn't help much. Then she punched in the number. "Okay, Richard. It's ringing. Just try to relax."

She tried very hard to take her own advice.

THE PHONE RANG shrilly in the silence. A sense of unease prickled Judd's skin. He hesitated before answering the call. The same instinctive feeling had stung him the night he walked toward the café and found Erika bound and gagged. It was the same feeling that had knocked him for an emotional loop when Steve had caught a bullet that should have had Judd's name on it.

Something was wrong; he could feel it to his bones.

Gritting his teeth, trying to prepare himself for the worst, Judd snatched up the phone. "Foster here."

"Sylvie? Hi, it's Erika."

Judd frowned, bemused. "Erika? Where the hell are you? You know perfectly well I'm not Sylvie."

"Oh, I'm fine," she said a little too cheerily.

Something was going down and it wasn't good. Judd's previous training clicked in immediately. "Tell me where you are and describe the situation as best you can."

She chuckled, as if he had said something amusing. "I'm at my apartment, of course. Where did you think I was?"

"Everything is going to be okay, sweetheart," Judd said reassuringly. "Tell me what's going on and I'm *there*. Whatever is wrong, I'm going to fix it. Guaranteed."

He heard a male voice mumbling in the background and his senses went on high alert. He clenched his fingers tightly around the cordless phone and wished the hell he could get his hands on whoever was upsetting Erika.

Soon, he promised himself. As soon as she gave him the facts he was going to be all over this situation.

"Here's the deal, Sylvie. Richard flagged me down in the rain after I left your house," Erika explained.

Oh damn, the jealous ex-husband, Judd thought. "Is he armed?"

"Yes, as a matter of fact. He jumped into the pickup with me," she replied. "He wants to talk to you about getting back together. Naturally, he wants you to come over here alone. Don't bring Dave or Matt."

"Is he intoxicated?" Judd asked as he sped down the hall to retrieve his handgun.

"Yes. I know it's pouring down rain and that will slow you down, but could you come over and talk to him?"

"I'm on my way. You're doing great, honey." Judd snatched his pistol from its secluded place on the top shelf of his closet. "I'll insert through your bedroom window. I'll also call Dave for backup from my cell phone. Give me the last four digits of Sylvie's phone number in reverse so I can make the call in transit."

"Calm down, Syl," Erika cooed. "Don't get rattled. You know my address. It's seven, eight, three four Fifth Street, remember? You were just here this afternoon. Just take a deep breath and think of an excuse and give Dave the slip so he won't know what's going on. Richard just wants to talk to you privately."

"Nice work, sweetheart, I've got it," Judd praised her on his way back to the living room. "I'm on my way."

"Oh, and Sylvie? I love you. I'll see you when you get here… I hope."

Judd disconnected and hit the door running. He swore colorfully when he remembered Erika had his pickup and all he had for transportation was the rattletrap wheat truck that had belonged to his father.

Dashing through the rain, Judd headed to the open shed attached to the old cedar barn. He piled into the vintage truck and cranked the engine. It sputtered to life momentarily, then died.

"Hell!" Judd erupted, then tried again. And again.

On the third try, the truck rumbled and vibrated. The worn-out muffler reminded him of a hot rod equipped with glass packs, which wasn't good when you were relying on the element of surprise. You could hear him coming a block away. But if the damn thing got him close to where he needed to go, Judd could jog to the apartment.

The truck lurched forward, backfired, then putt-putted from the shed. The wipers, so brittle with age, scraped the windshield ineffectively, making it difficult for Judd to see where he was going in the downpour. Especially since only one headlight was operational. Talk about driving blind!

Once he was underway he punched in Sylvie's number. "Sylvie," he said abruptly. "I need to talk to Dave. Now. He can explain to you later. Just put him on the horn."

"What's wrong?" Dave questioned.

Good instincts. He was a good cop, Judd mused. "Erika just called me from her apartment and pretended she was talking to Sylvie. Richard is over there, holding her at gunpoint and demanding that Sylvie come over so they can get back together before you marry her," he explained in a rush.

"What? Holy—" Dave howled, then shut up immediately when Judd cut him off.

"Do not show your face over there until I'm inside. You aren't on Richard's list of favorite people and he's armed," Judd warned.

"Damn it, when I locked him up I should have thrown away the key," Dave muttered.

"I plan to come through the bedroom window to surprise him. ETA is seven minutes." Judd shifted gears and caromed around the corner. "The sound of pouring rain should make it easy for you to take your position by the front door without being detected. Hopefully it isn't locked and you can come barreling inside when you hear my signal."

Judd disconnected, then crammed the cell phone in the breast pocket of his chambray shirt. He reminded himself, as he streaked through a residential area, that he had been in worse situations than this plenty of times. But he could recall only one other time that he had been overwhelmed by such helpless frustration that it clogged up his rational thought processes.

The last image he had of Steve flashed across his mind and threatened to steal his breath. That hellish night had haunted his dreams for months. Judd wasn't sure he could handle it if Erika ended up in the same condition.

The dismal thought caused his heart to twist inside his chest like a pretzel. Erika had become his trusted confidante, his friend and lover. He didn't want to lose her after she had taught him to live and hope again.

He didn't want his hometown acquaintances to lose their beloved do-gooder, either.

He was *not* going to lose her, he told himself resolutely as he squinted to see where he was going. He had made this run through town to the grain elevators hundreds of times while he had helped his dad with wheat harvest. He knew the way, even if he couldn't see clearly.

After what seemed forever Judd located Erika's apartment complex and noticed his pickup sitting in the parking lot. He stamped on the brake, shifted into reverse and wheeled back around the corner. With his pistol tucked in the waistband of his jeans, he shifted his mind into commando mode and jogged down the alley in the pouring rain.

"WHAT THE HELL is taking her so long?" Richard growled impatiently as he staggered from one end of the living room to the other. "She should be here by now."

"She's probably upset," Erika speculated, then let out her breath in a whoosh when Richard shoved her down on the sofa and loomed over her. "You caught her off guard and it rattled her. She couldn't even remember my address for a moment. Plus, Dave is over there with her and she has to dream up an excuse to leave. So you need to take it easy and be gentle and understanding when she gets here."

"I told you that I don't need your misguided guidance," Richard growled at her. "I know exactly how to handle my own wife."

"*Ex*-wife," she said carefully. "You have a lot to make up for, Richard. Sylvie needs stability and security. She needs to know—"

"Hush up!" Richard yelled at her. "You always could influence *Sylvie,* but *I*'m not listening to your useless lectures." He frowned. "In fact, I don't want you around to interfere while Sylvie and I work this out."

Erika stopped breathing altogether when Richard looked at her as if she was dispensable, then jabbed his pistol at her. "*Think,* Richard," she wheezed. "I'm Sylvie's oldest and dearest friend. If something happens to me, she won't be the least bit receptive to what you have to say. And you better get rid of that gun before she gets here. That is not a good way to start your conversation."

Richard whipped his dark head around. Looking for what? Erika had no idea. He seemed to have arrived at some sort of decision. Whatever it was, Erika appeared to be part of it because he shot out his hand and grabbed a handful of her hair. He jerked her abruptly to her feet and held her head at a painful angle while he prodded her into the kitchen.

"Pick up the chair," he demanded gruffly.

Grimacing at the excruciating pressure on her hair, Erika did as she was told.

He rammed the pistol into her rib cage. "Carry it back to the living room."

When he shoveled her toward the coat closet beside the front door, Erika realized that he intended to lock her out of sight, using the chair as a barricade to keep the door shut securely.

This was her one and only chance to make a break for it. Although she had called Judd and she knew he was coming to her rescue, she had no intention of putting his life in jeopardy. She loved him too much to see him injured while trying to help her. Richard had gone berserk after he discovered he was about to lose his ex-wife. No telling what he would do when Judd arrived on the scene unexpectedly.

Now is definitely the time, Erika told herself—and mentally crossed her fingers, hoping she could escape unscathed.

Richard directed her attention to the closet. "Get in there. I don't want to hear a peep out of you while I'm talking to Sylvie," he barked. "If I do, it'll be the last peep you make—"

Erika exploded into action. She sideswiped Richard with the chair and sent him stumbling off balance. With a roar of outrage he braced himself against the wall and swung the handgun toward her.

Chapter Thirteen

Judd had dealt quickly with the lock on the bedroom window. Then he thrust one leg over the sill and eased into the darkened room. He sank into a crouch, pricked his ears and tried to determine exactly where Richard and Erika were.

When he heard the pistol discharge his heart stopped beating for several vital moments. Half a dozen worst-case scenarios bombarded his thoughts as he sprang to his feet and lurched into the hall. If that maniac had hurt Erika— or worse—he was toast! Judd vowed vengefully. And if Dave came barging through the front door, thinking that gunshot was the signal to charge, there was no telling who else might get hurt.

Praying nonstop, Judd clung to the shadows and inched down the hall. He hesitated to crane his neck around the corner, for fear he would have to deal with the emotional blow of knowing Erika had been the victim of a gunshot wound. Swearing profusely, Judd *made* himself look around the corner to assess the situation.

To Judd's everlasting relief Erika wasn't lying in a pool of her own blood. She was wielding a chair and Richard was trying to fend her off, while simultaneously trying to retrieve the pistol that she must have knocked from his grasp and caused to discharge.

Judd shot across the room, but he couldn't reach the weapon before Richard latched on to it. He did, however, divert Richard's attention before he could turn the gun on Erika. Lowering his head, Judd tackled Richard and slammed him into the wall. The pistol went skidding across the tiled floor.

Snarling, Judd buried his fist in Richard's jaw. "That's for scaring Erika half to death," he growled vindictively. He cocked his arm, then punched Richard squarely in the nose. "And that's from me, you moron!"

Judd was still crouched atop Richard when the front door splintered, then burst open—and hit him in the back. He grimaced, but he didn't shift position. He had Richard down and he planned to keep him that way.

"Sorry," Dave said as he poked his head around the door. "I thought I heard a shot on my way up the sidewalk."

"You did," Erika said shakily as she scraped herself off the floor. "It discharged *accidentally* when Richard and I got into a tussle."

Judd whipped his head around to peer incredulously into her peaked face. What the hell was she doing? Letting this imbecile off the hook?

Damn it, the man had almost shot her—whether accidentally or on purpose. For certain he had held her hostage at gunpoint and threatened her. For that alone, Judd wanted him placed under arrest.

While Dave and Erika stared meaningfully at one another, Judd focused his attention on Richard and his bloody nose. The man peered up at him, then glanced at Dave—as if sizing up the cop and finding himself lacking in comparison.

Judd hauled in a calming breath and reminded himself that he was face-to-face with a man who'd had too much to drink and had felt desperate and threatened when he discovered that he was about to lose free access to his ex-wife and his son. That didn't excuse his rash actions, but it explained his motivation.

"Richard didn't want to lose Sylvie," Erika told Dave. "He wanted to talk her into coming back to him. But he didn't think he could get her alone without going around you, so he tried to use me as his go-between." She shifted her attention to Richard. "Isn't that right, Richard?"

Richard slumped on the floor and nodded his head jerkily. The fight went out of him then. Judd stared down at him and felt himself transported back to that awful night six months ago. Richard had that same defeated, fatalistic look that Steve had been wearing. It was over and he knew it.

"Are you telling me that you aren't pressing charges?" Dave asked Erika in total disbelief.

"I'm not pressing charges." Erika inhaled a steadying breath and stared at Richard—miserable excuse of a human being that he could be sometimes.

She couldn't—*wouldn't*—bring this down on Matt's head. His father had serious problems, but the poor kid was already going to have to deal with the fact that his stepfather-to-be had arrested Richard. In a town this size it would be difficult to keep the situation under wraps.

She knew Dave had used discretion during the DWI arrest, but if this hit the newspapers Matt could suffer the same kind of misery Erika had endured when her mother abandoned her and her schoolmates teased her unmercifully.

Matt was not going to suffer through that kind of torment, not if she could help it. She didn't know exactly what to do about Richard, but she wasn't filing a complaint.

"Are you sure about this, Erika?" Judd asked as he loomed over Richard.

She let out a sigh and said, "I'm sure."

Judd stared at her for a long moment. "Okay, if that's what Erika wants then we'll do it her way." He sank down cross-legged, then pulled Richard into a sitting position. "Since Erika is going to let you off the hook—" he shot her a disgruntled glance "—because she's too caring and kind-hearted for her own good, then this is how things are going to play out for you, Richard."

Judd stared at the broken, bleeding man—and saw another face superimpose itself. *I'm paying it forward, Steve,* Judd mused. *I couldn't do a good deed for you so I'm going to compensate by doing a good deed for Richard and his son.*

"I lost my best friend during a mission in the Middle East. He didn't survive to return to his wife and young daughter," he told Richard grimly. "They will never know how much Steve loved them because he won't be there to remind them, to guide and support them for these next fifty years."

"Oh, Judd…"

He heard Erika's voice catch. He could feel her sympathetic gaze on him, but he didn't take his eyes off Richard. "Fortunately for you, you aren't going to lose your ex-wife and child forever. But you *are* going to have to accept the fact that there is a new man in their lives. Someone who has proved that he is ready, willing and able to commit to their best interests."

When Richard glanced sideways at Dave, then muttered under his breath, Judd snapped his fingers in his face. "Pay attention here. Don't force me to knock some more sense into you."

He stared Richard into submission. "After your divorce you lost the right to involve yourself in Sylvie's life. And I will be *damned* if I'm going to stand aside and let you hurt or embarrass that adorable kid of yours. A good friend of mine told me how much it hurts to be the subject of ridicule and I don't want Matt to have to deal with that."

Blotting his nose, Richard glanced at Judd briefly, then looked the other way.

"I couldn't save Steve, but I *am* going to save *you* from *yourself.* I intend to see that you get professional help. No more booze," he told Richard sternly. "You're going to dry out and wise up. You're going to check yourself into a clinic and you're going to learn from your mistakes."

He clutched the lapels of Richard's shirt and got right in his face. "If I ever hear that you're hassling Dave or Sylvie or upsetting Matt, then you will deal directly with me. Dave is a cop and he has to play by the rules. But I was trained to fight in places where the only rule was that there are no rules, just survival of the fittest."

He gave Richard his best don't-mess-with-me-when-I'm-good-and-mad glare. "You with me so far, Richard?"

Richard nodded warily.

"Good." He glanced over his shoulder. "Erika, would you mind getting Richard a cold cloth so he can clean himself up?"

"Be glad to," she said, then hurried off.

"Dave, is there some place Richard can go for the night so he won't be a problem for himself or anyone else?"

"Sure. I'll make the arrangements." Dave strode off to use the phone.

When they were alone, Judd said, "You're going to be my good deed for the year. You're also going to learn to treat women with the respect and courtesy they deserve. And if you *ever* try to take your frustration out on Erika and place the blame for your shortcomings on her, you do not want to know what I will do to you. Don't screw this up, Richard."

Judd stabbed his forefinger in Richard's chest. "You are getting a second chance. Not everyone is that lucky. Steve wasn't. If you care anything at all about that bright, lovable kid of yours, you'll do this for *him*. Don't make him ashamed and embarrassed to call you *Dad*."

Richard dropped his head and nodded humbly. Whether it was the physical threat or the thought of humiliating his son that got through to him Judd didn't know. Maybe it was both. It didn't matter. But Richard was finally regathering his senses, and he looked as if he regretted his desperate ploy to get his wife and child back.

"Here, Richard," Erika murmured as she hunkered down beside Judd.

"Would you make Richard some coffee so he can sober up?" Judd asked.

While Erika was brewing coffee, Richard wiped his face. Judd picked up the discarded weapon, then surveyed the hole in the closet door. He wanted to pop Richard in the chops again for good measure for waving a weapon at Erika. He also wanted to strangle her for resisting Richard. She had scared Judd half to death with her escape attempt.

Why had she done that? She knew he was on his way over here. Didn't she trust him to resolve this crisis? Damn it, she knew he was trained to handle all sorts of tricky situations. Why hadn't she waited for him to defuse this crisis?

When Dave strode up, Richard cast him a disgruntled glance, then concentrated on stemming his nosebleed.

"You probably don't want to hear this, Richard, but I will take good care of them," Dave promised in a calm, nonthreatening voice. "When you get your head back on straight we'll make the necessary arrangements for visitations. But you need to understand that you won't be allowed to see Matt alone until you have proved yourself trustworthy with him."

"You can bring Matt to my ranch and we'll plan some activities together," Judd offered. "I took Matt horseback riding this afternoon and he loved it. He wanted to go fishing, too, but the storm forced us to cut our outing short."

"Thank you," Richard mumbled, his head downcast.

Dave reached down to haul Richard to his feet. "I have a friend on the force who agreed to let you bunk with him tonight. We'll get the arrangements at the clinic squared away tomorrow."

When Erika handed Richard a cup of coffee-to-go, he sighed audibly. "I'm sorry. I went a little crazy."

Erika smiled wryly. "You went a lot crazy. I understand why and I forgive you. But let's not do this again sometime." Her expression sobered. "Just make this work, okay? If there is anything I can do to help, just give me a call."

When Dave and Richard walked off in the rain, Judd rounded on Erika. "What the hell were you thinking by taking on Richard when you knew I was on my way? Damn it, woman! I nearly suffered heart seizure when I heard that gunshot!"

Judd tried to rein in his pent-up frustration, but it wasn't easy. Now that the worst was over, he needed to vent. As usual, Erika didn't look the least bit intimidated by his tirade.

"Didn't you trust me to help you?" he demanded.

"Of course I did," she said, looking calmer than he felt. "I didn't want to have to call you at all, but I knew it would be a disaster to call Sylvie as Richard ordered me to do. Dave wouldn't have allowed her to come alone and he was the last person Richard needed to see while he was upset."

She stared meaningfully at him. "But that did *not* mean that I intended to risk having *you* get hurt while trying to rescue me."

"You didn't…?" He gaped at her. His breath gushed out like a deflating balloon. *"What?"*

Oh, now he got it. She had tried to protect *him* from harm, even if it meant risking personal injury in her attempt to escape from Richard before Judd showed up. Noble but hardly necessary. This was his forte and she knew it.

Annoyed, he wagged his index finger in her face. "Do not ever do that again," he lectured sternly. "You scared ten years off my life."

"I'm not planning to get into any more scrapes, so you should be safe." She picked up the chair to return it to its proper place in the kitchen. "Maybe it would be best if I spent the night here. After all, what else could possibly go wrong this weekend?"

Judd reflexively ducked when lightning flashed and thunder boomed directly overhead. He didn't take that as a good sign. "Don't even ask," he muttered, staring skyward. "Just grab your raincoat and some more clothes for the week. You are not staying here. Bad things happen at this apartment. It's jinxed. You are coming home with me and you are staying there indefinitely, too."

"No. It's time for me to get back to my own life and stop disrupting yours." Erika pivoted to stare into his ruggedly handsome face, wanting to fling herself into his arms and take what he was offering, even if he was offering for all the wrong reasons.

"You don't need me anymore. You have adapted to civilian life. What you did for Richard just now assures me that you have put the trauma of your friend's death behind you and have channeled it in a positive direction. I will always be grateful to you for that. Richard needs help and you're seeing to it that he gets it. He might make something of himself yet, thanks to you."

"Forget Richard for a minute," Judd said with a dismissive slash of his hand. "Whaddya mean I don't need you anymore? What about Juanita? I thought you agreed to help me convince her that I'm not the new flavor of the month."

Erika grinned wryly. "After seeing you in action tonight, Captain Commando, I'm convinced that you can fend off Juanita if you really want to." She wrinkled her nose at him. "I found myself in the middle of this mess between Sylvie and Richard. I don't want to become Juanita's scapegoat. She might decide to pull a gun on me, too. That has happened enough lately for me to realize that I don't like it very much."

Feet apart, arms crossed over his broad chest, Judd narrowed his eyes and stared her down. "So basically you're telling me that you've had your fun with me. You seduced me, just to see if you could. Now that the challenge is gone, you're brushing me off? Is that what's going on here?"

Erika smiled ruefully. Avoiding future contact with him was the last thing she wanted. But she knew she was going to get her heart broken in a zillion pieces if she didn't get out while the getting was good. She needed some distance, some perspective. She also needed to remember that he wasn't going to be a part of her future.

It would be so easy to go home with Judd and roll with the flow until he tired of her. He would eventually, she predicted. She refused to watch his attitude toward her wither into indifference. He wouldn't admit it, macho man that he was, but she had become his emotional crutch. She had been the place he came to vent his anger and frustration that resulted from the loss of his dearest friend.

Judd didn't need her now. He didn't need to be nudged, prodded and pushed into making a contribution to his hometown. He was back on track.

"I think it's best if we get back to business as usual," she insisted. "We've had our fun. Plus, I encountered enough dangerous excitement to last me a lifetime. I'm ready to be done with all that and get back to normal."

"That's it? Sayonara? I'll see you around?" He shook his head. "I'm not buying that. Things were going good between us. Now tell me what went wrong?"

"Nothing."

"Nothing?" he repeated dubiously. "Then why did you tell me over the phone—and I quote: 'I love you and I'll see you when you get here… I hope'?"

Erika shifted uncomfortably beneath his intense gaze. Darn it, why did he have to throw *that* back in her face? "That was nervous tension talking," she explained, wishing she hadn't blurted out that confession on the phone. But she hadn't known how the ordeal with Richard would play out. She had wanted Judd to know that he had her heart ..just in case.

"Well?" he prodded when she didn't meet his direct gaze.

"I was scared, okay? I was trying to act like I was talking to Sylvie while Richard was pointing his pistol at me. That just popped out of my mouth, so you shouldn't hold me accountable for what I said under duress."

"So it was just about sex?" he demanded. "That's it?"

"It's been a harrowing evening." She turned her back on him to grab a cup of coffee. "Could we not do this right now? I need a hot, soaking bath and a good night's sleep. I need to focus on getting my life back to normal. I have to focus on my professional obligations of running the café. I'll be helping with the arrangements of two more upcoming weddings. And tomorrow is the day I visit my friends at the retirement—"

She stopped talking when she heard the front door slam shut. She sagged heavily against the kitchen counter for support as she stared at the empty space Judd had left behind in her apartment, in her heart, in her life.

He was gone and it was for the best, she consoled herself. But knowing that didn't make the hurt easier to bear.

Erika felt tears welling up in her eyes as she poured a cup of coffee. This was it, she told herself. The fantasy weekend was over. She couldn't go on loving Judd and trying not to let it show. It was too hard.

Carrying her mug with her, she strode into the bathroom to fill the tub. *I'm back where I started,* she mused as she sank into the steamy water. *Alone. Still loving a man who is only interested in the physical attraction between us.*

They had shared an incredibly wonderful sexual interlude this weekend. But Judd was never going to love her the way she loved him and she had to accept that.

Erika rested her head against the edge of the tub and sighed raggedly. This had been one hell of a weekend. She had blazed through the entire gamut of emotions and landed with a resounding crash. Her good deed had nearly backfired in her face—literally. The love of her life had walked out because she had refused to continue their superficial affair.

If he loved her, even a little, he could have said so. He could have said *something*. But he didn't. He simply left.

Erika cupped her hands over her face and bawled her head off. She was entitled, wasn't she?

If she wasn't, she damn sure should be, she decided as she vented the jumble of emotions that roiled inside her.

JUDD STALKED BACK to the jalopy farm truck, oblivious to the cold rain that pounded down on him. He was angry with himself for letting Erika push him away. Angry with himself for taking an emotional nosedive after being scared to death that he was about to lose Erika to a flying bullet.

Just as he had lost the best friend he had ever had.

Judd whipped open the door of the truck and clambered into the cab. Damn it, Erika had said she loved him over the phone. Whether he was worthy or deserving of a woman like her or not, she *had* said the words. When he had confronted her with it she had written it off to the stressful situation.

She had been lying when she said it was just about sex, Judd concluded as he cranked the engine. He could see it in those expressive blue eyes, in the way she looked at him. She had told him once that she didn't lie convincingly.

Well, she was right. She didn't.

Plus, you didn't go to the wall to protect someone who was physically and mentally equipped to deal with those kind of dangerous situations unless you cared personally or professionally. And what was between them was very intimate and personal.

So, what was she hiding from him? What was she afraid of? Why would she back out of his life if she loved him?

Judd was sorry to say that he didn't get it.

Muttering, he shifted into first gear and lurched off. Maybe he didn't understand what made a woman tick. Didn't understand why a woman said one thing when she meant something entirely different. But he did have enough sense to quiz someone from the perplexing feminine gender and ask her to explain things to him.

Sylvie was Erika's closest and dearest friend. Erika had protected her by calling Judd instead tonight. If anyone could tell him why Erika was holding out on him, surely Sylvie could.

Determined, Judd veered down the side street, then cruised toward Sylvie's house. Even through the pouring rain he could see the lights ablaze in the house. He rumbled into the driveway and noticed the front door swing open immediately. When he reached the porch Sylvie flung herself into his arms and squeezed the stuffing out of him.

"Oh, thank God you're okay! Where's Dave and Riki? Are they all right?" she asked in a worried rush.

"Everyone is fine," Judd assured her as he gave her a comforting squeeze. "Erika didn't press charges so Dave took Richard to a friend's house to cool down. Erika is at her apartment."

Sylvie reared back and stared at him in astonishment. "She's *by herself?* You left her by herself after the weekend she's had? Are you *insane?*" She whirled around to grab her coat. "Matt is asleep. You stay here with him and I'll go over to comfort Riki."

When she tried to whiz out the door, Judd clutched her arm and steered her back into the house. "She asked to be alone, even when I insisted that she come back to the ranch with me. She more or less told me to get lost."

Sylvie frowned, confused. "That makes no sense. I know she enjoyed being out there at the ranch with you. I haven't seen her that happy and content in years."

"I thought she was happy there, too, but obviously I don't know what it takes to make a woman happy." He stared hopefully at her. "That's why I came to you."

Sylvie smiled approvingly. "Well, finally! A man who has enough sense to come right out and ask. First off, a woman wants to be treated as an equal and she needs to know her feelings and opinions are important to you."

Judd made a mental note. "Got it."

"Secondly, she wants to be romanced and told how appealing she is to you," Sylvie insisted.

Judd made another mental note. "What else?"

"Thirdly, when you ask a woman what's wrong and she says *nothing,* then you can bet it's *something.* But she expects you to be smart enough to figure it out all by yourself, because *you* were probably the one who did something to irritate her in the first place."

Judd winced. "We have to be mind readers?"

Sylvie snickered. "Yep, and if you're tuned into her and look at the situation from her perspective, then you can puzzle out what went wrong. Which makes you look even more caring and conscientious so that earns you Brownie points like you wouldn't believe."

"This is all very enlightening. And confusing." Judd

frowned thoughtfully. "Nothing means something. Little things are important. Read her mind." He threw up his hands. "Jeez, military training was easier than this."

Sylvie grinned. "You bet your combat boots it is. You didn't have to have a meaningful relationship with your enemies. But this is serious stuff. And if you want to be my friend then you need to explain all this to Dave so he can be a considerate, conscientious husband."

"Sure. Be glad to," Judd said—and wondered if he would do Dave more harm than good. For sure, pleasing and understanding a woman was going to take dedicated effort.

"I was really hoping that something might come of this thing between you and Riki," Sylvie said, breaking into his thoughts. "*Did* something come of it? Is that why you're asking me these questions?" She stared accusingly at him. "What did you do wrong?"

"Me?" Judd hooted. "I didn't do anything." When she raised her brows at him he sighed, then shrugged. "At least I didn't think I did anything to upset her. All I did was invite her to come back to the ranch after that fiasco was over."

"And?" she prompted.

He shifted beneath Sylvie's probing stare and decided that she had perfected her death ray glare after years of dealing with difficult students. "And we were getting along fine so I can't figure out what went wrong."

Her brows snapped down into a sharp V. "That is exactly the same thing Riki told me when I asked her the same question. I don't want to hear *fine*. I want to know if you two hit it off or not?"

Judd averted his gaze. "Mind if I sit down?" he asked, hoping to delay Sylvie's version of the Spanish Inquisition.

"Sure, make yourself comfortable." She parked herself in the armchair directly across from him. "Do you want something warm to drink before you tell me what's going on with you and Riki or shall we get this over with?" She stared sternly at him. "One way or the other you *are* going to tell me, you know."

Judd chuckled. "No Chinese water torture? Going easy on me, are you?"

"Yes. After all, you did defuse a tense situation tonight." She leaned forward and stared intently at him. "But I *will* roll out the heavy artillery and blast away at you if you don't spill the beans."

"She told me she loved me on the phone, then she tried to take it back after the furor died down," he blurted out. "She told me it was over between us and she was going back to life as usual. Why did she do that?"

Sylvie slumped back in her chair and gave him such a pitying look that he felt his stomach drop to his boots. And his heart went right along with it.

"I'm really sorry, Judd. I don't know exactly what kind of hang-up Riki has going, but I do know it's chronic. She's never dated anyone for more than a couple of months. Then she backs away before things get serious."

Judd didn't comment, just waited for Sylvie to elaborate.

"I don't know exactly what happened way back in grade school. We became close friends after my family moved here when I started seventh grade. But occasionally Riki mentions this special guy. Not by name. But I think he's her Prince Charming, the one that got away." She shrugged. "Whether he is real or imagined, it's as if no mortal can measure up to him. The situation never changed through high school or college. Whoever this Mr. Right is, or was, she can't seem to get past him and she won't give herself a chance with men."

Judd half collapsed on the sofa when he remembered what Erika had told him during her third visit to the ranch. She had confided that he had been her hero when he rescued her from the cruel taunts of classmates.

"Well, I will be damned," he said with a burst of laughter.

Sylvie stared curiously at the wide smile that spread across his lips. "Do you know something about Riki that I don't know? How is that possible?"

It was possible all right. He knew lots of things about Erika. He knew how and where she liked to be touched. He knew her more intimately than any man alive.

He also knew he was competing against himself.

Well, not himself exactly, he amended. He had been her childhood hero and she hadn't allowed another man to disturb that perfect fantasy she had going. All he had to do was figure out how to merge that image of her hero with the reality of whom he had become. It might take some doing, but at least he knew what he was up against.

Feeling ten times better and far less befuddled, Judd jetted to his feet. "Thanks, Sylvie, you've been a tremendous help."

She blinked up at him. "I have?"

"Definitely. Thanks for clearing all this up for me."

Before he reached the front door, she hurried over to detain him. "Thank you for handling the situation with Richard. I'm truly grateful and relieved."

"Glad to have helped."

"Will you do me one more favor?"

Ah, that sounded like Erika. He had never been able to turn her down, either. "Sure, what is it?"

She dimpled and grinned up at him. "Stop by sometime and tell me what it is that we just resolved. I'm completely in the dark."

Judd chuckled on his way out the door. "I'll be in touch. I might need you and Dave to return the favor *soon*."

He walked out into the rain, smiling like a fool, no doubt. But he didn't care. He felt good. Really good. Really focused and alive again. Plus, he was armed with the facts and he was prepared to launch his campaign to get his life completely in order.

His assignment was Operation Erika Dunn. And she was *done* running and backing away, he told himself firmly. He knew exactly what he wanted and needed and he was calling in the troops. They were going to take his side, too. The do-gooder of Moon Valley was in his sights—and he had an exceptionally high success rate when he accepted a mission.

Send him away, claiming it was just about sex? Judd smirked. Who did she think she was kidding? He knew for a fact that Erika had never fooled around. That was Juanita Barlow's forte.

Erika was going to be back where she belonged very soon. She was not going to stand there and tell him she didn't care about him, Judd vowed as he drove home.

He was getting down to business. When he got through with that infuriating, adorable woman she was going to tell him exactly what he wanted to hear!

Chapter Fourteen

Erika was grateful that Judd had left his pickup at her disposal, even though he had left angry a week earlier and she hadn't seen him since. This morning—like most mornings—she had places to go and things to do. First on her list was to purchase transportation that wouldn't cause a serious financial setback.

She skidded to a halt in the apartment parking lot when she saw Dave drive up in her stolen car. She smiled in relief. Maybe her streak of rotten luck was easing up, she mused as she watched Dave slide off the driver's seat.

Dave handed her the keys. "The California highway patrol arrested the criminals driving your car," he reported. "You can rest easier knowing they will be transported back to Texas and prosecuted. The missing items from your apartment haven't turned up, but these have…"

Erika smiled in satisfaction when Dave poked his head inside her car to retrieve her purse and wallet. She noticed that her driver's license was among the items. Although her credit card was gone Murph had canceled it and had replaced it with a new one.

"This takes an enormous load off my mind." Erika breathed a gusty sigh of relief, then peered curiously at him. "What's the latest on Richard? Sylvie said you were making arrangements."

Dave nodded his sandy-blond head. "Judd and I escorted him to a clinic in the city and he's receiving counseling. I squared it with his employer so he can have a leave of absence." He grinned broadly. "Hell of a nice guy, that Judd Foster. I like him a lot. You should marry him," he teased playfully, then winked.

Erika smirked at the unexpected advice. "Last week you were warning me to watch my step with him. Now you're suggesting marriage, just because the love bug bit you and Syl?"

"No, because he's one hell of a good guy and he's exactly what you need," Dave insisted.

That was true. Judd *was* exactly what she wanted, but he hadn't indicated that he wanted her to return to his ranch for any other reasons except keeping her safe from harm and exploring the sexual attraction between them. She was not going to settle for less than his love because that would be the final straw that would shatter her long-held dream of him.

Erika wanted the whole dream. Or none at all.

"Maybe you and Judd can come over for dinner some night this week," Dave suggested as Erika handed him the keys so he could return Judd's pickup. "He's going to be my best man."

"When did you decide that?" she asked, startled.

"When Judd showed up to resolve the situation with Richard and offered to help get him lined out." Dave opened the pickup door, then tossed her a smile. "Marry the guy before Juanita Barlow sinks her claws into him. You would be doing him a tremendous favor. That woman has been dogging his steps for days."

Exasperated, she watched Dave cruise off. She had vowed to set aside all thoughts of Judd and get back to business. It wasn't easy when her friends kept tossing his name in her face every chance they got.

Erika piled into her old car, then grimaced at the thought of those thieves sitting where she sat. The car was due a good cleaning, too, she decided. When she returned home this evening she was going to disinfect this vehicle as thoroughly as she had wiped down her apartment last week.

When Erika arrived at the café Frannie tossed her a greeting smile. While her aunt fired up the griddle to serve the breakfast special, Erika walked through the back exit to clean the smoker so she could cook chickens for the evening special. She purposely avoided the shed where she had been accosted a week earlier. Finally, Erika worked up the nerve to return to the scene of the attack.

Sure enough, unpleasant memories bombarded her the moment she stepped out the back door and veered around the corner. She steeled herself against the remembered fear and panic and vowed not to allow that ordeal to upset her all over again.

Inhaling a steadying breath, she surged into the shed— and stopped in her tracks when she saw the arrangement of yellow roses sitting beside the smoker. What in the world? Bemused, she walked over to remove the attached card.

"I miss you. Come home. Judd," she read aloud. That dear, sweet, considerate man anticipated that returning to the scene of the attack might rattle her. He had left an unexpected gift to take her mind off the bad experience.

He missed her? Truly? That was nice to know. But why couldn't he have written, *Love,* Judd? Not just *Judd.*

"Infuriating man," she grumbled as she got the fire

going in the smoker. "There is only one thing I want from you. The one thing you can't give."

Whirling around, Erika reentered Blue Moon Café to help Frannie serve and deliver breakfast to their customers.

"Why did you stay at your apartment all week when you could have stayed with Judd?" Frannie wanted to know. "I purposely delayed in having the locks on your apartment replaced so you would have an excuse to be with him."

Erika's mouth dropped open at the confession, then she frowned suspiciously. "You also neglected to pack my nightgown and decent clothes *on purpose,* didn't you?"

"Guilty as charged," Frannie said unrepentantly. "I was trying to give you a nudge in the right direction and you fouled it up. Now it's time for you and Judd to get back together. For your own good. And his."

"Can we talk about something else, please?" Erika requested as she cracked eggs on the hot griddle.

"I know he's your Mr. Right," Frannie said. "I found mine and I hear that Sylvie found hers." She stared pointedly at Erika. "And it *is* June, you know."

Erika rolled her eyes, then playfully tossed back the words of the repetitive lecture Frannie had delivered to her during her school days. "And if everyone decided to jump off a cliff, would you do that, too? Being one of the crowd doesn't mean you shouldn't have a mind of your own. You have to make wise personal decisions."

Frannie shrugged casually. "That was different. That was then. This is now. Seize the moment is my new motto and it should be yours, too."

Erika had seized the moment with Judd. Unfortunately, he hadn't fallen head over heels in love with her.

She wanted head over heels.

When the usual breakfast crowd had been fed, Erika untied her apron and grabbed the box of cigars from under the counter. "I'm headed to the retirement center to play cards with the seniors," she announced.

Frannie gestured her head toward the box. "How long are you planning to support their habit of one cigar a month?"

Erika smiled dryly. "They are over eighty. If you think they should give up their monthly cigars and pinochle games, then *you* can tell them."

"Okay, I suppose they are old enough to make up their own minds, but you should still go after Judd," she said in the same breath.

Erika rolled her eyes, shook her head and left.

FIFTEEN MINUTES LATER, Erika was in the courtyard of the retirement center, sitting beneath the covered pavilion. Her four guardian angels were puffing their cigars and she was dealing cards. Here, at least, she wouldn't have to hear Judd's name mentioned every time she turned around—or so she thought.

"So…when is that handsome rascal gonna make a respectable woman of you?" Hilda Watson asked before she blew a lopsided smoke ring in the air.

"You should marry him," Freda Lawrence and Wanda Jamison said in unison.

Erika's hands stalled in mid-deal. She gaped at the foursome that had pinned her with narrowed stares. Before she could ask what brought on the outburst she noticed that one of the employees from the center was striding toward her. He was carrying a bouquet of yellow roses.

With a smile, the attendant handed the flowers to her. "These came special delivery."

"What's the card say?" Annabelle Burton wanted to know.

Erika opened the card. "I still miss you. Come home. Judd," she read aloud.

Still no *Love,* Judd.

"You should go back to his ranch," Wanda advised. "He obviously wants you to. Better than hanging around your burglarized apartment."

"That place is barely big enough to provide room to change your clothes," Freda remarked. "Wide open spaces are the ticket."

"You need fresh country air," Hilda added.

"That is a big, spacious house," Annabelle piped up. "Plenty of rooms for kids. You need kids, Riki."

Erika couldn't take it anymore. This was pure torture. Her guardian angels kept listing material benefits of hanging out at Judd's ranch. None of those things were important if Judd didn't love her. Which he didn't. She had just become a habit he wasn't quite ready to break.

"We'll have to cut the game short. I have to get back to work." Erika scooped up the bouquet, then bolted from the table.

"Okay, but we still think you should ask Judd to marry you," Wanda said. "It's the new millennium, you know. Women shouldn't have to wait around for a man to propose. Just go for it, hon."

Erika walked swiftly to her car and buzzed back to the café. She arrived in time to help Frannie with the noon rush hour. There on the counter were another dozen yellow roses and another card.

"'Have you taken the hint yet? I still miss you and I want you to come home. Judd'," she read to herself, and scowled.

Apparently he was missing his daily-recommended dose of sex and this was his attempt to lure her back to him. He was trying to *buy* her willing participation.

Fuming, Erika ripped up the card then tossed it in the trash. If all he wanted was a fling for the sake of flinging then he could look up Juanita, for all she cared.

But you do care, the voice inside her head said.

"This is a sign, you know," Aunt Frannie said philosophically as she gestured toward the flowers. "You should pay attention to it." She dished up an order of burgers and fries and wrapped them up. "The man is trying to tell you something."

Right. Unfortunately he was saying the wrong thing. And that was *not* a good sign.

"This is a delivery." Frannie packed the food in a paper sack. "I'll hold the fort while you deliver it."

That suited Erika fine. She scooped up the sack and made for the door. "Where am I headed with this?"

Frannie beamed in amusement. "Where else? Foster Ranch."

"No," she said stubbornly. "*You* take out the food and *I'll* hold the fort."

Frannie's shoulder lifted in a nonchalant shrug. "Okay, but I thought you might want to see for yourself that Judd is cleaning out the old cedar barn. He told me that he has decided to tear down the old barn and sell the property to a tractor supply outfit from the city. They contacted him last week."

"He can't do that!" Erika railed. "That's my barn. I made the first offer!" Annoyed, she stormed toward the door. "So that's what all these flowers are all about. He was trying to soften me up before he gave me the bad news himself. That sneaky, underhanded, back-stabbing…oh!"

"You go, girl," Frannie cheered her on. "After you rake him over the coals for double-crossing you, convince him to marry you so you'll acquire half ownership in that old barn. That will show him—but good."

Erika stamped over to her car, plunked down on the seat, then sped off. That did it! It was bad enough that all Judd had to say was that he missed her. Now he was shattering her second dream by spitefully selling the barn so she couldn't expand the café business. Well, he was going to hear about this, believe it!

Still fuming, Erika wheeled into the gravel driveway. Her jaw dropped open when she saw the stack of antiques—cream separators, milk cans, single trees used to hitch horses to wagons and outdated farm tools—stacked in the back of the old wheat truck. And there he was, the jerk, looking like every woman's dream come true in his faded, physique-hugging work clothes and gloves, toting more stuff outside to stack in the truck.

She wanted to hug him and shake the stuffing out of him simultaneously.

Stiffening her resolve, determined to let him have it with both barrels blazing, Erika bounded from her car and stalked toward him. She clenched the paper sacks of food in her fist, and wished she could wrap her fingers around his neck instead. She girded herself up to lash out at him, but she had to bite her tongue when young Kent Latham emerged from the barn, carrying another load of priceless relics.

She manufactured a smile for Kent and ignored Judd for the time being. She would get to him later. "Here's lunch, Kent. Will you take it up to the house for me? I need to have a private word with Judd."

When Kent jogged off, Erika rounded on Judd. "I told you that I would pay a premium for this property. I will match the price the tractor supply company offered," she snapped.

"Hello to you, too, Erika," Judd said congenially. "Thanks for bringing lunch. Kent and I are starved."

She scowled at him, then realized that they had exchanged roles. Now *he* was Mr. Cheerful and *she* was the grouch. And it was *his* fault. He was making her crazy.

"That is supposed to be *my* barn," she said bitterly. "It was the one dream I might actually have been able to attain, if you hadn't double-crossed me. How could you do that? You know how much this place means to me!"

He calmly removed his leather work gloves, then stuffed them in the hip pocket of his jeans. "Of course, I know what it means to you. More than I do, obviously. You wanted the barn so much that you tried to *seduce* me out of it. If that isn't deceptive and underhanded, I don't know what is."

"I did nothing of the kind!" she howled in outrage. "That is the dumbest thing you have ever said. And believe me, pal, you have said some pretty stupid things!"

"At least I didn't use *you* for sex," he countered. "Now, three dozen yellow roses and the threat of losing the barn later, you finally show up." He stared at her in offended dignity. "How do you think that makes me feel?"

"I know how you feel," she sputtered. "You're ticked off because *I* said exactly what *you* were thinking. You didn't like it because I'm the one who said it first!"

Her face flushed angry red. She stood before him, rigid as a fence post, hands fisted on hips. Judd loved seeing her livid and huffy. He was pushing *her* buttons for a change. It felt damn good. For all the times she had prodded him, bullied him and pushed him around—with her own unique brand of style and charm that made her impossible to refuse—she was discovering how it felt to have the boot on the other foot.

"A word to the wise, darlin'," he drawled. "Don't ever try to put words in my mouth or accuse me of thinking." He crossed his arms over his chest and narrowed his gaze. "Why don't you just admit it so we can get this over with?"

She frowned. "Admit what? That you're an idiot? Now there's the understatement of the century."

"No," he said, summoning his patience. "Admit that you are in love with me. You said it over the phone. Now say it face-to-face. Then I want you to tell me why you won't come back here to stay. Everyone in town thinks you should."

She opened her mouth, then snapped her jaw shut. A wary frown puckered her brow. "You went to my friends behind my back and had them gang up on me, didn't you?" she accused. "That's why Aunt Frannie, Dave, Syl and my guardian angels have been hounding me, isn't it? You put them up to it."

"Hey, they are my friends, too. At least that's what you keep telling me," he reminded her. "Now *say* it."

"No," she snapped stubbornly. "If you want to hear the words so badly then *you* say them."

"Is that what it's gonna take?" he asked, suppressing a grin.

She crossed her arms over her chest and elevated her chin. "Yes. I need a good reason to come back here and you have yet to provide the most important reason of all. I miss you isn't going to cut it, cowboy. You'll have to do better than that."

Judd sighed melodramatically. "Fine. We'll do it your

way. So what else is new?" He got down on one knee and looked up into her lovely but bewildered face. "Erika Dunn, you are one stubborn, headstrong woman, but I love you anyway. I want to be with you more than I have ever wanted anyone or anything in my whole life. Will you please marry me and come back where you belong before I go crazy without you?"

He grinned when her jaw scraped her chest and her blue eyes bulged from their sockets. Ah, he loved it when he left her speechless. For once, he had the honor of being several mental laps ahead of her.

"Okay," he added, while she tried to recover her powers of speech. "Just to make sure you can't turn me down, I'll sweeten this deal. If you agree to marry me, you can remodel the barn into your new restaurant. I'll give it to you as a wedding present."

Erika finally emerged from her paralyzed daze and stared intently at him. "Do you mean it? Truly?"

Judd stared sincerely at her. "Erika, I have never been more serious in my life."

With a whoop and holler she flew right at him. They tumbled in the grass while she showered him with kisses.

The apprehension of putting his heart on the line and taking the risk of being shot down gushed out of him. The gratifying pleasure of finally having Erika back in his arms again swept through him, bringing with it the urgent need to share the intimacy he had been missing like nobody's business.

"I need you, sweetheart," he said in between desperate kisses and caresses. "I'm absolutely nuts about you. Nothing was the same when you left and nothing is going to be right in my world until I have you back again. I want you like crazy. I want the right to touch you, to make love to you whenever I feel like it. Or when you feel like it. I want to have babies with you. I want us to be a family and I want to grow old with you."

He cupped her face in his hands and stared into her luminous eyes. "I want to be the hero from your childhood and I want to be the man of your present and future dreams." He smiled hopefully at her. "Say *something. Please.*"

The smile she bestowed on him outshined the summer sun that was beaming down at high noon. "I never stopped loving you, Judd. But you already knew that, didn't you?" An impish sparkle lit up her blue eyes as she grinned at him. "That's what I'm supposed to say, isn't it? That's what it will take to get my hands on that old cedar barn, right? And I get all the rock-my-world sex I want in this package deal, too?"

He chuckled good-naturedly, because the expression on her face told him everything he needed to know. She had loved him for years and she still did. She belonged to him and he belonged to her forever and ever.

"That's right, sugar britches," he agreed. "It's definitely a package deal and you can have whatever you want if you say yes."

"Then *yes!*" she yelped before she covered his face with another dozen smacking kisses. "Definitely yes."

"Ahem…"

Startled, Judd and Erika glanced up to see Kent grinning down at them. A good lesson for the boy, Judd decided. The kid needed to know that you didn't always have to be dignified and mature when you were head over heels in love.

"Are you guys gonna come up to the house to eat lunch or not?"

Judd squinted up at the gangly teenager whose pride and self-confidence had improved by leaps and bounds at the ranch in the past month. "How old did you say you were?"

"Still thirteen," he replied, still grinning.

"Darn, you're too young to drive yourself into the café for lunch." Judd rolled to his feet, then pulled Erika up beside him. "Guess we'll do lunch." He glided his arm possessively around Erika's waist, then leaned in and said confidentially, "But I definitely want you for dessert. You're even better than slice-of-heaven pie."

Erika didn't walk to the house; she floated. "I never would have taken you for a romantic," she murmured with a marveling shake of her head. "First roses? *Three* dozen of them? Then a down-on-one-knee traditional proposal?"

He smiled confidently. "Mr. Romantic. That's me all right. I've made it my new mission in life to figure out what a woman wants and to keep her happy." He waggled his brows suggestively. "Just wait and see what I have in store for you tonight."

"Sounds intriguing. I'll be there with bells on," she promised enthusiastically.

The smoldering look he flashed at her made her toes curl. Her body went into instant meltdown.

"Just wear the bells, babycakes. And nothing else…" he whispered seductively.

And that's *exactly* how she showed up in his king-size bed that night.

Epilogue

The triple ceremony was held at Moon Valley Park because it was the only place in town that could accommodate the guest list that included the entire town population. It was held at the end of June. Aunt Frannie's idea, of course.

Being the practical soul that she was, Frannie decreed that since everyone in town was invited to the shindig, they might as well save the guests from tying up three separate weekends to attend the weddings.

Three brides. Three grooms—and no extra expense for tuxedo rentals for three separate weddings. One wedding buffet catered by the café. It was practical and sensible, and that's the way Aunt Frannie conducted business.

Erika sighed happily as well-wishers milled around her. She glanced toward the local band that struck up a lively country tune. Hand in hand, couples ambled onto the cordoned area of the lawn that served as the dance floor.

"Now this is what I call a humdinger of a wedding," Frannie said. "Good music, good eats and three good-looking grooms."

"But three separate honeymoons," Sylvie said wryly. "We have to draw the line somewhere."

Erika glanced across the lawn to see Judd, Dave and

Murph in conversation. She frowned in annoyance when Juanita sashayed up to Judd and draped her arm over his shoulder.

Possessive jealousy spurted through her, but she quickly reminded herself that Judd's heart, and that incredibly masculine body belonged to her and her exclusively. He insisted that he only had eyes for her and he had thoroughly and repeatedly convinced her of that.

She actually pitied Juanita because she would never know or understand the bond of love that existed between the newlyweds. Juanita had set a pattern of acquiring and discarding husbands for all the wrong reasons.

Her thoughts trailed off when Judd detached himself from Juanita and moved deliberately toward her, an intimate smile playing on his sensuous lips.

Her mouth went dry. The murmur of conversation and the sound of music faded into oblivion as Judd approached. His onyx eyes were teeming with seduction and promise, and the look he directed at her made her knees go weak.

She still couldn't believe that her dream really had come true. Judd Foster loved her. Wasn't that something? He had married her and they were going to be together for the rest of their lives—and she had the license to prove it. In Erika's book, life just didn't get any better than this.

Sylvie sighed audibly. "Isn't he the handsomest groom you ever laid eyes on?"

"Absolutely, positively," Aunt Frannie agreed.

"The perfect husband," Erika chimed in, knowing that they were individually discussing three different men. She, however, had married the best groom of all.

"I love you," Judd whispered as he waltzed Erika around the dance floor. "Great party...so how long before we can shed these fancy digs and head down to the Gulf? I want you all to myself, Mrs. Foster."

"Mmm…I like the sound of that, Mr. Foster," she murmured, staring starry-eyed at him, feeling her love for him shimmering in every part of her being.

"And I like the feel of you in my arms. In my very soul," he said huskily.

Erika smiled in amazement. "How is it that you always know the right thing to say to melt me into sentimental mush?"

He twirled her in a circle, then pulled her tightly against him. "It's easy when you speak right from the heart."

You gotta love this guy, she mused as he swept her away into a fast-tempoed two-step. Judd was every romantic dream she had ever dreamed come true—and then some.

* * * * *

Turn the page to read excerpts from next month's Harlequin American Romance selections. You'll find a range of stories and styles.

In March, we're offering books from some of your favorite authors— Judy Christenberry, Leah Vale and Linda Randall Wisdom— and from newcomer Lisa McAllister, a delightful new addition to our lineup.

The Marine by Leah Vale
(Harlequin American Romance #1057)

This is the third title in Leah Vale's miniseries THE LOST
MILLIONAIRES. In these books, four men—the secret
offspring of millionaire Joseph McCoy's son, Marcus—are
contacted by the family's lawyers. Marcus is dead—and his
sons are now millionaires.... You'll enjoy this fast-paced,
humorous and yet emotional story! (And watch for the
fourth book, *The Rich Boy* in May.)

> Dear Major Branigan,
> It is our duty at this time to inform you of the death
> of Marcus McCoy due to an unfortunate, unforeseen
> encounter with a grizzly bear while fly-fishing in
> Alaska on June 8 of this year, and per the stipulations
> set forth in his last will and testament, to make for-
> mal his acknowledgment of one USMC Major Rick
> Thomas Branigan, age 33, 7259 Villa Crest Drive,
> #12, Oceanedge, California, as being his son and
> heir to an equal portion of his estate.
>
> It is the wish of Joseph McCoy, father to Marcus
> McCoy, grandfather to Rick Branigan, and founder
> of McCoy Enterprises, that you immediately assume

your rightful place in the family home and business with all due haste and utmost discretion to preserve the family's privacy.

Regards,

David Weidman, Esq.

Weidman, Biddermier, Stark

"My life just keeps getting better and better," Major Rick Branigan grumbled at the letter he held in one hand....

Rachel's Cowboy by Judy Christenberry
(Harlequin American Romance #1058)

Rachel's Cowboy is the next installment in Judy Christenberry's popular new series CHILDREN OF TEXAS. You'll find Judy's trademark warmth here, and her strong sense of family and community—not to mention her love for Texas, her home state!
A Soldier's Return, the next CHILDREN OF TEXAS story, appears in July 2005.

For the first time in her life Rachel Barlow had time on her hands.

After working nonstop for the past six months, she stood in Vivian and Will Greenfield's spacious home feeling at loose ends, trying to rest. She didn't know how. Her constant worries and her hectic schedule had caused her to lose weight. Still, she couldn't stop fretting about her future.

Thanks to her adoptive mother, who'd stolen all Rachel's savings and even borrowed money in her name, she'd been forced to take on one modeling assignment after another, with the hope of repaying the debt and building a nest egg. But she was about to crack.

Her two sisters—Vanessa Shaw, Vivian's adopted

daughter, and Rebecca Jacobs, who was Rachel's twin—
were concerned about her. They'd persuaded her to move
into Vivian's home, where she could be taken care of.

She looked around the lavish Highland Park home that
after six months she still wasn't used to. It was strange not
only living in such luxury, but also having a loving family.

When the doorbell chimed, she called out, "I'll get it."
Knowing the housekeeper would be in the kitchen, she figured she'd save Betty the trip.

She swung open the door and stared at the one man
she'd never wanted to see again.

J. D. Stanley.

Frozen with horror, she said nothing.

Neither did he.

Then, when he took a step toward her, cowboy hat in
hand, she asked, "What are *you* doing here?"

At the same time he demanded, "What are *you* doing
here?"

Neither of them answered.

Single Kid Seeks Dad by Linda Randall Wisdom
(Harlequin American Romance #1059)

Clever, fast paced and charming, this is a story about matchmakers—with a difference. Take one young boy with a single mother and one older man with a single son and see what kind of plan they come up with!
A delightful story that's guaranteed to make you smile.

The small, dimly lit room was a dark contrast to the bright lights and merriment going on in the nearby reception hall. It was the perfect meeting place for the two conspirators who faced each other.

"I have to say, young man, that your note was intriguing. Are you now going to reveal why we're having this meeting in private?" The older man settled back in a chair and studied the boy facing him. He was impressed that even with the stern eye he kept on him, the kid didn't waver.

"It's very simple." The boy kept his voice low. "I have a single mom. You have a single son. We both want to see them married off. There's no reason we can't work together to accomplish our objectives."

The man chuckled. "I suppose you have a plan?"

"Yes, I do. We're already ahead, because your son's hot for my mom."

The older man shook his head. "I've also heard that she's told him she isn't interested."

The boy shrugged off his statement. "Yeah, but that can change. I did some research on your son, and what I've learned tells me he's perfect for my mom. All she needs is some time to really get to know him."

The man chuckled. "How do you expect to bring them together?"

Nick Donner smiled. "I worked up what I feel is a fool-proof plan." He then proceeded to explain the idea.

The older man's skepticism soon turned to interest as he listened to Nick. "I'll admit that I'm impressed. Do you honestly think something that wild could work?"

"There is absolutely no reason it won't, as long as you're willing to do your part," Nick said with unshakable confidence.

An hour later their plan was mutually agreed on with a handshake. The two participants slipped out of the room separately and returned to the reception hall just in time to watch Nora Summers Walker and her new husband, Mark Walker, cut the wedding cake.

For the balance of the evening the young man and his older partner didn't do anything to betray that they had come up with a plan that if successfully carried out meant another wedding would occur in the near future. That of Lucy Donner and Judge Kincaid's son, Logan.

Baby Season by Lisa McAllister
(Harlequin American Romance #1060)

Welcome to Halden, North Dakota! This small prairie town
has always been home to midwife Genevie Halvorson.
Veterinarian Josh McBride and his son, Tyler, are new
here—and despite his differences with Gen, Josh soon
finds himself falling for her.

You'll be enchanted by Lisa McAllister's characters. And
you'll enjoy visiting Halden and its nearby ranches. This
is American country life at its best!

"Dr. Connolly said you're a midwife. What's a midwife?"
Tyler asked from the back seat.

Josh answered before Gen had a chance to reply. "It's
a person who helps ladies have their babies."

"Do you do anything else besides help ladies have
babies?" Tyler directed this question at Gen.

"Well, helping deliver babies keeps me pretty busy," she
replied, "but I'm also an herbalist."

"Oh, that explains it," Josh murmured as Tyler asked,
"What's a herbalist?"

"Explains what?" Gen turned to Josh, puzzled. To Tyler
she said, "An herbalist is someone who uses plants to make

medicines for people and animals." She looked back at Josh, waiting for an answer.

"Are you into all that New Age-y junk or just giving people false hope when there's nothing that can be done?"

Where had that come from? Gen wondered. She bristled at the implication that she was some sort of charlatan. "It's hardly New Age, Dr. McBride. Midwives and herbalists have been around a lot longer than doctors and veterinarians."

"So have witch doctors," he said coolly.

Gen had encountered such bias before. This was the first time, though, that she'd felt compelled to defend herself. What was it about him that made her want to change his mind?

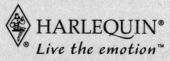

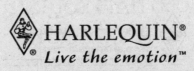

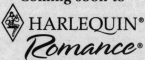
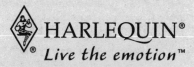

If you enjoyed what you just read,
then we've got an offer you can't resist!

Take 2 bestselling
love stories FREE!

Plus get a FREE surprise gift!

Curl up and have a

Heart *to* Heart

with

Harlequin Romance®

Just like having a heart-to-heart
with your best friend, these stories
will take you from laughter to tears
and back again. So heartwarming
and emotional you'll want to
have some tissues handy!

Next month Harlequin is thrilled to bring you
Natasha Oakley's first book for Harlequin Romance:

For Our Children's Sake (#3838),
on sale March 2005

Then watch out for....

A Family For Keeps (#3843),
by Lucy Gordon, on sale May 2005

Available wherever Harlequin books are sold.

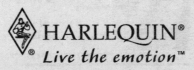
HARLEQUIN®
Live the emotion™

www.eHarlequin.com   HRHTH

SILHOUETTE *Romance*®

TRADING PLACES WITH THE BOSS
by **Raye Morgan**

(#1759) On sale March 2005

When Sally Sinclair switched roles with her
exasperating boss, Rafe Allman, satisfaction
turned to alarm when she discovered Rafe was
not only irritating...he was also utterly irresistible!

BOARDROOM BRIDES:
Three sassy secretaries are about
to land the deal of a lifetime!

Be sure to check out the entire series:

THE BOSS, THE BABY AND ME
(#1751) On sale January 2005

TRADING PLACES WITH THE BOSS
(#1759) On sale March 2005

THE BOSS'S SPECIAL DELIVERY
(#1766) On sale May 2005

Only from Silhouette Books!

HARLEQUIN

AMERICAN *Romance*®

COMING NEXT MONTH

#1057 THE MARINE by Leah Vale
The Lost Millionaires
When lawyer Lynn Hayes's career depends on keeping one of the long-lost McCoy heirs out of jail, she's ready for a skirmish in the courtroom. But her first battle is with the defendant, who's a perfect officer and a gentleman. In this case, her worst enemy might be herself....

#1058 RACHEL'S COWBOY by Judy Christenberry
Children of Texas
When Rachel Barlow needs a place to recuperate, it turns out that the best alternative is J. D. Stanley's ranch. J.D.'s a friend of the family—and the man with whom Rachel spent one passionate night six months ago. After a few weeks in this cowboy's company, Rachel discovers she wants to make love with him again...but can she make a life with him?

#1059 SINGLE KID SEEKS DAD by Linda Randall Wisdom
Motherhood
Thirteen-year-old Nick Donner has decided it's time for his mother, Lucy, to remarry, and he's chosen local vet Logan Kincaid as the prospective husband and father. Nick (a very bright kid) takes some unusual measures to get Logan and Lucy together....

#1060 BABY SEASON by Lisa McAllister
Fatherhood
Josh McBride is in Halden, North Dakota, for one reason—to fill in for another vet at the local animal hospital. Then Josh and his eight-year-old son, Tyler, will move on to the next town, the next assignment—anything to avoid putting down roots. But Josh begins to see that his transient lifestyle might be hurting his son. And when Ty becomes attached to local midwife Gen Halvorson, Josh realizes that putting down roots might not be such a bad idea.

www.eHarlequin.com

Cupid, Meet Your Match

Judd Foster is the perfect new project for Moon Valley's resident do-gooder, Erika Dunn. After serving in Special Ops, Judd has returned to his family's ranch, seeking solitude to overcome the traumas he's endured. But sweet-talkin' Erika intends to wipe away this cowboy's pain with a dose of her irresistible small-town charm.

Of course, Erika's interest isn't purely selfless—not when Judd's been the man of her dreams since she was a little girl. Sure, he's a bit gruff and withdrawn now. But when the two are forced to pretend they're a couple, Erika knows that Judd is still the only man for her. And this Texas Cupid isn't above using every arrow she's got to capture the heart of her cowboy!

www.eHarlequin.com

ISBN 0-373-75059-5

75059

UPC

S

0 65373 00499 4